Bad Advice

CARRIE JACOBS

Welcome to Hickory Hollow!

Each novel in the Hickory Hollow series is a stand-alone, and can be read in any order. There are some character appearances across books, so there may be some very minor spoilers if you read the books out of order.

For details about all of the Hickory Hollow books, visit my website at carriejacobs.com

For exclusive sneak peeks, behind-the-scenes information, and much more, sign up for my newsletter at carriejacobs.com.

For Bethany
and the best "advice" we've ever gotten...
Philippians 2:14

Chapter One

Lincoln Foster thought he might throw up. He clutched the flowers in his sweaty hand and had to remind himself not to crush the stems. This was his first date in six long years. He couldn't screw it up.

He got out of his car and touched the bit of plastic in his ear, making sure it was secure. One of the voices instructed him, "As soon as she opens the door, tell her she looks beautiful."

A second voice chimed in, "More beautiful than the last time you saw her."

He pursed his lips and blew three bursts of breath out into the chilly autumn evening air.

"You've got this," a third voice encouraged.

He nodded, even though the voices couldn't see him. He stood straighter, made sure the flowers weren't crushed, and forced himself to stride up the sidewalk and climb the three steps to the front porch, and then cross to the front door. He swallowed hard, then lifted his fist and knocked. The cellophane crinkled obnoxiously loud in the quiet of the evening.

A moment later, the door opened.

Lincoln's eyes fixed on a pair of feet clad in fuzzy red socks. "You... you look even... more beautiful than... than when I saw you last." It came out in a stilted mess, but at least the words were understandable.

"You've never seen me before, idiot."

Lincoln's throat constricted as his gaze snapped up to her face. This must be Lisa. His date's sister. He squawked, "*Ohno-Iamsosorry,*" as a single word.

"Maybe you should just go." She crossed her arms over a well-worn sweatshirt emblazoned with the Penn State logo.

Sue, his actual date, came up behind her. "It's fine." Her weary tone dashed any hope that she hadn't heard his mistake. "Come in."

He thrust the bouquet in her direction as he stepped through the door. The carnation's stems were no match for his white-knuckled fist. *"Theseareforyou."* A Yorkie eyed him suspiciously from the sofa.

Lisa snorted. "Not for me?" She rolled her eyes and snatched the flowers from him before Sue could make a move. "I'll put these in water. You kids have fun." She shot him one more filthy look before turning on her heel.

"Thanks for the flowers." Sue didn't look at him as she pulled her coat on.

"Dude. Tell her she looks nice." One of the voices said.

She did look nice in her sky blue dress and carefully done hair and makeup, but he ignored the suggestion. Opening his mouth would produce nothing good at this point.

"We should get going." Sue clearly wanted to get this over with.

Lincoln stepped back, catching his heel on the door. He yelped, sending the resident Yorkie into a hysterical barking frenzy. It charged at him, four pounds of raging fury. He slipped his hand into his pocket and pulled out a treat, which he tossed to the dog before it got close enough to sink its teeth into his ankles.

"You just randomly carry dog treats in your pockets? That's… interesting."

"Uh, I, um, it's, yeah. My job… uh…"

His earpiece said, "Linc, just go. Out the door."

This time, he listened. He held the screen door open until Sue came through and pulled the main door shut behind her. He let go of the screen door and it crashed against its frame with an awful racket.

Sue walked ahead of him to his car, a little hybrid. "Cute car."

He hurried to open her door for her. "Thanks. This was better than one of those ridiculous, giant, environment-destroying trucks." He closed her door and went around to the driver's side. At least he'd managed to get one sentence out normally.

He pulled his seatbelt on and heard a rumble. The garage door directly in front of his car rolled up.

Sue pointed to a massive truck. "You mean like that?" A four-door Ford Super Duty F350. Diesel. Black with lots of chrome.

He audibly gulped.

She pressed a button on her keyring and the garage door lowered. "Let me hide my environment-destroying shame."

"I…" He went hot and cold.

Her voice was about as cold as the shiver sliding down his spine. "Kidding. I love that truck. It was either that or a Prius, but I had to go with the *slightly* better towing capacity. Made more sense for my landscaping business."

"Oh, crap," one of the voices muttered in his ear.

She huffed an annoyed sigh. "Shall we? I'm hungry."

"Of course." His voice quietly croaked out. He pulled onto

the road and headed for the restaurant. They'd agreed on Carmine's Italian Restaurant, which was an unfortunate thirty-minute drive away.

They'd gone at least ten minutes in uncomfortable silence when Sue spoke up. "Does this thing top out at thirty-five or something?"

"Huh?"

"Speed limit is fifty-five."

He glanced down at the speedometer. "I'm going fifty."

"Not feeling the other five?"

"I, uh, don't tend to speed?"

"Going the speed limit is speeding now? Did they change that recently?" She turned back toward the window and sighed something that sounded like, "The ravioli better be worth it."

A few more torturous moments passed and Lincoln couldn't think of a single thing to say. The voices in his ear were quiet. Not that they'd been particularly helpful anyway.

He tried, "So, um, you do landscaping. Do you like doing that?"

She seemed to relax a little. Very little. "I love it. I think the design aspect is what I enjoy most."

One of the voices in his ear said, "Design? Isn't landscaping just planting flowers and mowing grass?"

Lincoln parroted the words exactly.

The more reasonable of the three voices groaned, "You did not say that."

"No, *Lincoln*, landscaping isn't just planting flowers and mowing grass. Unbelievable." She crossed her arms and turned her head to the window.

It took a thousand years, but they arrived at Carmine's. Sue was out of the car and on the sidewalk before he had a chance to open her door.

The host raised a snooty eyebrow when Lincoln had difficulty choking out his name for the reservation. He gave another snide look before he led them to their table. Sue said, "I'm going to the restroom. If the waiter comes, I'd like ice water."

"Okay." He sat in his chair and half-expected her to make a beeline for the front door.

"Now's your chance to redeem yourself," the earpiece told him.

"Yeah. Order for her. It shows you're thoughtful and in control of the situation. It'll make up for putting your foot in your mouth."

"That's not a great idea," the third voice said.

The first two shushed him. "It's perfect. Get back on track. Order a nice appetizer and meal."

Lincoln's hands shook a little as he held the thick leather menu. The words swam across the cream-colored parchment.

The waiter approached the table with a tight smile. "Would you like to wait to order?"

"You can do this," the voice encouraged him.

"No, thanks. We'll have a bottle of this wine." He pointed to a name on the menu that meant nothing to him. "We'll have the stuffed mushrooms for the appetizer, and for the entrée, we'll both have the mushroom lobster fettucine in alfredo. Thank you."

"Good job!"

The waiter nodded. "Excellent choice, sir."

A few minutes later, Sue came back from the restroom. The waiter brought the bottle of wine and turned to leave.

"Excuse me, could I get a menu, please?" she said. "And some water?"

Lincoln's heart thumped in his throat. He couldn't believe he'd forgotten the water.

The waiter looked confused. "Your order was already placed?"

"What?"

Lincoln said, "I took the liberty—"

"Liberty indeed." She looked at the waiter. "I'll have the shrimp ravioli. With the special red sauce, please."

"The first order is already in." He spoke with an undisguised tinge of annoyance.

Sue matched his energy and carefully enunciated each word. "*I* didn't place an order. Shrimp ravioli. Red sauce. Please."

"Certainly. I'll be right back with your water."

He disappeared and a moment later, a different server appeared with a glass of water and a small tray holding the appetizer. He placed the dish in the center of the table.

Sue's glass paused halfway to her lips. Her nose scrunched. "What is that?"

"I'm sorry," Lincoln said. "I was trying to... I don't even know." He stared dismally at the mushrooms.

Neither of them had touched the appetizer when their alfredo dishes arrived.

"I appreciate the attempt at chivalry. Wait." She flicked her cloth napkin across her lap. "You know what? I actually don't. Ordering for someone you've just met is presumptuous and rude. I was looking forward to the shrimp ravioli, and I don't like mushrooms."

He sent a panicked glance at her plate. Big chunks of mushroom sat atop the creamy noodles.

The waiter came by. "How is everything?" He didn't sound hopeful.

Lincoln gestured to Sue's plate. "Could we get this boxed up and get the shrimp ravioli, please?"

He blinked like this was the first he'd heard anything about shrimp ravioli. "Right. We're out of red sauce. Would you care for the white sauce instead?"

"No, thank you," Sue managed.

"Would you like to order something else?"

"Do you have lasagna?"

"Certainly. Tonight's lasagna is spinach and mushroom. It's delicious."

Her left eye twitched. "No regular, plain old lasagna?"

"I'm afraid not."

"Just a box then, please."

As soon as the waiter walked away, Lincoln shook his head. "I'm so sorry."

"It's fine."

He knew it wasn't fine. "I'm sorry, Sue. This is a disaster."

"I won't disagree." She sipped her water and shrugged. "It couldn't be much worse, that's for sure."

The waiter returned with the check and boxes.

Lincoln couldn't hand over his card fast enough.

They boxed up the food.

The waiter returned with an irritated expression. "Sir, your card was declined." Then he sighed. Actually sighed.

Sue shoved her own card at him. "Here."

Lincoln stared at his card like it was covered in hiero-glyphs. "That can't be." He'd checked his account and paid bills before he left to pick her up. This didn't make any sense.

"Obviously I'll pay you back. I'm so sorry." Sweat rolled down his back, and no doubt beaded across his forehead.

The waiter returned and handed Sue her card. "Sign the top, bottom is your copy. Have a lovely evening." His tone suggested that he did not, in fact, want them to have a lovely evening.

Lincoln stood quickly, taking a step toward Sue, intending to pull her chair out for her. At the same moment that she stood. His foot bumped the chair leg, and he stumbled. He reached out to catch himself on the edge of the table, but his hand grazed across Sue's wine glass. Sue's untouched, very full wine glass. Which splattered in every direction.

In slow motion, the dark red wine arced upward, then down, creating a red slash down the entire front of Sue's pretty light blue dress.

He made a strangled noise as the earpiece launched from his ear and landed on the table. He wasn't sure if he was going to vomit or cry. Or both.

She eyed the earpiece with a hint of sympathy, like maybe she thought it was a hearing aid. He shoved it back into his ear with violently shaking hands. Not that it mattered, because the idiot voices had gone silent.

The drive back to Sue's house was excruciating. Every quarter of a mile, he issued another desperate apology. His knuckles were white on the steering wheel. It was forever before he pulled into her driveway.

"Sue, I'm—"

She snapped, "If you apologize one more time, I'm going to scream."

"I, uh, I'll walk you to your door?"

"NO. I've got it from here." She jumped out of the car and practically sprinted to the front door.

Chapter Two

Lincoln rolled to a stop for a red light and smacked the steering wheel. "Oh, *now* you jerks are quiet? Thanks a lot."

"Dude. Sorry. That was bad." Noah's sympathetic voice filled his ear.

Alex agreed. "Yeah. You're right. You suck at dating. I had no idea how much."

"You guys were supposed to help me!" He waited for the light to change. "I told you how important this was. She's never going to talk to me again."

"She has to," Oren piped up. "You owe her money."

"Aaaaahhhhhh! I never stopped at the ATM." Lincoln made an abrupt right-hand turn and drove around the block to backtrack to the bank. He slid his card into the ATM machine, where it was promptly declined. "I have plenty of money. What is going on?" He glared at the card, willing it to give him answers.

A moment later, it did.

"Oh, no."

"What?" Alex and Oren asked in unison.

"Today's November first."

"So?"

"My card expired yesterday. I got the new one last week and didn't think anything of it." He leaned forward and banged his forehead on the steering wheel a few times.

"You don't have another card?"

Lincoln sighed. "No. I only use my debit card."

Noah snorted. "Yeah, you're forgetting he's Mr. Responsible, who never uses credit cards."

"Come on, man, get off my back."

Oren made a grunting noise. "You won't get any flack from me. I'd love to be out of debt."

"It's been a long night, guys. I'm signing off." Without waiting for a response, Lincoln tugged the earpiece out, pressed the button, and tossed it onto the passenger seat.

What a disaster. His one shot, and he'd blown it. There was no way he could ever look Sue in the eye again, and every eligible woman in town would probably know all about his stupidity by morning.

Every minute of the evening replayed in excruciating detail. Every time he insulted her, every stupid idea he'd gone along with from the buzzing in his ear. Why? Why had he ever thought it would be a good idea to order her food for her? It was only chivalrous in the movies. Old, old movies.

He parked the car in the driveway and carried his takeout containers—all three of them—into the house. The heavy containers mocked him as he put them in the fridge, a reminder of his stupid stupidity.

He'd been so sure his friends would be able to help him. After all, they were all in great relationships, so they had to know something about dating, right? He could only imagine what Gretchen would have to say.

Speaking of which, might as well get it over with. He dialed her number.

She picked up right away. "It's only... 8:02. Why are you calling me? Are you stuck in the bathroom? How's it going? Do you need rescued?"

Lincoln sighed heavily. "It *went* horribly."

"Oh, geez. What did you do?"

He immediately bristled and went on the defensive. "Why are you assuming I did something wrong?"

Gretchen didn't bother dignifying that with a response. "Tell me you did not go ahead with your stupid plan to let those idiots talk you through the date on an earpiece."

Ouch. She nailed it. "Those idiots are your friends, too."

"If you think being my friend exempts anyone from being an idiot, think again. Now what exactly did you do?"

Lincoln flopped onto the couch. Edith and Pickles jumped up on either side of him and demanded pets. Jerry was across the room, sprawled on the top level of their cat tower, satisfied with his own company. "It doesn't matter. It was a complete disaster."

"It matters so you learn from it and do better next time."

"There will be no next time. I'm going to die alone. I'll end up being a sad crazy animal dude living in a one-room shack with nineteen mangy cats and fifty dogs and I'll spend my day in a rocking chair on the front porch screaming at people to get off my lawn."

Edith purred loudly, in total agreement with this plan.

Gretchen didn't miss a beat. "I'm glad you've got it all figured out. What do you need me for?"

"I need to borrow your car to haul the cats."

She laughed at that. "Tell me everything. Leave nothing out."

So he did. Every humiliating detail.

And then he waited.

For several long minutes.

"Let me get this straight," she said slowly. "You called her sister beautiful, insulted her truck, belittled her profession, ordered her meal while she was in the restroom without having a clue what she'd want, and then stuck her with the bill for food she didn't eat."

"It sounds so bad when you put it all together like that."

"Wow."

He heard the secondhand irritation in her voice.

"Wow. I mean… wow."

"Please don't say 'wow' again." He felt bad enough as it was.

"Woooooooooow. Lincoln. Wow."

"Are you done?"

She was not. "I'm glad those geniuses in your ear didn't tell you to rob a bank. Although, if you had, you might not have stuck her with the bill."

Lincoln listened to her barbs for a few more minutes. "Gretchen. What I need to know is what to do about it *now*."

"Now? Nothing. Leave her alone. Forever."

"I need to reimburse her and apologize." And definitely explain himself.

"No."

"No, what?"

"That tone. Like you're having an idea."

"I wouldn't call it an idea, exactly."

She said more with her lengthy sigh than she could have with words.

"I was thinking about a letter or something. Or maybe flowers." He hurried to clarify. "Not to ask her out again, strictly to apologize and explain that I acknowledge all the ways I was an idiot. I'm not stupid enough to think she'd give me another chance."

"I mean, you were stupid enough to put a bug in your ear and let those idiots tell you what to say."

He could imagine her squeezing her eyes shut and sending her red curls into a frenzy as she shook her head and contemplated the fates that put a whole passel of men in her life who existed without a single functioning brain cell among them. Which she regularly told them.

"If I were her, I'd probably appreciate a short note of apology and cash. No letter. You're not Mr. Darcy. No flowers. Nothing fancy."

"Mr. Darcy? Is that from one of the Shakespeare plays?"

When she groaned, he could imagine her face with her eyes squeezed shut and her jaw clenched as she tried to summon a sliver of patience. "Mr. Darcy. *Pride and Prejudice.* Jane Austen. He wrote letters. You know what, never mind. Just listen to me. No letters, no flowers, just cash and an apology."

Lincoln couldn't blame himself for his assumption. She ran a Shakespeare troupe and a theater, so of course his mind immediately went to Shakespeare. "Why not flowers?"

There was a long pause. A really, really long pause. "Are you kidding me?"

"Because she might not like them? Or maybe she's allergic?" Lincoln guessed.

"Now you're worried about allergies? But not when you ordered her—never mind. No, Lincoln. Because flowers are romantic. If you give her flowers, she'll probably toss the card without looking at it."

"Oh." Yup, that made a lot of sense.

"Trust me on this."

Of all his friends, she was probably the one to listen to. Which he should have figured out before subjecting Sue to the worst date of her life. He ran a hand down his face. "I trust you on this."

"Okay. See you tomorrow."

Lincoln tossed his phone onto the couch cushion. Pickles pounced on top of it and wrestled it into submission.

Lincoln scratched his back. "Good job, ferocious protector."

Chapter Three

Gretchen Ross was still thinking about Lincoln's date when she pulled into the busy parking lot at Hickory Hollow Animal Rescue early Saturday morning. Lincoln had roped her into volunteering to help with the photo shoot they'd set up. Hopefully the calendar they were creating would be a big fundraiser for the cause.

She jumped out of her car and jogged over to Megan Caretti's SUV. "Here, let me help you!"

Megan was pulling props and equipment out of the back of her vehicle. "Thanks. I probably shouldn't have brought everything, but once I got started with sorting the props I couldn't make myself pare it down." She set a small velvet armchair on the ground.

"I totally understand that." She reached over to pull the dolly out of Megan's vehicle and pointed to the plastic bins stacked to the ceiling. She said, "Do these all go inside?"

"Yeah," Megan said with a chuckle. "I told you, I brought everything and the kitchen sink."

Gretchen stacked bins on the dolly, then pushed it up the

ramp to the main entrance while Megan pulled a cart piled high with a mountain of even more bins.

Lincoln was already inside and hurried to push the door open for them. "Is there anything else to bring in?"

Megan waved a hand toward her vehicle. "Lots. You'll want to use the dolly."

"What on Earth did you bring?"

"Props."

"We're only taking twelve pictures, right?"

She stopped and eyed him.

Gretchen bit her lips to keep from laughing at Megan's stunned expression.

"Wrong. We're making a calendar that will feature at least twelve photos. In order to get twelve photos to put in the calendar, we'll need to shoot a lot more than that."

He held his hands up in surrender. "Sorry, sorry, you're the expert." He looked to Gretchen for help.

She shrugged. "Where are we setting up?"

He seemed grateful for the change of subject. "In the common room."

The rescue was housed in a building that was originally a tiny elementary school with ten classrooms, one huge common room that had served as a cafeteria, and three offices. When the school was closed two years earlier and absorbed into a larger district-wide elementary school, the community banded together and raised money to secure the building for the rescue. Lincoln, despite his social anxieties, had been instrumental in making that happen.

It was the perfect setup for the rescue. The classrooms had been converted with kennels and cages to house the dogs and cats in separate spaces. The fenced-in playground area was perfect for daily exercise, and for potential adopters to play with the dogs. And the common room was a great space to hold fundraising events. The smallest of the three offices had even been converted to a makeshift hotel room so a staff member or volunteer could stay onsite in the event of impending snowstorms or other emergencies. Best of all, the floors in the entire building were designed for easy cleanup.

Gretchen helped unload the cart and the dolly. She said to Megan, "You start setting up. We'll go get the rest of the stuff."

Lincoln grabbed the cart and Gretchen pushed the dolly back to the entrance. Outside, the air was chilly and brisk. Fall had firmly taken hold of Hickory Hollow. The trees clung to the last of their colorful leaves against the brilliant blue sky.

They loaded up the last of the bins from Megan's vehicle and lugged it all inside.

In the common room, Megan had already attached white sheets to a frame and set up the backdrop. She spread another sheet on the floor to set the stage.

"How can we help?" Gretchen asked.

"The bins are labeled with months. If you could set them up in order along those tables, that'd be great."

It took a few minutes for Gretchen and Lincoln to get the bins in order, and after that, Megan was busy setting her scenes, so they mostly stayed out of her way.

They stood off to the side, watching Megan work her magic when Gretchen asked, "Did you decide how you're going to handle last night?"

"Already done. I stopped and got cash to cover the bill plus tip, and a Carmine's gift card. I just wrote a generic 'sorry about the terrible evening and here's a gift card so you can go back and get the shrimp ravioli.' I left it on her front door this morning and sent a text to let her know it was there."

"That was thoughtful."

"I hope she thinks so. She read my text but hasn't responded. Not that I expect her to."

Gretchen hoped this disaster of a date didn't set him back. It had taken a lot of nerve–six solid months–for him to gather the courage to try dating again after his therapist gave him the green light. Not that he'd ever dated much to begin with. "I'm sure she'll appreciate the gesture."

"Where do you want us?" a voice boomed from the doorway.

She turned toward the entrance. A group of Hickory Hollow's finest volunteer firefighters came in with their gear, ready to pose with the animals.

Gretchen jumped to action. "You can hang out over here and I'll find out where Megan wants everyone."

A few minutes later, Megan called, "Okay, ready to go!" and began directing the firefighters. When she was satisfied, she said, "Ready for the cats."

Lincoln gave a nod and said, "I'll be back with the stars of the show."

From there, the morning flew by in a flurry of activity, with scenery changes and cats, then dogs, and even a snake posing for the rescue's annual calendar.

As the finale, each of the six firefighters was assigned an animal. Leashes and harnesses were attached for safety, and they went outside and posed as a group in front of the firetruck for the calendar's cover. The bright red truck against the orange and yellow leaves and perfect cloudless sky would make a stunning photo.

Lincoln helped the rescue volunteers keep an eye on the animals until they were back inside, safe and secure.

"I'll order pizza," Gretchen offered. She ordered, then helped Megan pack all the props back into their boxes and bins. "That was amazing."

Megan beamed. "We got so many great shots. It's going to be hard to narrow it down to twelve. Of course the ones that don't make it to the calendar can be used for social media, so it's a win either way."

"Good thinking."

One of the rescue volunteers came up and shyly said, "Mrs. Caretti?"

Megan whirled with a big smile. "Please call me Megan. Mrs. Caretti is my mother-in-law."

"Sorry."

"No need to be sorry. What's up?"

"I was wondering…" The young woman twisted at the hem of her t-shirt. Her nametag read Alyssa. "I know you're very busy, but I was thinking that maybe…"

Gretchen found herself holding her breath. Alyssa's nervousness was apparent.

"Maybe, if it's not too much bother, could we maybe take some pictures of the lifers?"

"Lifers? I'm sorry, I'm not sure what that means." Megan's voice was gentle.

"It's the animals who have been here for a year or longer, that just seem to get overlooked because they're old or have health issues and people gravitate toward the kittens and puppies and cute animals." She sounded more confident the more she spoke. "We have several senior cats and dogs that would be wonderful companions if the right family would just give them a chance."

Megan turned to Gretchen. "Would you be able to help a while longer?"

"Of course."

"Alyssa, that's a wonderful idea. Maybe we can even do a second calendar. Or spotlights on social media." As she talked, she refastened the backdrop to the frame. "Gretchen, would you grab the December bin? I think we'll just use the Christmas props and we can do a big push with these guys. Maybe a whole 'Home for the Holidays' sort of campaign."

"Sounds good." Gretchen retrieved the December bin while Alyssa watched.

"What needs taken out?" Lincoln came back into the common room and stopped, frozen in place. He lifted his hands, confused. "I thought we were done?"

"We were," Gretchen said, "but Alyssa had a fantastic idea, so now we're not." She filled him in.

Lincoln's brows rose as he listened, impressed. "I wish I'd have thought of it myself. Great job, Alyssa."

Megan pointed. "These bins can go ahead out. We're just going to use all the Christmas stuff."

They took a lunch break, inhaled the pizza and sodas, and spent the early afternoon doing photo shoots with the senior residents of the rescue.

It was mid-afternoon by the time Gretchen helped Lincoln carry the last of the items to Megan's SUV. She said, "That was a super productive day. The calendar is going to be amazing, and Alyssa's idea to showcase the other animals was a great idea."

"It really was," Lincoln agreed. "She's a great volunteer. I wish we had the budget to put her on the staff. She works really hard and she's so good with the animals."

"That's great."

He shut the hatch on Megan's SUV. "She reminds me a lot of myself. Dealing with the animals is easy. People? Not so much. Obviously."

"Hey." She put her hand on his arm. "If you're talking about last night, don't get down about it. It was your first date in ages. And now that you've got the disaster out of the way, you know you can handle anything that comes your way next time."

"There's not going to be a next time, at least not for a while."

"Why?" She hoped he wasn't retreating back inward.

"It's the holidays. Getting up the nerve to go on a date is bad enough, but add in all the holiday stress and it's a million times worse. I think I'm going to just pump the brakes until after the new year."

A thought occurred to her. "Are you sure you're not using the holidays as an excuse to stay in your comfort zone?"

He shrugged one shoulder. "Maybe? I don't know. I've asked all my friends for advice, but they're no help."

Gretchen rolled her eyes. "You've asked all your *guy* friends for advice."

"It's not like I have many woman friends I can talk to."

"What the heck am I?"

"No, I know, but you're really my only woman *friend*. I have a handful of woman acquaintances, and I don't want to make you my emotional support human and lean on you for all my questions about dating. That doesn't seem like being a very good friend to do that." He sighed. "It's too bad there's not some kind of coaching service where you can hire someone to teach you how to date. Like for practice."

She jerked to attention. "That's brilliant. It's the perfect solution."

"Yeah, except it doesn't exist."

The idea took hold. "No, but I do."

"What?"

It made perfect sense. He needed help getting his confidence up, and she just wanted to get out of the house sometimes and do grown-up things instead of always doing six-year-old friendly activities. Before she could think better of it, before she could consider any possible downsides, the words popped out of her mouth.

"You could date me."

Chapter Four

Lincoln nearly dropped Megan's keys onto the ground. He juggled them awkwardly and finally grasped them firmly. "What?" he managed to wheeze out.

Gretchen's hands waved and her red curls bounced enthusiastically as she talked, a sure sign she was excited about a new idea. "This is perfect. You said it yourself. Trying to date around the holidays is a nightmare. It's the beginning of November. We'll practice date through New Year's and then you'll be ready to go off on your own and date for real."

"Practice date." His pounding heart slowed to normal. Okay. That made a little more sense than actually dating his good friend Gretchen. "What if you find someone?"

Gretchen snorted. "Not gonna happen. I keep finding frogs but none of them ever turn into princes. It'll be nice for me, too. A few evenings out, someone to do stuff with, and none of the awkward getting to know you crap because we're already friends. It'll be fun."

"Fun," he echoed.

"I mean, obviously it's just an idea. You said you wanted a coach."

His attention snapped back to her. "Yeah." The idea was growing on him. "It makes a lot more sense than listening to the guys in my ear."

"I still can't believe you went along with that. Whose idea was it? Alex?"

Lincoln shrugged. He would never throw anyone under the bus, but of course it was Alex's idea. He was in the security business, and it wasn't a far leap to surveillance. Alex wanted to try out a new earpiece, Lincoln needed some help, and a disaster was born. Oren hadn't exactly been the voice of reason, either. Noah tried, but in the end he was just as helpful as the other two. Which was exactly zero.

Lincoln had assumed since three of his best friends were in successful relationships that they'd be solid mentors to guide him through dating.

Obviously he'd overestimated them.

Gretchen eyed him with a smirk. "I knew Alex was the ringleader. Oren and Noah came along to witness the train-wreck, and Nate stayed as far away as he could."

He mumbled, "Something like that." Exactly that.

"Think about it. Can you even imagine if Alex tried ordering Avery's dinner without checking with her? That'd go over like a lead balloon, and he knows what she likes."

"I know, I know. It seemed like a good idea at the time."

She nudged him with her elbow as they headed back for the entrance. "Well, 'the time' was less than twenty-four hours ago, so excuse me if I'm not convinced you've learned your lesson."

He reached past her to open the door and let her pass through ahead of him.

"See? That was good."

"What was?"

"Opening the door."

"I do that for everyone." This was going to be complicated, wasn't it?

"Exactly. Stick with regular old manners. Nothing fancy like ordering her dinner."

They turned into the common room where Megan was snapping photos of Fred, a ten-year-old basset hound whose entire body was wagging.

"Who's the goodest boy?" Megan asked as she shifted this way and that, directing Fred's attention for the best angles.

Fred happily brayed, loud and long, his tail whipping back and forth, because he obviously knew the answer to that question.

Lincoln couldn't help but smile. Fred was such a character, and it was a shame he hadn't found his forever home. Yet.

Alyssa came over with her tablet and tapped the screen. "Here are some of the bios I've been working on. What do you think?"

Lincoln scrolled down through the bios. She'd done one for each animal as if they were writing it themselves. The best part was that each bio's tone matched the animal's personality. Upbeat and funny for Fred, low-key for shy Mittens, who wouldn't do well in a home with children. "These are amazing, Alyssa." He pointed to the screen. "There's a typo here, but otherwise these are just perfect. Great job."

"Thanks. I'll make sure to proofread before I add them to the photos." She headed toward the offices.

They finished the project much later than he'd planned, but Alyssa's idea to showcase the lifers was pretty brilliant, so he had no complaints.

Once Megan's car was packed and the next shift of shelter workers was in place, Lincoln breathed a sigh of relief. He took one last look around the common room.

Gretchen joined him. "I'm starving. Do you want to grab something to eat?"

"Yes. That one slice of pizza didn't do much for me."

"Me, either."

He followed her out to the parking lot. It was only four o'clock, but the sun was already heading down for the night, giving in to the growing clouds, and the temperature had dropped. "Is it supposed to snow?"

Gretchen shrugged. "I haven't looked at the weather. Probably."

"Sonny's?"

"Of course."

A little while later, they slid into a booth at Sonny's Diner. Gretchen set a notebook and a pen on the table.

"What's that for?"

"So we can lay down the ground rules for this project we're about to embark upon."

"Ah."

After they ordered their food and got their drinks, Gretchen opened the notebook and smoothed the page. "We've already established our timeline, right? Starting now until New Year's."

"Yeah." He chuckled. "Maybe we can do family dinners so I won't have to answer the four hundred billion questions about whether I'm dating anyone."

She cocked her head. "Is that something we want to do?"

He immediately felt like he'd suggested something wrong. "Oh. Are family things off limits? That's fine. I..." His tongue felt too big for his mouth. He pressed it against the roof of his mouth, working to control it before it twisted and he started babbling incoherently.

"I'm just making sure. Families can be complicated."

He sat back against the booth and tried to relax. This was Gretchen. Not a random woman he was trying to impress. She'd witnessed some of his worst moments and she was still here, one of his very best friends. There was no need for his anxiety or insecurity to make an appearance now. "That's true. My family's pretty laid back, they're just ready for me to find someone. They mean well, but boy do they not know when to stop asking personal questions."

"Ha. Tell me about it. I swear Seth hadn't even been gone a month before I started getting comments about raising Abby without a dad and was I interested in being set up with one person or another."

"That's awful."

"And on the flip side, I went on my first date two years after he took off and then I got comments about moving on too fast. Point being, someone will have something to say no matter what you do."

"True." He fidgeted with his glass. "Was that mostly from family?"

"Depends on which family you mean. My immediate family has been amazing. Most of my extended family is fine. His family? They were horrible."

"How so?" He quickly added, "If you don't mind my asking."

"Let's see. When Seth found out I was pregnant, he proposed. I was excited at first, but when he started asking questions about 'managing the baby's funds' I got a little suspicious. Then his mother, Carla, called me and demanded to know how her son would be provided for if we ever got divorced because he was already accustomed to my lifestyle."

"Whoa."

"My parents, bless them, gently but firmly insisted on a prenup to protect not only me, but the baby. As soon as I suggested it, he blew up. Threw a coffee cup through the kitchen window, then insisted it couldn't be his baby." She made an absentminded doodle on the paper. "He took off and after Abby was born he and his parents tried to sue me for custody. I don't like using my financial situation as an advantage, but let me tell you, I didn't feel the least bit bad paying for the best lawyers in the country."

"You shouldn't."

"When it came time for a paternity test, Seth decided to skip town. I haven't seen him since. I had several more run-ins with Carla, to the point where she tried breaking into the house–she had a baby seat in her car, so I'm pretty sure she was planning to kidnap Abby–and we were granted permanent restraining orders. I hired security. About a month after that incident, she moved across the country, but I kept the security staff for a whole year."

"I'm so sorry." He knew she'd had issues with them, but it all went down a few years before they became close friends, so he had no idea it had been this bad.

"Then there was a social media smear campaign. She even went to the toy company who owns *Mister Miser* and said some crazy stuff. Because my family has money and they don't, they felt I had some sort of moral obligation to support them."

He felt his eyes bug. "What?" He knew she got royalties from her great-great grandfather's *Mister Miser* board game, but someone would have to have a screw loose to think the toy company and the family had anything more to do with each other.

"Oh, yeah. I blocked the whole lot of them."

"I had no idea it got that crazy."

She shrugged one shoulder. "It's not something I like to talk about. Despite my lengthy ramble."

"You didn't have to tell me all that."

"I know. Sorry I went waaaaaaaaay off track."

He watched a parade of emotions cross her face as she stared down at the paper and drew some random lines. "You okay?"

"Yeah. I'm really not sure why my head went there. I go the longest time not thinking about it, then it just creeps up at weird times." She shook her head, sending her red curls flying. "Okay. Done with that. Family events. Would you be introducing someone to your family this soon?"

He thought about it. "Probably not. But we've already met each other's families. Does that make it different?"

"Maybe? But if we started dating for real, it would probably still be too soon for the big family holiday events, wouldn't it?"

"How about we leave it open. We don't plan on it, but if it comes up and it makes sense, it's okay."

She made a note. "Sounds good. How often should we schedule something?"

"Is once a week too much? That'll be about eight dates between now and New Year's." That seemed like a solid number of dates to learn how to do it right.

"That's what I was thinking. Now. How are we defining dates? Actual formal dates, or any sort of activity?"

He thought about it for a minute. "Maybe we should do a time limit instead of activity. Like, if whatever we're doing lasts longer than an hour or ninety minutes or whatever, it counts?"

"Perfect." She wrote another note, then clicked her pen and set it down. "Since we talked about family events, what are we telling people? Is it going to embarrass you to have everyone know it's essentially fake?"

Lincoln hadn't thought about that, but she'd hit on a very real issue. People were bound to ask questions. "Well, I'm not comfortable lying, and I don't think we need to. If we tell our friends it's for practice, it'll be easier for them to support us in the process. And I don't want my family to get their hopes up. I guess I'm saying that I think we should be up front about it to the people who matter."

"I agree."

He leaned back in the booth. "Seems like we're off to a good start. When should our first date be?"

Gretchen opened the calendar on her phone. "It's November second. Let's say next weekend?"

"How about Friday night?"

"Sounds good."

"What do you want—"

She held up a hand. "Nope. I'm helping you practice, not giving you step by step instructions to follow. You'll have to get ahold of me this week and ask me out."

"I get it. You want me to do everything like I would for a real woman."

Her eyes narrowed. "Yeah, Lincoln. Just pretend I'm a real woman."

His face flamed. Maybe he should find a coach to help him keep his foot out of his mouth.

Chapter Five

Gretchen pulled up to her parents' house. There was nothing about the two-story brick home that would suggest the occupants were anything other than middle class. In fact, Gretchen's great-great-grandfather had invented the *Mister Miser* board game that had been purchased by a massive toy company in 1907, and was now in nearly every American home. He'd been a shrewd businessman and had the foresight to include language about any current and future versions of the game—which meant the estate drew significant royalties from video game and app versions that could never have been conceived of when he made the deal.

When her grandmother inherited the estate, she made some wildly lucrative investments that had paid off in spades. Then Dory, her mother, the only child of an only child, inherited everything. She made wise investments of her own, and the fortune had only grown under her watchful eye.

Still, her parents' money philosophy had always been "easy come, easy go" and as such, they always expected Gretchen to work for what she wanted. Growing up, she had chores and part time jobs like the majority of her peers did.

Gretchen was very conscious of how fortunate she was, not only to have grown up never wondering where her next meal might come from, but also to have parents who instilled a solid work ethic in her.

She breezed through the front door. "Hello?"

Footsteps thundered down the stairs. "Mommy!"

Gretchen reached out and caught Abby as she leaped off the bottom step. "Hey, speed racer, your hair's all wet."

"I just took my bath."

Dory appeared at the upstairs railing. "We were just about to blow dry."

Abby scrunched up her face. "It's too loud."

"Yes, but if you go to bed with wet hair, you'll end up with a tangled rat's nest in the morning."

"So?"

"So then it'll hurt when we brush it out."

Abby shrugged dramatically and declared, "Then we won't brush it."

Dory clucked her tongue. "You sound exactly like your mother did when she was your age."

"Ugh, not another boring story about Mom."

"Hey, now." Gretchen shook her head and looked at her mom. "Thanks for watching her today. We weren't expecting it to take so long, but one of the new volunteers had a great idea for showcasing the senior animals. Hopefully we can find some of them their forever homes."

"Like Walter?" Abby asked.

"Exactly." Gretchen smoothed Abby's wild hair back from her forehead.

Walter was the nine year old pug they'd rescued a year earlier after an elderly client of Lincoln's was moved to an assisted living facility and could no longer care for him. He was the sweetest gentleman, and Gretchen gladly sent him updates and pictures of Walter regularly.

Abby danced away, toward the kitchen, singing a song about snacks. Definitely a kid after Gretchen's own heart. "Snacks?"

"We made Rice Krispies treats," Dory said.

"My favorite." She followed Abby to the kitchen and helped herself to a huge marshmallow treat with miniature chocolate chips sprinkled over the top. "Yum."

"Grandma let me put the chocolate chips on."

"Good job."

Abby side-eyed her grandmother and added, "She made me use a spoon."

Dory put her hands on her hips and cocked her head. "Because you wanted to dump the whole bag on them."

"So?"

"So that would have been a mess."

Gretchen popped the last bite in her mouth. "This was just the right amount of chocolate chips."

Abby grumbled, "I guess."

The front door opened and closed, followed by a loud exclamation of, "BRRR!" from Gretchen's dad.

"Grandpa!" Abby scrambled down off the chair and raced down the hall.

Dory called out, "Brian, blow dry her hair, would you, please?"

"Sure," he called back.

"So, Mom," Gretchen said as she put her dirty glass in the dishwasher.

"Yes?"

"Can you hang with Abby Friday night?"

Dory immediately perked up and raised an eyebrow. "And why might you be asking?"

"Don't get your hopes up."

"Yes, we can watch her, what do you have going on?"

She glanced toward the hallway. "I sort of have a date." She held up a hand before her mom got the wrong idea. "But it's not really a date."

Dory leaned her hip against the counter and crossed her arms. "A date that's not a date. How exactly does that work?"

"Because it's with Lincoln."

Dory's head jerked slightly with surprise. She stood up straight and crossed her arms. An eyebrow inched upward. "Lincoln? You're going out with Lincoln? Really?" She was entirely too excited about this.

"Not really-really. You know he's been getting a lot better with his anxiety and he actually went on a date last night but it crashed and burned in a most spectacular fashion. Mostly because he had Alex, Oren, and Noah in his ear. Literally. He wore and earpiece and they told him what to say."

Dory put a palm to her face and shook her head. "Oh, no. Which one of them thought that was a good idea?"

"They all went along with it, so apparently all of them. It was bad." She gave her mom a few of the highlights.

"Oh, poor Lincoln. That poor girl."

"So we were talking about it and he said he was going to give up trying again until after the holidays. That's when I suggested we go on some practice dates from now until New Year's. That'll give us both someone to do stuff with, and I'll give him feedback from a dating perspective."

"That's a much better idea than wearing an earpiece. Why on Earth would they tell him to order her dinner? That's a risky proposition when you've been with someone forever, let alone on a first date. What were they thinking?"

"Something about chivalry."

Dory snort-laughed. "Chivalry! More like stupidity."

"We're not blabbing to everyone that it's basically fake dating. We're just going with the basic truth. We're dating casually, nothing serious, no plans for the future. I'm not sure his family is going to like the idea. Now that more he's comfortable talking to people, particularly women, they think he should have no problem being a social butterfly and finding a perfect wife."

"Hmm. I'm sure they mean well. They know he's a great guy so it's hard to imagine not everyone can see it. It's got to be frustrating for him, though."

"It is." Gretchen reached over and slung her arm around her mom's shoulders. "They're not cool like you and dad. No pressure to find a new husband from you guys."

Dory narrowed her eyes. "Only because we have outstanding self-control. You know we want to see you find someone."

"Eventually, maybe. It's hard to think about dating and romance with my schedule."

Dory squeezed her middle. "You mean Abby's schedule."

"Both. Speaking of which, I need to stop by the theater and make sure the ballet dancers don't need anything."

"Ballet dancers?"

"Didn't I tell you? The dance school is using the theater this year for *The Nutcracker* since we have more seating."

"I don't think you mentioned it. You're not doing *A Christmas Carol* this year?"

"Nah. Attendance was way down last year, so I figured people are tired of doing the same thing year after year. We'll take this year off and maybe even next year, and then we'll revisit adding it back onto the schedule. Besides, it'll be nice for our players to have some time off before we start prepping for *The Merchant of Venice*."

"Time off? Do you even know what that is?"

"Do you?" Gretchen fired back with a laugh.

"Touché."

Abby skipped into the kitchen.

"Grab your stuff, kiddo. We're heading home."

"Fiiiiiiiine." Abby groaned and hunched over, letting her arms flop like she was too weak to stand, then lurched out of the room like Quasimodo.

Dory snickered. "Gee, I don't know where she gets her flair for the dramatic."

Gretchen flung her arm across her eyes and wailed, "How dare you attack me so viciously! And unprovoked. Oh, my heart, my soul. The pain. Oh, the searing pain. You have wounded me, wounded me such that I shall never heal! I beg for your mercy. Pull thy dagger from betwixt my shoulder blades."

"Like I said. No idea where she gets it. Baffling, really."

"It's a mystery," Gretchen laughed.

After Abby was in bed, Gretchen curled up on the couch with her cozy afghan and texted Jody.

> You'll never guess what happened today.

> You and Abby adopted six more dogs.

> LOL No, she was at Mom's or that might have happened.

> You finally cleaned out the back closet.

> If that ever happens, assume I've been abducted by aliens.

I give up.

I have a date Friday.

A what???? NOW I think you've been abducted by aliens. Are you signaling for help? Blink twice if you need me to save you.

She was still typing a reply when the incoming call buzzed. "Ha, ha, you're very funny."

"Do we need to do a video call so I can see if you have lizard eyes? Tell me something only Gretchen would know."

"How about that I love you even when you drive me crazy."

Jody abruptly change the subject. "By the way, that case of extra dark roast you ordered came in today."

"Dark roast? That stuff is disgusting, what are you even talking about?" For a second she thought Jody was on the phone with the wrong person.

"Whew, it really is you."

"Very funny."

"Just checking. Now fill me in. How did you get a date today? Weren't you helping at the shelter?"

"Yes."

"Did some really cute guy come in and adopt a dog and you just couldn't resist?"

"Not exactly."

"Ooooh, so a really cute guy came in and he couldn't resist you."

"No. You're getting farther away."

"You're killing me here. Spill. Leave nothing out."

"The date isn't for me."

"What?" The confusion and impatience was ramping up, if Jody's voice was any indication.

"I was talking to Lincoln. He had a disaster of a date last night. Like epic, sell everything and move to a monastery in Tibet, monumentally, awfully bad. Like… *bad*."

"It couldn't have been that bad."

"Alex and Oren and Noah were guiding him through an earpiece."

"What?!" Jody's shriek was so loud she half-expected it to wake Abby up.

"Yeah."

"Oh, no."

"He was pretty discouraged. So I suggested I help him."

"Please tell me you're not using the earpiece."

"No. I'm going to go on a few dates with him and sort of coach him on how to date."

"Huh? Won't that be super awkward if you go along on his dates and coach him through? Where did you come up with that cockamamie scheme?"

Gretchen couldn't figure out where her explanation had gone so wrong. "No, no. That would be really weird. This is just me and Lincoln. Essentially dating. Each other."

The silence stretched so long Gretchen pulled her phone away to make sure the call hadn't disconnected.

Jody finally said, "Let me get this straight. You're going to date Lincoln. In some bizarre fake practice dating thing that you both think sounds like a good idea?"

"It is a good idea."

She blew out an audible breath. All teasing left her voice. "It's a terrible idea. You should not do this."

"Too late. Our first date is next Friday."

"Date," she scoffed.

"It's a good thing. Lincoln gets some practice and I get to go out and do stuff. It's going to be great."

"Yeah, until one of you forgets it's supposed to be fake."

"Don't be ridiculous." That wasn't even a possibility.

"Hmm."

"No hmm. I'm serious, Jody, it's going to be fine."

"If you want my advice, I'd cancel and call this off. Something is bound to go wrong."

Jody's hesitation gave her pause, but only for a moment. "I think it's going to be great."

Chapter Six

Lincoln adjusted the plate Corinne had just placed in front of him for his weekly late breakfast, early lunch, definitely not brunch, with the guys. Sonny's Diner had the best bacon cheeseburger and fries. But before he could start to eat, he had to tell the guys what was up. "I'm taking Gretchen on a date." He regretted the words as soon as they blurted out of his mouth.

Three pairs of eyes swiveled and lasered onto him. Beside him, Oren's jaw dropped, and across the table of their booth, Noah and Alex wore the same stunned expression.

"Don't take it the wrong way."

"Yo, how many ways can we take it?" Alex demanded.

"She's helping me." He held up a hand. "Let me back up and fill you in."

Noah dropped his fork onto his plate. "Yeah, man, spill all the tea."

Alex rolled his eyes. "Spill the tea? You watch too much reality television."

"Only two more episodes of *Single No More* until we find

out if Jordyn chooses Mack or Drake. Becky's hooked on the stuff."

Oren snorted. "Yeah, blame Becky."

For half a second, Lincoln thought they'd forgotten about his comment.

Noah tapped the table. "Enough of that. Lincoln, what the heck are you talking about?"

He took a deep breath to calmly explain. "It came out wrong. Gretchen's going to help me figure out how to date. We're going to go on a few dates between now and New Year's and she'll give me feedback on how I'm doing."

"What do you need her for? I thought *we* were helping you learn how to date." Alex looked offended.

"You guys suck," he said with a laugh.

"Pffft. We had a few minor blips, but you can't blame us for your card being expired."

Lincoln conceded the point. "No, I can't blame you for that. But the rest of it?"

Oren held his hands up. "You got what you paid for."

Lincoln laughed. "I don't think I did. You guys got pizza, and I got my butt handed to me."

"We are all in successful relationships, so we do have some expertise to share." Alex grumbled.

Noah snorted. "Expertise? Come on, man. We all got lucky."

Oren nodded in agreement. "I think 'expertise' is over-selling it."

"How's this Gretchen thing going to work?"

Lincoln shrugged. "I'm taking her out Friday night. I asked where she wanted to go, but she told me I had to plan everything like it was a real date." He scrubbed a hand down over his face. "Which is when I asked her if I should act like she was an actual woman."

Oren snickered. "Bet she loved that."

"I don't think I'll ever figure out how to stop saying stupid stuff. I mean, I knew what I meant, and I think she knew what I meant, but it came out all wrong."

Oren shook his head. "Bad news. Saying stupid stuff is part and parcel of life. You can get better at it, but it never really goes away. Just ask Chandler. She wants to strangle me on a weekly basis."

"Yep," Alex added. "The other day Avery asked me how I manage to tie my own shoes after I said something stupid. Like really stupid."

"What'd you say?" Noah asked.

Alex's cheeks turned red. "We're talking about Lincoln here."

"Nah, man, you brought it up. What'd you say?"

"I made the colossal error of saying out loud that I like my mom's meatloaf better than hers."

Noah and Oren groaned and winced. Lincoln wasn't sure why that was so awful. He said, "Okay, tell me why that's wrong. If your mom's meatloaf tastes better, then what's the issue?"

Oren blinked at him a few times. "It's saying her time and effort isn't good enough. What she did doesn't measure up."

Lincoln caught on. "So you should just eat it and not say anything?"

All three of the men chorused, "Yes!"

Alex told them the rest of the story. "I knew better. Her meatloaf was fine, but I mentioned that my mom puts onions in her meatloaf and makes some kind of sauce she puts on top. I should have stopped there, but Avery said maybe she'd get the recipe from my mom. I did not realize she was being sarcastic and that I'd hurt her feelings, so stupid me, I gushed about how that was a great idea because Mom's meatloaf is delicious."

Noah nodded. "Implying that Avery's was not."

Oren agreed. "Exactly."

Lincoln sighed. "Why is everything so complicated? It shouldn't be a big deal if you like your mom's meatloaf better."

"It's not," Alex said. "The big deal is that I dismissed Avery's effort. A week or so ago, I mentioned I was hungry for meatloaf. She went to the effort of finding a recipe online and making it just because she wanted to do something nice for me. She wasn't upset because I ultimately prefer my mom's meatloaf, because she wasn't even crazy about this particular recipe herself. She was upset because I didn't show her the appreciation she deserved for her thoughtfulness."

Oh. That made a lot of sense. "What I'm hearing is that I shouldn't say anything to anyone at all, ever."

"Pretty much." Alex drained the last of his soda.

Noah snickered. "Nah, don't listen to him. Just be yourself. Be nice, and if you say something wrong, own up to it and do better."

Oren added, "This is a cakewalk next to all the hard work you've done with your anxiety. It's gotten to the point where it mostly feels natural to small talk with people, right?"

"Yeah."

"Same idea. As you figure out a sort of rhythm of how dating works, you'll get more comfortable. I think practicing with Gretchen is a great idea. She's really good at constructive feedback. I'll be honest. We've had some players I didn't think could cut it in the theater, but with Gretchen's coaching, they've ended up being really good actors."

Corinne refilled their drinks and left the check.

Alex snatched it. "It's on me this time." As he fumbled with his wallet, he said, "Just don't forget you've got us, too. Practicing is great, but you'll still need some good advice from a guy's perspective."

Lincoln laughed. "I've got two mushroom fettucine dinners in my fridge to remind me how 'good' your advice is." He made air quotes with his fingers.

"You aren't going to let that go, are you?"

"Not a chance."

On Tuesday, he texted Gretchen.

> I was thinking we could do Carmine's Friday night and maybe catch a movie?

He attached a screenshot of the movie times and showings, then sent the message.

> Carmine's?? Returning to the scene of the crime?

Lincoln's face heated. That had exactly been his thought. Exposure therapy of sorts. Go back to the place he'd gone so wrong and have a do over. Hopefully with a different waiter, and a much, much different outcome. Before he could think of a response, his phone dinged again.

> I love Carmine's. Do you want to see this one?

She sent a picture back with a movie and time circled.

Lincoln didn't even bother to check which movie she'd picked. If she was willing to spend her time helping him out so he could be a functional dating adult, he'd go see anything she wanted.

Sounds good. Pick you up at five thirty?

She sent back a thumbs up emoji and a smiley face and he breathed a sigh of relief. He'd actually expected her to give him a hard time, just to see how he'd handle the situation. Then again, Gretchen wasn't taking a boot camp approach like his friends. At least he hoped she wasn't.

Chapter Seven

When Friday rolled around, Gretchen was a little surprised at how much she was looking forward to the evening with Lincoln. It was almost like getting ready for a real date. She stared into her closet, willing it to toss out the perfect outfit.

Her phone vibrated with an incoming call from Jody that she immediately answered. "Hello to the world's most awesome coffee shop owner and most perfect bestie a girl could ask for. What's up?"

Jody laughed at the greeting. "I keep getting asked how you're feeling about tonight."

Gretchen cocked her head. "Who's asking? How did anybody hear about it?"

Jody snorted. "Oh, please. There are no secrets in Hickory Hollow. Corinne overheard Lincoln at Sonny's with the boys and told Derek, who told Rowan, who told Sarah, who confirmed it with Avery and then told Megan, who told Eric, who told Stewart, who obviously had to run home and tell me. Even the Ladies' Society caught wind of it. Ruth made a special trip in, pretending she was after lemon bars."

"Impressive game of telephone there. What other intel did you get?"

"Unfortunately there were a lot of men in the mix, so most of the critical details were dropped. Basically I heard you and Lincoln figured you might as well date each other since he sucks at it."

"That's... not too far off. I don't want to say he sucks at it—"

"He really does. Or shall we get Sue's unvarnished opinion?"

"Fair."

"Speaking of opinions, I still think this is a terrible idea."

Gretchen stopped flipping hangers back and forth. "I appreciate that, but it's going to be fine. We're just practice dating until New Year's. Then I can give him some feedback and he doesn't have the extra pressure of meeting new people over the holidays."

"That is a good point, I suppose. Who wants to have a second date the week before Christmas? Like, do you have to get them a Christmas gift then? How much do you have to spend on it? So messy."

"Exactly."

"Where are you going?"

"We're going to a movie and to Carmine's."

"Be careful. They're talking about a possible snowstorm blowing in, but I don't think it's supposed to start until late. We could see up to a foot of snow by morning."

"You're kidding."

"I wish. Hopefully they're overpredicting otherwise our Saturday morning crowd will stay home. It's too early for this crap."

"I'm not a fan of the slush and ice, but I do love a good snowstorm."

"And I love you despite that," Jody laughed. "On to important stuff. What are you wearing?"

"Probably jeans and a sweater."

"You should wear those tall black boots with the silver side buckle. They're cute with jeans. Ooh, wear those with your black jeans. Which sweater?"

"I hadn't gotten that far."

"What about that super cute soft gray sweater? Add some of those long silver chains and you'll be good to go."

"Perfect. Now stop by and organize the rest of my life, will you?"

"Ugh, Stewart's blabbing something about me going out to help make coffee. I'll organize your life later, okay?"

"Deal." As soon as she hung up, she opened her weather app. Sure enough, Jody was right. Incoming snowstorm, likely to start around midnight. To emphasize the forecast on her screen, a massive truck roared past the house, spraying pretreatment on the road.

She sighed and turned back to the closet.

"Walter, what do you think?" She held up the gray sweater Jody suggested and a pink one she hadn't had a chance to wear yet.

Walter looked up from his cozy dog bed and sneezed, then went back to sleep.

"You're not very helpful." She ignored Jody's advice and went with the pink sweater. She did, however, put the long silver necklaces on top of her dresser and pulled out the black jeans and tall boots before heading into her office to get some work done for the day.

Walter got up with a huff and followed her to the office, where he immediately plopped down onto his doggie bed. Yes, he had one in pretty much every room in the house.

She was in the middle of adding the first product to the client's website she was building when Walter waddled over and nudged her leg. That was his way of letting her know it was potty time. It also reminded her it was lunchtime.

"Alrighty, let's go for a walk."

For Walter, a walk meant a stroll around the back yard, where he investigated the same bushes and trees he'd been sniffing since he moved in. A cardinal squawked when Walter got too close to the bush his mate was in.

The air was chilly, and Gretchen bit her lip instead of encouraging Walter to stop dawdling. It wasn't his fault she hadn't grabbed her coat. Eventually he did his business and they headed back inside.

"I think it's a sandwich for lunch. What do you think?"

Walter snuffled and cast a longing gaze at the treat jar.

"Oh. Sorry." Gretchen tossed him a treat.

He flopped down on his kitchen doggie bed, right next to the heater vent, where he stayed for the rest of the afternoon.

Gretchen checked the mirror a thousand times. She snapped a selfie and sent it to Jody.

Thoughts???????

Jody's response was almost immediate.

You look gorgeous.

You have to say that.

LOL I'd say it even if I weren't obligated to because it's true. When did you get that sweater??? I LOVE IT!!!

Last time I had Kohl's Cash to use up. LOL

Good choice.

A second later, Jody sent an eye-rolling emoji.

Apparently there are customers who want service from me. So rude.

Gretchen ended her reply with a string of laughing face emojis. Jody adored her customers and loved every minute of interacting with them. Okay, maybe not *every* minute, but most.

She slipped her phone into her back pocket and checked the mirror for the zillionth time, then caught herself. It's not like this was a real date.

When he knocked on the door, she was ready to go.

"Hi." He thrust a fistful of flowers toward her. "I got these. For you. I figured I was supposed to…"

"Thank you. Very nice gesture. I'll put them in water." She carried them to the kitchen. Since she wasn't sure where there might be a vase, she trimmed the stems and stuck them in a big cup.

"You look nice." His voice was loud and high.

"Breathe. You look terrified."

He pulled in a loud breath and pushed it out. Then he did it again. And again.

Gretchen put a hand on his forearm. "That's what we call hyperventilating."

"Sorry. I'm not… I wasn't sure… I don't know how to act."

"Act like my friend Lincoln."

He choked out a humorless laugh. "Your friend Lincoln has issues."

She grabbed her coat and opened the front door. "Don't we all."

Chapter Eight

Lincoln couldn't argue with that. Everybody had their own stuff they had to deal with. He opened the car door for Gretchen, then went around and got in the driver's seat. "Ready?"

"Ready."

He backed out of her driveway and onto the road. "I figured you'd have a clipboard or something."

She laughed heartily. "No. I'm not using a clipboard. I don't have a checklist, and I'm not grading you. If something note-worthy happens, I'll tell you."

He swallowed hard. "Well… I was thinking…" Right now he was thinking that he sounded like an idiot, but he pressed on. "I was thinking that specific feedback would be helpful. Like… written feedback."

"Oh?"

"So, um, I, uh, if it's okay…" He felt her curious gaze burn into the side of his head. "I made a form," he almost shouted.

"A form." She clearly had no clue what he was talking about.

A bead of sweat made its way down his back. "Never mind, forget it."

"Lincoln, breathe. I'm not going to forget it. Just take a second." She reached over and touched his forearm. Her voice was calm, without a trace of judgment, which helped calm his racing heart.

"Sorry."

"Nothing to apologize for."

"I made a form. Sort of like a post-date evaluation. I thought, like, if you have time, maybe we could do feedback that way. I thought it might be... less... awkward."

"Okay."

"I know it's weird."

She squeezed his arm and put her hand back in her lap. "It's not weird. It's very analytical. It makes a lot of sense. Then you can look over it at your leisure."

"I tried to make the questions open-ended."

"Good thinking."

His heart rate was mostly back to normal. It didn't seem like she thought the idea was completely bizarre. Then again, she *was* an actress, maybe she was just really good at hiding what she really thought.

Before he could latch onto that negative thought and ride it to a downward spiral, she said, "Anything interesting going on this weekend?"

"Yeah. Megan called and said the photos are ready, so Ruby, Alyssa, and I are going over to her studio to pick out the pictures for the calendar."

"That was fast."

He nodded. "I almost feel like we're taking advantage of her services. I know she rushed and put in a lot of extra hours for us."

"Megan's amazing. And I am one hundred percent certain she does not feel taken advantage of. She loves giving back."

"And believe me, we appreciate it. She went to the printer on our behalf and got us a big discount. With the sponsors that are advertising on each month, we're actually already in the black for this project, and that's before we've sold a single calendar."

"That's fantastic!" She shifted in her seat. "Be sure to use that in the marketing. Like, one hundred percent of the cost of this calendar is going straight into the rescue. It'll make people feel like they're doing more than if only a dollar or two of the price was actually going to you guys."

He hadn't thought of that. "Every dollar from your purchase of this calendar... Hmm, I'll have to see if we can word it better, but yeah. That's a great point."

"If there are any calendars left, maybe we can put them in the lobby during the *Nutcracker* performance on December fourteenth. But I'm betting you'll sell out right away."

"I hope so." He paused. "Wait. You're doing the *Nutcracker* this year? What happened to *A Christmas Carol*?"

"We put it on hiatus for this year. The dance school asked if they could use the theater for the *Nutcracker* because their stage is getting some much-needed upgrades to the floor and it won't be ready."

"They'll have more seating in your theater, too, won't they?"

"Almost triple. They're doing a good job of promoting it already, so hopefully they get a packed house."

"Is Oren disappointed about not being Scrooge this year?" Lincoln chuckled.

"I think he's more disappointed that Finn won't be Tiny Tim. Chandler, however, is thrilled she doesn't have to do any costumes this month. She's neck-deep in the new pioneer series Nate and Kim's production company is doing."

"I keep wanting to reach out and ask Nate and Kim if they'd do something for us, but I'm sure they gets requests all the time."

"I'll put a bug in Chandler's ear. Isobel works for her, so we can subtly get the word to them. Maybe they'll even think it's their idea."

A smile spread across Lincoln's face. "You're an evil genius."

"You're just now realizing that?"

"I'm just now realizing how deep it runs."

Her warm laughter filled the car. This had to be a good sign, right? He must be on the right track, at least for now. Some of the tension released from his shoulders.

Gretchen pointed through the windshield. "What's that say?"

Up ahead, a blinking sign warned, ROAD CLOSED BAKER ST NO ACCESS.

"Baker Street? Isn't that where we're going?"

"I think it is. Let me check."

Lincoln pulled over to the side of the road as she got her phone out of her purse and tapped to open the most efficient news source ever–social media. A minute later, she said, "Whoa. Look at this."

He leaned over to look at her phone. Photos showed plumes of water shooting three stories into the air from a water main break.

Right in front of Carmine's parking lot.

Which was cattycorner from the movie theater.

His shoulders dropped and he could feel himself starting to get sweaty again. Disappointment bloomed in his chest. "Figures."

"What?"

"Everything was going so well. Now... I guess we have to call it a night."

She stared at him with one eyebrow raised. "Why?"

He gestured to the phone. "Because of that. The restaurant, the movie theater. That was our whole plan."

Gretchen sat back and crossed her arms. "Lincoln. What was the point of this evening?"

He didn't understand the question. "To go to Carmine's and then see a movie."

"No."

Now he *really* didn't get it. Embarrassment and frustration twisted together and made it harder to figure out what she was trying to make him understand. "I don't know what you mean. That was the plan. Eat at Carmine's. See a movie."

"That was the plan, but what was the *point*?"

It felt like he was missing something obvious. "They're the same thing?"

"No. Drill deeper, Lincoln."

His racing thoughts refused to make sense of her request. He stared out the windshield at the blinking sign. What was the point? To go to dinner and a movie. To go on a date. Ah, he suddenly got it. "Okay, the point was to go on a date. To spend time together. I get what you're saying."

"Tonight's lesson is how to roll with the punches. Don't just give up because there's an obstacle."

"But what if a real date wanted to give up and go home?"

"Then it probably wasn't a great match anyway. You say, 'Are you sure? We could do whatever instead.' And if she still says she wants to go home, take her home. But you don't have to give up right off the bat, because nine times out of ten, the date–especially a first date–is about getting to know each other and not the actual destination."

That made a lot of sense.

"I think it all goes back to pause and breathe instead of making snap decisions."

"Yeah." He felt like he'd gotten a demerit on his report card.

"For all intents and purposes, this is a real date. Instead of what iffing, talk to your date."

His tongue felt too big for his mouth. It took a few breaths to focus on the fact that this was Gretchen. His friend, who had his best interests at heart. Not a stranger sizing him up as a potential partner. The tightness eased a bit. "It looks like we're not going to Carmine's. I didn't have a plan B in mind. Is there somewhere in particular you'd rather go?" The words felt stilted.

Gretchen smiled and gave him a wink. "I had my heart set on Italian."

He wracked his brain for a solution. It came to him and he said, "It's only another ten minutes to Olive Garden. How about that?"

"Oooh, unlimited salad and breadsticks. Sold."

The rest of the tension in his neck melted away. He'd half expected her to issue some sort of follow up challenge. Maybe that wasn't fair. He was assuming she was planning to test him along the way, but that didn't make sense. It's not like she caused the water main break to see how he'd react.

He put the car back into drive and pulled onto the road. Instead of driving toward Carmine's, he made a left and headed to Olive Garden.

They changed plans on the fly.

That wasn't so bad, was it?

Chapter Nine

She had to admit, after his initial freak-out, Lincoln handled the change of plans better than she'd expected. Sometimes it was almost a disadvantage to have known him for so long because it was hard to separate Lincoln now, who could talk to almost anyone with just a hint of anxiety, and Lincoln a few years ago, who could barely speak to anyone outside of his closest friends. Including one event where he almost got arrested because he couldn't explain his situation to the officer. Thank goodness Avery had arrived and helped.

The Olive Garden parking lot was packed. Lincoln found a parking space at the far end of the lot. Despite the cold, people were waiting on the sidewalk for their tables to be called.

The area was lit up with bright signs as far as the eye could see. Gretchen's attention landed on a marquee sign at the entrance of the mall across the street. "Hey, check it out. Five dollar movies."

"Where? Oh. I haven't been in the mall for years."

"Really? Abby loves the mall. It's a shame, though. Lots of vacant stores. I wonder how much longer it'll last." She could remember spending a lot of her teenage years hanging out at the mall.

He asked, "Did you want to see what's playing? I bet the wait is at least an hour here."

Look at him, rolling with another slight inconvenience. "Sure." She pulled out her phone and searched the movies. Triumphantly, she held up her phone. "Check it out. The one we were planning to see is here for five bucks and it starts in twenty minutes."

Lincoln drove over to the mall and parked as close to the theater entrance as he could. They jogged across the parking lot, bought their tickets, popcorn, and soda, and made it into the theater just as the lights went down and the previews started.

Gretchen nudged his arm and pointed up the sloped seating. "Up there."

They made their way to an upper row and settled in the sweet middle seats. Barely a dozen people shared the theater with them, and most of them sat on the lower level, closer to the screen.

"This is great," Gretchen stage whispered. She popped a few kernels of buttery popcorn in her mouth.

Lincoln nodded his agreement, carefully opening his box of Jujyfruits.

Before long, they were both laughing at the on-screen antics of a straightlaced (male) lawyer and an elderly (female) petty criminal who switched bodies during a freak lightning storm on the courthouse stairs. Utterly implausible, and utterly hilarious.

Gretchen tossed her popcorn bag into the trash can in the hallway. "Oh, my goodness. When she was in the lawyer's body and whacked that guy with the cane I thought I'd pee myself."

"How about the really, really confused dog? Those expressions were priceless."

She reached over and touched his arm as they exited the theater into the main mall. "Do you mind if I stop and grab some pretzels? Abby will be over the moon if I give her cinnamon pretzels for breakfast."

"That sounds pretty great."

"I'll be honest, it's only partly for Abby. I will also be over the moon to have cinnamon pretzels for breakfast," she said with a laugh.

"Now that you mention it, that sounds like a great way to start the day."

They walked down the hall to the pretzel kiosk and a few minutes later were heading out the door with their bags of warm cinnamon pretzels.

At the car, Lincoln opened Gretchen's door and closed it when she was in. As he slid into his seat, he said, "Hopefully the Olive Garden crowd is gone."

Gretchen checked her watch. It was just after eight o'clock. "I bet we'll get right in."

The traffic was much lighter, and the parking lot was half-empty.

As she'd expected, they were ushered directly to a booth. A while later, when they'd polished off their desserts, Gretchen tapped the bill. "It wasn't quite Carmine's, but it was much less expensive, and the movies were less than half the price. So plan B turned out to be a pretty good bargain."

Lincoln snatched the bill and put his debit card in the black folder.

"I can pay my half."

"I got it. You can pick up something else later on, okay?"

"Okay."

She wasn't going to make a big deal out of the bill. Everyone knew she had money to burn, and she knew he didn't. But she also knew that money was deeply connected to a person's perception of their strength or whatever, so she was always very conscious of not flaunting her wealth. Especially since it wasn't like she'd earned it herself. Thank you, *Mister Miser*.

They were both quiet on the ride back to Gretchen's, but comfortably. The unlimited salad and breadsticks could have been a meal on their own, but she'd also gotten a delicious fettuccini alfredo and on top of the popcorn, it was pleasantly heavy in her gut and made her sleepy.

She yawned as he pulled into her driveway. "I had a really nice time."

"Me, too. I'll try to do better rolling with the unexpected."

"You did fine. And when the Olive Garden was packed, you rolled with that perfectly."

"I'll, uh, send you the link for the form?"

"Sounds good. Have fun picking the pictures for the calendar tomorrow."

He sat upright, rigid in his seat, and gripped the steering wheel. "Oh no. I'm so sorry."

Confused, Gretchen let go of the door handle and turned in her seat to look at him. "What?"

"I never asked what you were doing this weekend. You asked me and I told you about the pictures, but I never asked you."

She put a hand on his forearm. "Lincoln, it's okay. The conversation just naturally flowed onto different topics."

He didn't look convinced.

"Seriously. I didn't even notice until you said that."

He sighed heavily, his shoulders drooping. "I'm so bad at this."

She squeezed his arm. "No, you're not. You just need some confidence. That's why we're practicing."

"Okay."

"I'm serious. This evening was a lot of fun." She touched the door handle again, which seemed to energize him.

"Hang on!" He jumped out of the car and raced around to her side to open the door.

She stepped out and smiled at him. "Thank you." She'd bring it up later that he didn't need to risk an ankle sprain to open her car door.

"I'll, um, walk you to your door?"

"Sure." She wasn't about to mention that it was unnecessary to escort her to the door. Hopefully it would only take another date or two to help get him out of his head and relax.

As they stood on her porch, she could see him trying to figure out how to end the date, so she took the initiative. "Can I have a hug?"

"Of course."

She squeezed him and stepped back. As she unlocked her door, she said, "Thanks for a great night."

"Yeah, thanks, uh, thank you."

She pushed the door open. "Drive safe."

"Will do. Good night." He gave a little wave and walked back to his car.

Gretchen's phone dinged before he pulled out of the driveway. He'd sent her a link to the form.

She called her mom to see if Abby was ready to be picked up.

"Your dad just made popcorn and started another movie. Can you just get her in the morning?"

Like Gretchen was going to argue with that.

"How was the date-that's-not-a-date?"

"Good. There was a water main leak in front of Carmine's, so we ended up going to Olive Garden instead."

"Ooooh, unlimited salad and breadsticks."

"Exactly." She filled her mom in on the movie and the rest of the evening.

With Abby spending the night with her parents, she decided to treat herself to a bubble bath and a glass of wine. As she soaked, she scrolled through the form on her phone. Holy cow had he been thorough. He had questions about whether he'd been dressed appropriately, whether he'd greeted her correctly, if his conversation had been acceptable... All in all, there were twenty-five questions with spaces for feedback on each.

She clicked the button to turn her phone's screen off. His anxiety came through loud and clear on his questionnaire, and it was making her anxious by proxy. She'd deal with it in the morning when she was rested and refreshed.

Chapter Ten

Lincoln thought he might barf when his email notification popped up early Saturday morning, letting him know Gretchen had filled out the evaluation form for their date.

Scout, Margo and Connor's black Labrador, nudged his leg then looked expectantly at the treat container on the counter. They'd just come back from Scout's morning walk, where he'd done his potty business, chased a squirrel, barked at the neighbor's cat who always antagonized him through the window, greeted a jogger, ate something questionable from underneath a bush, and sniffed every square inch of the entire neighborhood. He obviously deserved a treat after that much hard work.

"Sorry Scout. Here you go." He handed him a treat and scratched his head. "Good boy."

Scout wagged his tail in agreement and leaned against Lincoln for more head scratches before running off to find one of his many tennis balls.

Lincoln pulled the money off the clip on the fridge and smiled at the note.

Thanks so much for getting Scout last minute!

It was definitely no bother. Scout was one of his favorite clients.

He decided not to look at the feedback until he'd finished the other two clients he had for the day. The next stop was an obnoxious little chihuahua with a Napoleon complex. He barked ferociously the whole time Lincoln attached his leash, and then talked a lot of smack at the pitbull in the fenced-in yard across the street. Lincoln nudged him along the sidewalk. Eventually he did his potty business and they headed back to the house, plastic bag in hand.

The last client for the day was easy peasy. He stopped at Caretti's Coffee Shop and got Mrs. Middleton's favorite flavored tea. She had a hard time getting out these days, so she hired Lincoln to come by once a week to refill her cat's automatic feeder and bring her food and litter from his aunt's store, For Pet's Sake. Luckily for him, she had a housekeeper that took care of the litterbox duties. Not that he wouldn't do it, but he certainly wouldn't complain that he didn't have to.

"Hi, Mrs. Middleton."

"In here," she called from the living room. When he held out the cup, she beamed. "You brought my fancy tea. You're such a good boy."

He checked the automatic feeder and spent a few minutes playing with the cat, until the cat got bored and curled up on the sofa, like he usually did.

"What do I owe you?"

"Same as always," he answered.

Mrs. Middleton fished in the drawer beside her chair and pulled a five dollar bill out of her wallet. "This can't be enough," she scolded.

She was right, especially when the tea set him back six bucks, but he couldn't dream of charging her more when she'd done so much over the years for the animal rescue. "Nope, that's right." He slipped the five into his pocket. "You can settle up the food and litter with Aunt Midge. For me, I charge a lot less for cats since I don't have to walk them."

She perked up. "Do you walk a lot of dogs?"

"I do. In fact, I just walked a Labrador and then a chihuahua before I came over here." He pulled out his phone and showed her a picture of Scout.

"Oh, what a beautiful dog."

"He belongs to Margo Lewis. The veterinarian."

She smiled. "She takes good care of my sweet boy. We're lucky to have her."

"We sure are."

"Too bad she's married. You two would make a good match. You're both so good with animals."

He made some kind of half-laugh, half-grunt awkward noise in response.

"Do you have a nice young lady? You should."

"Well, no, not, I mean, well, I had a date last night."

"You did?" She clasped her hands across her heart. "Tell me all about it."

He gave her a short version, leaving out the part where it was a fake practice date, and the part where there was a date evaluation form he was terrified to look at.

"That sounds lovely. Are you meeting with her again?"

"Yes, next Saturday."

She nodded and muttered, "Good, good."

Her daughter arrived, saving him from further conversation. He considered himself lucky at the interruption. A month or so ago, he'd ended up sitting in her living room letting her chat for almost two hours because he was too polite to leave, and she was too lonely to let him go.

Like he normally did on Saturdays, he finished his client visits, then went back home and made lunch to use up the last of the week's leftovers. He polished off his leftover meatloaf, a gift from his mom, who made the best meatloaf in the world, no matter how good Alex's mom's or Avery's was, and got settled on the couch with his laptop. His stomach rolled. He closed his eyes and took a deep breath. No more putting it off.

He opened the form.

He'd tried to cover everything he could think of. Gretchen had graciously responded to each question. Yes, he'd dressed appropriately. Yes, he'd arrived on time. Yes, his car was clean enough and smelled fine. Yes, he'd planned an acceptable date. Yes, yes, yes.

As much as he'd been terrified of the responses, he found himself a little disappointed that they were all answered in the positive. He knew he had a lot to work on, and how was he supposed to improve if he didn't have feedback? That was the deal, right?

Oh. Wait.

Yep, he'd gotten way too comfortable, way too fast.

There was a whole paragraph in response to his question: How did I make you feel on our date?

This is a really hard question to answer. I know you're hoping for Good! Great! and while yes, I had a good time, I guess my answer has to be... It's complicated. First of all, you aren't responsible for my emotions or anyone else's. It's not something you can control. I hope you don't take this the wrong way, but part of the time I felt... responsible. It wasn't just a date, which of course I knew going into it, but I spent a lot of time feeling like I had to constantly be "on" to coach you and be on the lookout for every little way I could give you feedback. I felt like I was there to—not babysit *exactly—but to stay hypervigilant to what you were doing/saying/feeling. Like I had to manage your feelings.*

Even now, I'm second guessing whether to keep typing or just delete this because I don't want to hurt your feelings. To me, dating should be relaxing. Getting to know someone. Especially when it's not a "real" date so there should be a lot LESS pressure for us, not more.

Lincoln stared at the screen. Ouch. He certainly hadn't intended to make Gretchen feel so responsible for him. He hadn't planned to put pressure on her. In his mind, he thought they'd go out and then maybe she could reflect and give him feedback afterwards.

It didn't occur to him that she'd be feeling like she had to monitor every moment, even though that made sense now that he considered it. He'd asked for help, so of course Gretchen would do her best to help.

Well, crud. Maybe this wasn't such a good idea after all. He didn't want this little experiment to adversely affect their friendship. Maybe he should dial back his expectations as far as getting feedback and just focus on the basics. How to listen. How to ask the right questions. How to not put his foot in his mouth.

That one was going to be a challenge.

Chapter Eleven

Gretchen worried about Lincoln's reaction to her responses to the form he'd created for all of five minutes until a frantic phone call from a client demanded all her attention.

"Gretchen, I don't *knowwhattodoitquitworking*," she sobbed.

"Whoa, whoa, slow down. Take a deep breath." She double checked the caller ID to make sure she was talking to Phoebe, because she'd never heard her so upset. "Okay, what happened?" She clicked into her master list of client files to grab the direct link to Phoebe's website.

"I don't have any orders. I haven't for almost a week. I thought it was a little weird, but I was so busy and then I got all these nasty DMs from people not getting their stuff and I don't know what to do."

Gretchen put on her soothing customer service voice. "We'll get it figured out, don't you worry."

Phoebe sniffled and apologized for bothering her on a Saturday.

"It's no trouble. I'm getting logged into the admin panel right now." She clicked and scrolled until she found the admin access she was looking for.

"Umm, Phoebe? Have you tried logging into your site?"

"No?"

"Who has administrator access to your site?"

"Just you."

Gretchen squeezed her eyes shut, calling on patience. Phoebe was a lovely woman with a very nice business selling custom candles and bejeweled tumblers, but she wasn't particularly tech savvy. "No, I'm the master admin for the site itself, but who is able to help you with your orders and day to day stuff?"

"Well… no one, now."

Gretchen saw the problem. Whoever had access to Phoebe's site had changed the email addresses and passwords. "Who *was* helping you?"

"My boyfriend. But we broke up."

"Did you go in and remove his access to your site?" She already knew the answer.

"I told him he wasn't allowed to go in it."

"But you didn't log in and delete his stuff?"

There was an uncomfortably long pause. "No?"

"Okay. I can fix it on my end this time." Gretchen reminded her, "Normally there would be a fee, per our contract, since this is outside my typical scope of work. What is your business email address?" She shook her head. The ex-boyfriend had changed it to screwyouphoebe@screwyouphoebe.com, which is where the order notifications had been trying to go.

Luckily, the backlog of orders was duplicated on the site and easily accessible.

Phoebe recited her email address, which Gretchen carefully typed in and verified. "Okay, you're going to get an avalanche of orders. If it were me, I'd reach out to everyone, let them know there was a glitch with your ordering system, and take it from there. I also went ahead and reset your password. You'll need to log in and change it to something new. Do *not* use any passwords you've already used." She bit her tongue before offering advice on allowing random people–specifically new boyfriends–to have access to her website. She deleted the boyfriend's access, and took a quick peek around the website to make sure he hadn't wreaked any other havoc. If she had a nickel for every time someone trusted their site to someone untrustworthy, she'd probably bring in more money than the *Mister Miser* royalties.

"Oh! My phone is pinging like crazy. Thank you so much. You're a genius." Phoebe sniffled again. "I didn't know what to do. I'm so sorry to bother you on a weekend."

"Phoebe. It's not a bother at all. It's all fixed, good as new." She waited while Phoebe stopped blowing her nose. "Guess you'll be busy packing orders for the rest of the weekend," she added cheerfully.

"I guess so." Phoebe managed a laugh. "Thanks to you."

She'd no more than hung up with Phoebe than the phone rang again. This time, though, it was someone trying to reach her about her car's extended warranty. She hung up and shoved her phone into her back pocket.

That was enough business for a Saturday morning. She hopped in the car and drove the not-quite-a-mile to her parents' house.

Abby was watching cartoons. Her two ponytails bounced as she jumped off the couch and ran over to throw herself at Gretchen. "Mommy!"

Gretchen scooped her up. "Good morning, sunshine."

"Good morning, rainbow."

"Good morning, puppy."

Abby giggled. "Good morning, fish."

"Good morning, cupcake."

"Good morning, pillow."

"Good morning, fuzzy blanket."

"Good morning, socks," Abby said.

Gretchen laughed and reached down to tickle Abby's bare foot. "What would you know about socks? You never wear them."

Abby screeched and yanked her foot back. "I do, too."

Dory leaned on the door frame. "You'd go barefoot in the snow if we let you."

"Would not!" She wiggled until Gretchen set her down, then ran off to the stairs.

"How was your date?"

"Good." She filled her mom in on the evening.

"Wait. An evaluation form? That's... thorough."

"Most of it was fine, but I felt bad being totally honest when I answered the question about how I felt on the date. I felt like I was spending a lot of energy managing his emotions."

Her mom shrugged and said, "Didn't you kind of expect that? Like you were going into it as kind of a dating coach?"

"Yes and no. I expected that if I noticed something, I'd point it out. I didn't expect there to be a quiz at the end."

"I think it's kind of cute. Very practical."

"In theory. In reality it was kind of odd."

Dory shrugged again. "At least you didn't have to write an essay."

Gretchen laughed. "That's probably next." She walked to the staircase and yelled, "Abby, let's go. We're stopping at Jody's."

Abby yelled back, "Does she have cupcakes?"

"No idea. We'll have to see what's left."

Dory said, "Oooh, tell her I need more of those amazing cream cheese lemon bars I got the other day. They're so good. Your dad only got one of them."

"One? Didn't you get a dozen?"

She snickered. "I might have."

Gretchen sighed and grabbed Abby's backpack. "Weren't you just telling me the doctor said you need to keep an eye on your cholesterol?"

She waved a hand dismissively. "I don't get bloodwork again for six months. They'll be out of my system by then."

Brian, her dad, came in the door and grinned. "Hey, kiddo."

"Hey, dad."

He leaned over and kissed Dory's cheek. "Car's inspected for another year." He looked at Gretchen. "How are your tires? I don't want you driving around on worn tires."

"Beats me."

Abby bounded down the stairs. "Is Lincoln your boyfriend?"

"What? No."

"Grandpa says you need a boyfriend."

"Dad!"

"Way to rat me out, kid." He tried to look innocent and pointed at the door. "I'm going to just run out and take a look at your tires."

"Dad. Don't be telling my daughter I need a boyfriend."

"Gotta make sure they're not worn."

"Dad."

He slipped out the door.

"Mom."

"Hey, don't look at me. I had nothing to do with it."

Abby giggled and sing-songed, "Grandpa's in trouble, Grandpa's in trouble."

When they got out to the car, Gretchen buckled Abby in her seat while Brian pretended to be busy inspecting her tires.

"Dad."

"That left front's looking a little worn."

She crossed her arms and cocked her head. "Father."

"Daughter."

"Don't be telling Abby I need a man. I'm doing perfectly fine."

He pulled her in for a hug. "I never said you need a man. I said it's nice that you're going on dates, even if Lincoln isn't your boyfriend. You could do worse, though, as boyfriends go."

"I'm not doing worse or better, because Lincoln's not my boyfriend and we're not actually dating." She breathed in her dad's comforting cologne. "Besides. Who could ever measure up to you?"

His laugh rumbled in his chest. "No mere mortal."

"I'm fine, Dad, really."

"Of course you are. But don't settle for fine instead of happy." He squeezed her tight. "You can spare me the lecture about being a strong independent woman who doesn't need a man. If I thought you were content and satisfied being single, I'd keep my mouth shut. But I know you'd like a partner and I just want you to know that your mom and I think it's time for you to focus on yourself a little. We're here to support you however we can. Maybe you should try Tingle or something."

Gretchen snorted a laugh as she pulled back. "Do you mean Tinder? I think that's more for casual hookups."

He made a face. "Oh. Well, what do I know? I haven't dated in forty-five years, and God-willing, I'll never have to."

"Thanks, Dad. Maybe after the holidays I'll try Tingle."

"Maybe there's a Christmas dating app."

"Don't say it."

"I have to. Jingle."

Gretchen pressed her hands over her eyes. "You did not."

"Maybe there are fat, jolly dudes on the on the Single Kringle app."

"Please stop."

"Fine, I'll stop."

That was too easy. She spread her fingers to look at him. "Why?" she asked suspiciously.

"I ran out of words that rhyme."

"Thank goodness."

"Oooh, maybe a nice roofer on Shingle?"

"Dad!" She smacked his shoulder. "I'm getting out of here."

He laughed and walked up to the front door, where he waited, waving, until she pulled away.

"Grandpa's funny," Abby said.

"He certainly is." Funny, kind, loyal, protective, loving, devoted to his wife after almost five decades… all the things a man should be for his family. He set the bar really, really high.

Chapter Twelve

At Sonny's Diner, Lincoln scooted across the booth until he was smooshed against the window. Oren and Alex slid in beside him, while Noah and Eric squeezed in beside Nate. They'd been discussing some social media promos for the shelter.

Corinne came by with menus. "Corner booth just opened up. More room if you want it." She jerked her thumb over her shoulder.

The guys looked at each other, then nodded and slid back out of the booth, heading for the corner.

Lincoln shrugged at Nate. "Sorry, I wasn't expecting a crowd."

Nate laughed. "Fine by me. I haven't had much guy time lately with the new shows in the pipeline." Nate and Kim's production company had taken off like a rocket. As much as he didn't want to, Nate capitalized on his fame as Qaaxaag, the alien character he'd played on the international mega super hit *Daystar Rising*. Before they met, Kim had been a local celebrity in her own right, with her web show *15 Minutes to Fabulous*, devoted to all manner of crafts, cooking, and lifestyle tips and hacks that could be done in fifteen minutes. When the two of them joined forces, success was pretty much inevitable.

Lincoln admired Nate's ability to be perfectly normal in the face of overwhelming fame. "So yeah, anything you guys could do for the shelter would be awesome."

"Who's your social media coordinator?" Nate asked as they crossed to the bigger booth. "I'll have my assistant get with her."

"Alyssa. I'll get you her number." Lincoln pulled out his phone to find her number. After he gave it to Nate, he made himself a note to make sure the production company got some extra shout-outs as a supporter of the rescue.

Once they were settled, Corinne handed out the menus and took their drink orders. "Refills?" She pointed to the cups Lincoln and Nate had carried with them from their original table.

"Yes, thanks," they both answered. Luckily, they hadn't been seated long enough to have ordered their lunch.

Oren drummed his fingers on the tabletop. "I'm anxious to hear how last night went."

Lincoln blushed and perked up simultaneously. "I figured you would have had all the details by now."

Alex blew out a sarcastic breath. "We're not the Ladies' Society, you know."

The guys laughed and joked about how the ladies always seemed to know everything about everyone. In real time. It could be a little disconcerting.

By the time their sandwiches were delivered, the guys were coming back around to grill Lincoln about his date-not-date with Gretchen.

Lincoln tossed a fry into his mouth. "We had a couple of hiccups. When the road was closed and we couldn't go to

Carmine's like we'd planned, I sort of panicked and offered to just call the whole thing off."

"Whoa."

"Kind of jumped the gun a little."

"Just go someplace else."

"Carmine's has the best shrimp ravioli." Alex added and everyone's attention turned to him. "What? They do. But anyway, go on."

"That was pretty much her reaction. She told me to work on going with the flow. We ended up going to Olive Garden and the same movie was playing in the mall theater, so we still got to see it, and we still had Italian."

Noah said, "Heck yeah, unlimited salad and breadsticks."

The entire conversation veered off into the obvious superiority of Italian food, and whether Olive Garden actually qualified as such. The consensus was not really, but close enough. And no matter what you called it, it was delicious.

"Anyway," Oren said, bringing them back to the topic at hand.

"Everything was good. I took her home and she said it was a great date. But then I read her comments on the form, and—"

"Form?"

"Comments?"

"Wait, like an evaluation?"

"Crimeny, you gave her a performance evaluation to fill out?"

"She actually filled it out?"

Lincoln held up a hand. "I told her it was completely up to her if she wanted to fill it out. I thought it might be helpful, in case she had some things to say she didn't want to say directly to me."

"I can't decide if it's stupid or genius," Nate said.

Alex said, "A little of both, I think."

BAD ADVICE · 79

"Anyway," Oren said, "what about her comments?"

Lincoln shifted uncomfortably. "It's awkward."

Noah chuckled. "A survey is awkward. What was on it, anyway?"

The rest of the guys murmured their agreement, which made Lincoln feel even more embarrassed. Why had he given her a form to fill out? And why, why, why had he ever mentioned it to these guys? "Never mind," he muttered.

"No, no, come on. We're here to help you."

He pulled a long sip of his soda. "Okay. It was basically just a bunch of questions about how I did on the date. Did I dress okay, did I act okay, did I do anything inappropriate, that sort of thing. And almost everything she said yes, yes, yes, no feedback on anything. But there was a question about how I made her feel on the date and that's the one that kind of went off the rails."

"Uh oh."

"What happened?"

"What did she say?"

He held up a hand against the flurry of incoming questions. "I don't know. I mean, I kind of... here. I'll just read it to you." He pulled out his phone, opened the form, and read her response to them. When he finished, he said, "I never expected her to 'manage' my emotions or whatever. I just wanted her to let me know what I was doing wrong since I've obviously never been very successful at dating."

The guys pondered her response and dissected it as they ate their lunch. In the end, they all arrived at the same conclusion.

Lincoln needed to follow *their* sage advice and everything would work out fine.

Chapter Thirteen

Gretchen and Abby went through the doors of Caretti's Coffee Shop as Jody handed the last customer of the day a to go cup. She looked over and grinned. "Stew will be back any minute. I sent him over to Guacamoles to get us lunch."

Abby made a face. "What's gua... guac... what is that?"

"Guacamole is that green stuff I put on nachos, but Jody's talking about Holy Guacamole. It's the name of that taco restaurant."

"Oooooh, tacos. I like tacos."

"Me, too." Mindy, Jody's nine-year-old daughter, agreed. "I like lots of salsa on mine."

Abby nodded vigorously. "Salsa is so good."

As the door closed behind the customer, Mindy darted over and locked it. Her ponytail bounced as she spun around. "You can help me wipe tables if you want."

Abby beamed and followed her behind the counter, where Mindy equipped her with a spray bottle of cleaning solution and a rag.

The girls wiped down the tables and chairs while Gretchen logged onto the store's website with her laptop, and Jody boxed up the few remaining baked goods in the case. "You want anything? Stew's mom is taking the leftovers to her bridge club."

"No thanks." Gretchen glanced over the trays. "Oh, wait, are those lemon bars? My mom is bananas for those lemon bars."

Jody said, "Her and everyone else. I had to triple–*triple*–my order this past time, and as you can see, there are only four bars left. I'm thinking the novelty is going to wear off soon, so I didn't order quite as many for next week." She put the lemon bars into a small box and set them on Gretchen's table. "It seems like they'd be a better seller in the spring, but no, it's my top seller in November. Makes zero sense."

"Thank you. Mom will love you forever."

"She already does," Jody scoffed with a laugh. She finished boxing up the few remaining baked goods, then settled in beside Gretchen. She pointed to the screen. "This is what I was talking about. The drop down menu doesn't want to work."

"Oh. I see what you mean." She shook her head as if clearing out the cobwebs. "For some reason I kept thinking the issue was with your food menu, and I was really confusing myself."

"Ack, I guess I wasn't very clear, was I?"

Gretchen logged into the admin panel and sussed out the problem. "That should fix it. Did you need anything updated while I'm in here?"

"I think we should add the honey mint tea to the front page. I've been pushing it on social media since we're in cold and flu season."

"Is that the one with rosemary and thyme in it?"

"Yes."

"I'll grab a pouch for mom before we leave. She loves it."

"Me, too. I like to put a lemon wedge in it."

"Which would go great with her unseasonal lemon bars."

"Bingo."

"Hey, Mom, should I erase the specials?" Mindy pointed to the a-frame chalkboard sign standing next to the front door.

"Yes, please."

Mindy skipped to the back room and came back a moment later with two damp rags. She handed one to Abby. "You can do the back side."

The girls had just finished cleaning the chalkboard when Stew pulled in. Mindy unlocked the door and let Stew in with his two bulging bags of food. He held them aloft and announced, "We've got tacos, empanadas, burritos, and nachos."

Jody said, "Did you get extra sour cream for Tess?"

"Of course." He leaned down to give her a quick kiss, then set the bags on the counter.

He spread the food out and set a stack of paper plates and napkins beside the feast. "Help yourself."

Abby looked at Gretchen, waiting for permission to dig in.

"What do I owe you for lunch?" Gretchen asked Jody.

"Don't be silly. You fixed my website last minute on a Saturday. Lunch is the least we can do."

Stewart overheard. "You got it fixed?"

Gretchen answered, "Yeah, it was something with one of the new plug-ins. Easy fix on my end."

"Thank goodness."

Samantha and Darren, their twins, showed up a few minutes later with their middle daughter, Tess, in tow. The kids inhaled their food, then got to work behind the counter.

"They're in charge of the weekly deep-clean. We pay them double, so they don't grumble too much. And Stew supervises, so I am officially done for the day."

Mindy put Abby to work refilling sugar containers with a funnel.

Jody poured two cups of tea and sat down across from Gretchen. "Try this. It's my apple cranberry Thanksgiving blend."

Gretchen inhaled deeply. "Smells amazing." She took a sip. "Tastes amazing. I don't think you've ever made a blend I didn't like."

"Good. Now tell me all about this date with Lincoln. How'd it go?"

"It was okay." She filled her in on pretty much every detail of the evening, including the feedback form. "I feel bad about that."

"Why? It was honest, and I know you weren't unkind. If he wants you to help him, he has to be open to hearing things that will help, right?"

"Yeah." She sipped more of her tea.

"Look. If it's stressing you out too much, don't fill out the survey thing. Figure out how you're comfortable giving feedback and stick with that. You're a friend helping him out, not an employee who has to do everything his way." She tapped the rim of her mug. "And that's a good lesson in and of itself. Especially with dating. Nobody gets their own way all the time."

Gretchen felt the urge to defend him. "It's not like he wants everything his own way."

Jody held up a hand. "Hey, he's my friend too, so I know he's not a selfish man-baby."

"Man-baby? Are you talking about me again?" Stew called from behind the counter.

Jody rolled her eyes. "Stewart…"

He chortled and disappeared into the back room.

"Anyway," she continued, "Lincoln's a great guy. I'm not

ripping on him. But he's so new at this that it's like training a teenager. Or a puppy. Sometimes they need a little whack on the nose to learn."

"I'm probably not going to whack him with a rolled up newspaper, but I get your point." She glanced at her watch. "We should probably get going."

"Don't forget that this isn't just for him. You get to have a good time, too."

"You're right." She really hadn't considered that.

Abby came over and leaned heavily on her mom.

Jody said, "My goodness, you did a lot of work, didn't you?"

Abby nodded.

Jody got up and went behind the counter. She came back with a small box of leftover chocolate chunk cookies and a twenty dollar bill. She handed them to Abby.

"Wow, thanks!"

Gretchen said, "That's not nec—"

"You hush." Jody winked at Abby, then said to Gretchen, "I'll grab that tea for your mom and get you a bag to put your goodies in."

Gretchen put her laptop in her bag and zipped it shut. "Let me know if you need anything else."

"You're on speed dial."

Gretchen took the paper bag with their baked goods and tea. Abby still clutched her twenty. They said their goodbyes and got in the car.

"What are you going to do with your money?"

Abby smoothed the bill across her leg. "I might buy a pizza. A whole big pizza just for me."

Gretchen chuckled.

"Well, I mean you can have a *piece*," Abby generously added, holding up one finger.

"Thanks."

"Or maybe I'll get Walter a toy."

"That's a good idea, too."

"Can I have money for cleaning our table? Then I can get a pizza *and* a toy for Walter."

"We'll see."

"That means no," she grumbled.

When they arrived home, Abby was still contemplating the injustice of having to choose between pizza or a dog toy.

"You could get a dog toy and a small pizza," Gretchen suggested.

Abby's face scrunched in disgust. "What is even the *point* of a small pizza?"

Gretchen tried to keep from laughing. Her daughter was truly her mini-me, because she felt the same way. "I'll give you five dollars to get your things picked up off your bedroom floor and put away. Neatly. In their correct places. Books on the bookshelf, clothes in the hamper, toys in the bins."

Abby sighed deeply.

"If you'd put them away when I ask you to, it wouldn't be a big job to do at once," Gretchen reminded her.

"Fiiiiiiiiiiiiiiiine." She heaved another weary sigh and trudged upstairs to her bedroom.

Gretchen vacuumed the living room, and after she put the vacuum back in the closet, she realized she'd missed a call.

From Lincoln.

Yikes.

This was definitely going to be an awkward conversation, wasn't it? Ugh. She gritted her teeth and tapped the phone. Might as well get it over with, right?

Chapter Fourteen

Lincoln's mouth went dry when Gretchen's name lit up his screen. When she hadn't picked up his call, he assumed she didn't want to talk to him. That stung, but he figured maybe the evaluation form had turned out to be a bridge too far.

"He—hello?" He cleared his throat and unstuck his tongue from the roof of his mouth.

"Hey. Sorry I missed your call. I was vacuuming and didn't hear my phone."

Okay, it didn't sound like she was mad. Or upset. Or anything he'd assumed. "No problem."

"What's up?"

He'd practiced a few things he wanted to say, but all his preparations went out the window now that they were actually speaking. "Uuuuhhh, so…"

After a long pause, she said, "Lincoln?"

He snapped to attention. "Um. So. The um… that form."

"Ah."

"I just, I was, I wanted to, um, like, thanks for taking the time to answer the questions."

"Lincoln. I'm sorry if it bothered you when I said about

feeling responsible for your feelings. After I sent it, I felt like maybe I was being a little harsh."

That made him feel even worse. He'd been feeling crappy about the form, but it hadn't occurred to him that she might be, too. "No, you weren't harsh at all. I wanted to apologize for putting you in that position. You're my friend, not a personal dating trainer. I was expecting too much."

"What do we do now?"

"I think it's safe to say we should nix the feedback form."

"Agreed."

He tried not to read too much into her response. Was she judging him for even coming up with such a stupid idea? Not that he could blame her. Although, it wasn't exactly his idea. Connor had sent him a link to a fun news story where a man did a pre-date form and the response seemed to be that the idea was adorable and quirky, especially since he and the woman ended up becoming a couple. Maybe that was the ultimate lesson. Stop listening to anything that comes from his friends, because their skill at doling out bad advice was top notch.

"About next weekend. I'll be volunteering at the food bank's Thanksgiving meal giveaway, so I probably won't be available at all on Saturday."

"I can't do anything Sunday. I promised Aunt Midge I'd help her do inventory. I could probably help with the food bank if they can use an extra set of hands."

"I'm sure they can."

"Maybe we can grab something to eat afterwards. I won't even ask for an exit interview this time."

"Deal. No exit interview." Her warm laughter soothed the edges of his concerns. Maybe she wasn't judging him after all.

He mentally smacked himself. That was a bad, bad habit–

assuming people were judging him when they most likely weren't thinking about him at all.

She asked, "How did the pictures turn out?"

"Amazing. Megan is a genius with her camera. We got so many great shots that we could make ten calendars."

"That's fantastic."

"She even gave us all the rights, so we can use them for pretty much anything we need. All she asked is that we tag her on social media when we use the pictures."

"Wonderful. A slideshow or gallery right on the front page of the website might get some attention. If Ruby needs help putting anything up, tell her to let me know."

That was another great idea. "I'll be sure to say something. Megan got the pictures for the calendar sent to the print shop. We're supposed to have them by Wednesday."

"Wow, that's super quick."

He'd thought the same thing. "I know. I couldn't believe the turnaround is that fast, especially since we're kind of running late in the year for a calendar. I assume they have it already laid out and just need to plug the pictures into the right month since we already picked the size and all that." It occurred to him that he'd been monopolizing the conversation with all the calendar talk. "Did you have a good day today?"

There was a slight pause and he realized it was a kind of weird way to ask what she'd been up to.

"Yeah, mostly. I had a client crisis to deal with this morning, but we got it all fixed, and then I had lunch with Jody. Abby helped her kids clean the shop and they paid her twenty bucks. She's over the moon trying to decide how to spend it. It's either a toy for Walter or a pizza."

"Tough call."

"I know. She asked if I'd pay her to do some extra chores so she can get both."

"Industrious."

"Right now she's supposed to be cleaning her room, but it's pretty quiet, so I'm guessing she's either playing with something she found under the bed or reading a book."

He could relate. "That's how I always end up cleaning. I find a book or something I haven't seen in a while and get distracted."

He heard Abby yell the background.

"My room's clean, can we go to the pet store now?"

"Sorry, hang on," Gretchen said to him before answering Abby. "They're closed. We can go Monday after school."

"Monday! But Mommmmm."

"I'm on the phone. Why don't you take Walter outside and play for a while before supper?"

"Fine."

"Sorry about that. The money's burning a hole in her pocket."

"Mom! Walter knocked over the water thing again!"

Gretchen sighed. "The fun never ends. I'll talk to you later."

Lincoln slipped his phone into his pocket. Abby was a character. He'd always assumed that by his mid-thirties, he'd have a kid or two of his own, but here he was with forty speeding ever closer, and only one serious relationship from his early twenties under his belt.

Life certainly had a way of not going according to plan.

Chapter Fifteen

The rest of the week flew by in a flurry of work, theater visits with Miss Judith for the dance school, school activities, and of course all the regular errands that never ended. All of a sudden, somehow, it was the Saturday before Thanksgiving. Gretchen got up early and woke Abby.

"Hey, pumpkin. Time to rise and shine. Today's the day we're helping with the food bank."

Abby stretched and groaned and mushed her face into her pillow. She said something that was too muffled to understand.

"What?"

She turned her face slightly. "Can I do the turkeys?"

"No, sorry, there's already a team of grownups doing that. Frozen turkeys are heavy and so super cold they have to wear special gloves."

"Why?" She moved so one eyeball peeped up from her Princess Poppy pillowcase.

"To protect their hands."

"From the turkeys?"

"Yes."

"Do they bite?"

Gretchen had no idea how the conversation had taken such a sharp left turn. "No, honey, it's because they're frozen and they're so cold that if you touch them with your bare hands long enough, it can hurt your skin."

"Why?"

Ah. It was a stalling tactic. Well played, kiddo. "Time to get up."

Abby groaned again and made a hugely dramatic show of flinging her covers back and getting out of bed. "Why can't I stay with Grandma and Grandpa?" she grumbled as she trudged to the bathroom.

"Because they're both helping, too. I'm going to make breakfast. Don't take too long."

The only response was the sound of toothpaste being spit into the sink.

By seven o'clock, they had picked up Lincoln and were at the Hickory Hollow Rec Center, where the local food bank was setting up for the annual turkey dinner distribution.

"Have fun," Gretchen said with a grin as Lincoln was recruited to sling heavy turkeys.

Prescott's Grocery had loaned fifty small shopping carts for the event. Long tables were set up with all the fixings for a Thanksgiving feast divided by category. Rolls, side dishes, condiments, dessert. Gretchen was on the team that loaded the carts with a full meal, which would be refilled as each set of groceries was delivered to a waiting vehicle.

At nine o'clock, the doors opened to an overflowing crowd. Half of the youth group from a local church was in charge of wrangling the younger kids and helping them with their work, which was handing out fliers outlining the food bank's services, as well as the services of other local organizations.

The line was steady, with the other half of the youth group

pushing carts to the parking lot, loading cars, then returning the carts to be refilled.

By ten thirty, Gretchen's shoulders ached from the repetitive motion of loading cans into bags, then bags into the carts. The cans weren't that heavy individually, but after an hour, lifting them over and over felt like lugging cement.

By eleven thirty, the line had dwindled to the last remaining handful of people who needed to pick up a meal before the event ended at noon.

She swiped a hand across her brow, pushing a stray strand of hair out of her face.

A blood-curdling scream came from the direction of the room where the kids were being entertained.

Gretchen ducked underneath the table and pushed forward, racing across the almost empty community room they were set up in. She and another mom collided as they reached the doorway, knocking shoulders painfully.

She came to a stop and tried to parse out the scene.

Abby stood with her fists clenched. Her beet-red face was scrunched in fury. Behind her, a little girl, probably three years old, sat on the floor crying and holding her arm. In front of her, a little boy about her age was bent over, clutching his stomach.

Two teenage volunteers stood nearby, looking surprised and confused.

Then, chaos. The boy screamed, pointing at Abby. "She hit me! She hit me!"

The little girl sobbed louder.

The teenagers started asking questions.

The other mom shouted at Abby. "Say you're sorry!"

Abby ignored her, her glare never leaving the little boy.

The other mom grabbed Abby's shoulders, spurring Gretchen forward. She reached around and pulled Abby out of her grasp. "No. You don't put your hands on my daughter."

The woman sneered. "Your precious daughter attacked my son!"

"We have no idea what happened!"

The small room filled with people, people everywhere.

The other mom shouted to someone, "Call the police! My son was assaulted!"

"What?" Trish, one of the food bank coordinators put her hands up. "Hang on, hang on. Let's all quiet down and see what happened."

"I'll tell you what happened. This spoiled brat attacked my son!"

The coordinator looked over at the teenagers. "You were supervising. What happened?"

They–a boy and a girl–looked at each other, then the floor. "We, um, didn't see?"

Trish shook her head. "We'll deal with you later." She first turned to the little boy. "What happened?"

Gretchen noticed he took a moment to see how many people were in attendance before his face crumpled and he started to cry. He pointed at Abby. "She punched me. She just came up and punched me. It hurts. It hurts so bad. She's so mean!"

His mom rushed over and tucked his head against her stomach, hugging him close. "Your daughter is a menace. I want her punished!"

Trish turned to Abby. "I'd like to hear your side. Did you punch this little boy?"

Abby's chin jerked upward. "Yes I did."

"See? She's a violent menace. Call the police!"

Gretchen leaned down. "Abby. You know better. Why did you hit him?"

"Clearly she's been taught that money is more important than being a decent human," the boy's mother snapped.

The other little girl's mother had scooped her into her arms. "Did she hurt you, too?"

The little girl shook her head and pointed at the little boy.

Gretchen put a gentle hand on Abby's back. "What happened?"

She crossed her arms, defiant, thrusting a finger in the little girl's direction. "He twisted her arm and pushed her on the ground."

The mother shrieked, "You liar, he did not!"

Trish snapped, "For Pete's sake, Gloria, you're speaking to a child."

"A spoiled little rich child with no consequences for her actions."

The little girl's mom said, "Honey? Did this little boy push you down?"

The girl shoved her thumb into her mouth and nodded.

Abby added, "He tried to kick her. I told him to knock it off but he didn't so I pushed him away from her and he kicked me so I hit him."

Gretchen felt like all eyes were on her. It was a fine line–no, violence wasn't the answer, but the sequence of events seemed pretty logical. "Abby, we don't hit."

"Tell it to him." She shoved a finger in the boy's direction.

The mother screeched again about calling the police and how Abby was a spoiled little rich girl who was getting away with assault. She narrowed her eyes at Abby. "You think you're so special just because you have money. You're just like your pathetic mother!"

Gretchen spun and moved Abby behind her. "Look, lady, I don't know who you are, but you need to stop speaking directly to my *child*."

"Oooh, are you going to punch me? And then lie about it?

Billy never touched either one of these brats. You'll be hearing from my attorney."

"Attorney? What are you talking about?"

"Assault and slander. Accusing Billy of pushing that girl. You didn't push her, did you?"

Billy shook his head. "No, mama."

"That's a lie! He's lying!" Abby's hands clenched into fists.

Gretchen knew Abby was no angel, but she had zero reason to doubt her story. Especially since little Billy's tears were dry and he couldn't quite contain his smirk when his mother looked away.

Trish, who had been working since the crack of dawn, heaved a frustrated sigh. "I don't know what happened, but it's over now, and there's still a lot of work to do. Let's just apologize to each other and be done with it."

Abby looked up at Gretchen expectantly. It seemed like the simplest solution. She nodded.

Billy stuck out his tongue and laughed. "You're stupid."

His mother shrugged. "He doesn't need to apologize. He did nothing wrong." She looked at Abby. "Well? Where's your apology?"

Abby looked up again.

Gretchen put a hand on her shoulder. "Look, this is just going around in circles and wasting everyone's time. He shouldn't have pushed anyone, Abby shouldn't have hit him, let's just go our separate ways and be done with it."

"Oh, this isn't over by a longshot. Come on, Billy." His mom picked him up and carried him out of the room. At the doorway, Billy gave Abby the finger over his mom's shoulder.

Abby's chin quivered. "I didn't lie."

"I know you didn't."

"He pushed her down." Abby reached down and yanked

her pantleg up, revealing a red mark on her leg. "See? He kicked me."

Trish scolded the teenage chaperones. "Any reason you missed this whole thing?"

Abby said, "They were kissing."

Both teenagers turned beet red and sputtered.

Gretchen almost felt bad for them. She felt worse for Trish, who looked like she was ready to explode.

"I'm sorry about all this," she offered to Trish.

Trish managed a tired smile. "It's always something. Let's get back to work." She scowled in the direction of the teenagers. "You can watch the kids out here. Separately." She gestured to the main hall where the giveaway was mostly done.

Dory checked to make sure everything was okay. "Your dad and I are taking the carts back to Prescott's. Talk to you later."

Gretchen helped tear down the tables and box up the unclaimed food that would be going back to the food bank. When that was done, she grabbed a utility knife and joined Lincoln, who was tearing down empty boxes.

"Hey, how's it going?" he asked.

"Did you miss all that?"

"Miss what?"

A third voice came from the doorway. "Miss Ross?"

Gretchen turned, frowning. "Yes?" The frown turned to surprise as she realized the voice belonged to Sheriff Grady. "Oh. Hi." She straightened and followed his gaze to the utility knife in her hand. "Um, let me put this down." She turned and set it on the table.

"We got a call there was a disturbance. Deputy Branson is looking at the video footage, but I thought I'd get your version."

Would it be overkill to call a lawyer? Gretchen considered

it for half a second. "I was in the main area, so I didn't see it myself. My daughter said a little boy was bullying another child, so she put a stop to it."

"How old is your daughter?"

"Six."

He blinked. "Six."

"Yes."

He gave one slow nod. "I'll go see what Deputy Branson's found out. I'm sure we'll want to talk to your daughter."

"I'll get her." She might not go as far as calling her attorney, but she definitely wasn't letting Abby get interrogated without her present.

As the sheriff walked away, Lincoln said, "Are you okay?"

"Yeah, this is ridiculous. I need to get Abby."

"I'll come with you." He was already rounding the pile of boxes.

Two minutes later, Billy's mother was screeching first about her son being videotaped without her consent, and second, the video being altered because there's no way he pushed a little girl, and three, it was probably altered by one of Gretchen's hired goons because she's rich and everyone knows rich people do whatever they want without consequences.

Gretchen stood with a hand protectively on Abby's shoulder. She asked the sheriff, "Are we free to go?"

"Yes."

Without waiting for another word from anyone, she hustled Abby to the door.

The air had turned bitter cold, threatening snow. She got Abby into her seat and buckled in. The freezing air cooled her anger and she realized their coats were still inside. Along with Lincoln, and she was his ride.

"Crap."

Before she could decide what to do, Lincoln burst out the

front door, holding their coats aloft. He pulled his own coat tight and jogged over to the car. He dove into the back seat and yanked the door shut. "Wow, that got cold."

He shoved Gretchen's coat over the seat for her, then tucked Abby's coat around her.

"Thank you so much. I really did not want to go back in there."

He leaned forward like he was going to try climbing over the seats, then thought better of it. He jumped out and got in the front seat. "Who was that, anyway?"

"I have no idea. Clearly she can't stand me, but I have no idea who she is."

"Too bad. She has such a sparkling personality."

She had to laugh at that. "I'll keep her in mind the next time we have a casting call. Her flair for the dramatic was top notch."

Abby sniffled in the back seat. "Why was that lady so mean to me?"

Gretchen popped her seatbelt off and twisted in her seat, all humor immediately gone. "Honey, I'm so sorry. I don't know. I know she was upset that you hit Billy—you shouldn't hit people—but she had no business talking to you like that. She had no business talking to you at all."

"Am I going to jail?"

"No."

"Are you mad?"

Gretchen twisted further so she could meet Abby's eyes. The position was awkward to the point of painful, but she reached back and put her hand on Abby's knee. "No. I am absolutely, one hundred percent, totally, completely, not mad at you. Not one bit."

"I did something bad."

"Sweet pea, I don't know how to explain it. Sometimes the

reasons are more important than the action. You didn't hit Billy to be mean. You were protecting the little girl–and yourself– from Billy pushing and hitting and kicking. A better choice might have been to start yelling for help, but it's hard to think of better choices when it's all happening really fast." Especially when the chaperones were making poor choices right across the room in front of the little kids, and should have intervened at the beginning. But she kept that part to herself.

Abby's chin quivered. "You're not mad?" Her voice was small.

Gretchen smiled at her. "I am not mad at you. Not even a little bit. I'm a little mad at Billy's mom, but I'm definitely not mad at you."

She sniffled. "Okay."

"Let's get home so we can make some lunch and snuggle under the fuzzy blanket with Walter. Okay?"

"Yeah."

Lincoln held his hands in front of the blasting heater. "Man, that air just goes right through you."

Gretchen pulled out and headed toward his house. "I'm not ready for winter at all."

A little bit later, she parked in front of his house. "I'll let you know about supper, okay?"

"Sure thing." He got out of the car and gave a quick wave before dashing to the front door.

Chapter Sixteen

Lincoln was disappointed, but not surprised when Gretchen texted him in the later afternoon that Abby was feeling clingy and she wanted to stay home and watch movies.

> Sorry about that.

> No problem.

He thought about it for a minute then texted again. Why not try another pivot?

> I have a coupon for pizza and wings that expires today. Since I'm going out anyway, want me to bring food?

Three dots immediately appeared while Gretchen typed her response.

> Are you serious???? That would be beyond amazing.

He grinned and let her know he'd be there around seven.

If there was one thing he'd learned by being Gretchen's friend for several years, it was that pizza was the way to her good graces. Nachos were even better, so he added those to the order, too. If there was another thing he knew, it was that she was very sensitive about having money. Sounds like a good problem to have, but people could be vicious when she didn't open her wallet when and how they thought she should.

He was concerned about Abby's run-in with Billy, but he was more concerned about Gretchen's run-in with Billy's mom. The woman had really gotten under Gretchen's skin.

At six thirty, he went into the restaurant and picked up the order, which was ridiculous for three people. Pizza, nachos, wings, breadsticks, a baked pizza cookie, lots of ranch dressing for the wings, and three two-liter bottles of soda. Definitely overkill, but they wouldn't be going hungry, that was for sure.

He pulled into Gretchen's driveway at a few minutes before seven.

She opened the door and her eyes went wide. "My good-ness, what all did you get? Come in, come in." She hurried to close the door behind him.

His face was freezing just from the short walk from his car to the front door. "I can't believe how cold it got."

"Yeah, the temperature dropped like a bowling ball from this afternoon even, and it was cold then." She ushered him to the kitchen and helped set the food on the island. "What kind of coupon did you have?"

He chuckled. "I'm not even sure, but they gave me one of the bottles of soda free, too."

"Nice."

Abby trudged into the kitchen, then perked up at the sight of the boxes. "Sweet!" She climbed up onto a stool at the island.

Lincoln listed the details. "The pizza is pepperoni. Honey

bbq wings with ranch, cheesy breadsticks, and this one is special, just for your mom." He tapped a smaller rectangle box.

"Oh?" Gretchen looked curious.

He popped the lid open.

"No way. That's amazing."

"Extra jalapeños, extra salsa, extra sour cream."

"Lincoln, you really are going to make some lucky woman the perfect husband. You're so thoughtful."

His cheeks heated at her compliment. He mumbled, "I don't know about that."

Abby piled her plate with cheesy breadsticks and a puddle of marinara sauce.

"No pizza?"

"Later," she said as she hopped off the stool and carried her plate to the living room.

Gretchen explained, "We were in the middle of a Princess Poppy movie."

He inclined his head toward her chair. "You're going to eat in here and miss it?"

She rolled her eyes and dropped her voice to barely more than a whisper. "I've seen it fourteen billion times. I can't stand Princess Poppy. I thought it was mainly for little-little kids, but Abby and her friends are still obsessed. I swear if I have to see one more stupid peacock feather tiara, I'm going to scream."

He nearly choked on his chicken wing, laughing at the vehemence of her declaration. "Stop holding back, Gretchen. Tell me how you really feel."

She laughed. "I know it's irrational to despise an animated character, but seriously. She's so annoying and awful."

"Speaking of annoying and awful, how are you doing after today?"

"Abby's still upset about it. She didn't even want to go to my parents' for the evening, which was unusual. It's so hard to explain how hitting is wrong but in this case it's not wrong-wrong because it was basically self-defense. I don't want her to think you can go around hitting people, but I also don't want her to ever think she can't physically defend herself if someone hits her."

He finished his bite and wiped his mouth with a napkin. "That has to be complicated. But I was asking how *you* are doing after today. Billy's mom really threw some low blows."

"Yeah, I don't know what her problem is. I've been wracking my brain all afternoon and I honestly don't recognize her at all. I'm more ticked that she was being a jerk to a six-year-old kid. I mean, gee, wonder where Billy gets his crappy attitude and bullying from."

Lincoln agreed. "No mystery there, that's for sure."

"I'm embarrassed that Trish had to deal with it. She puts so much work into these holiday meal giveaways and to have something like this happen..." She shook her head. "I'm just embarrassed to even be part of it."

"You didn't do anything to be embarrassed about. Neither did Abby."

"I know, but you know how it is. Feelings aren't easily swayed by facts."

Very true.

They ate in silence for a while.

Gretchen asked, "What are you doing for Thanksgiving?"

"Going to my parents'. You?"

"Same. We go over early in the morning and do all the cooking as a family. Then we eat and watch football and ninety percent of the time we fall asleep. Then we eat pie for supper and go to bed early because Mom and I get up at the crack of dawn to go shopping for Black Friday."

"Better you than me. I have yet to meet the bargain that

makes me even consider getting out of my nice warm bed and standing in a crowd before dawn."

"Oh, we've got a whole strategy."

He chuckled. "Me, too. My strategy is to stay home. I usually go out on Saturday and do my shopping since it's Small Business Saturday. Black Friday leans more toward bigger chain stores, and I like to do my shopping to support small business." He quickly added, "Not that there's anything wrong with shopping anywhere else. I do, too. I mean…" He felt like he'd put his foot in his mouth. Again.

She held up a hand. "No, I understand and I agree with you. I run a small business myself, so I totally shop small and local as much as I can." She cocked her head. "Should that be our next date? Shopping on Small Business Saturday? You can take me to your favorite small businesses and I can take you to mine."

He normally shopped alone, preferring to get in and out of wherever he was going. But shopping with Gretchen could be fun. "Yes."

"We'll start with caffeine from Caretti's."

"And finish with lunch from Holy Guacamole."

"Brilliant." She grinned.

Walter waddled through the kitchen and wheezed at the back door.

Gretchen groaned as she pulled on her coat. "Dog, you better make it quick. It's freezing outside."

While she took the dog out to do his business, Lincoln cleaned up the leftovers and put them in the fridge. He sliced the still-warm cookie pizza into wedges.

"Where's Mom?" Abby's voice startled him.

"Hey!" He jerked around. "She took Walter out."

Abby's brows scrunched. "How come you didn't take him out? Isn't that your job?"

"Uhhh, well, I mean, yes, that's my job, part of my job, but I'm not working right now."

"Oh. Do you have your own dog?"

"I don't. I have three cats and one of them is super afraid of dogs, so I can't have one."

"Oh." She put her empty plate in the sink. "Are you my mom's boyfriend?"

He swallowed hard. Such a casual interrogation. "N—no?" He had no idea what she'd told Abby about the situation. "We're friends."

"But you guys are going on dates. That's what girlfriends and boyfriends do, right?"

His throat felt thick. He had *not* been prepared for this. "Um, well, yeah, uh, they do, but, um…"

She stared up at him expectantly.

"I mean, friends hang out together."

"But you guys are going on *dates*," she repeated.

"Oh." He scratched his head and wondered what was taking Walter so long. "Sort of."

She crossed her arms.

"Your mom and I are going on some dates because I'm really bad at dating. So she's kind of teaching me how to date."

She scowled. "You don't know how to date? But you're *old*."

Ouch.

"Yeah. That's why I really need help."

"Mom should teach you how to act."

Double ouch. "I mostly know how to act."

She rolled her eyes. "No, how to *act*. Like on the theater. You should do Mommy's improv class. That's how come I got really good at kickball."

He wasn't sure how there was a connection. "How did improv make you good at kickball?"

She sighed like it should be obvious. "Mrs. Flannery made

us play kickball a lot in gym class but I couldn't hit the ball, like, ever, and it made me sad. So Mom had me pretend to be the super best kickballer in the whole world. Then in gym class I would pretend to be super great and then I kicked the ball sometimes."

"Sometimes?" That didn't seem like a huge improvement.

She scoffed like a seasoned teenager and set him straight. "Sometimes is better than no times."

Holy cow that was some big insight from a six-year-old. "Thanks, Abby."

She looked confused, but just shrugged and went back to the living room. A minute later, Gretchen and Walter came back inside.

She hurried to close the door, then hugged herself for a minute. "That. Is. So. Cold. And this guy," she pointed to Walter, "had to investigate every square inch of creation to find the perfect spot to do his business." She shivered and hung her coat up. "You should pivot your business to teaching dogs to use the toilet. You'd make a fortune in weather like this."

He chuckled and leaned down to scratch Walter's ice cold ears. "You'd miss going out, wouldn't you?"

Gretchen huffed. "He'd miss it. I would not."

Walter wheezed and trotted to the living room.

"He's going to burrow under the blanket with Abby."

They both watched around the corner as Walter used his doggie stairs to get up on the couch and push his way under Abby's thick, fuzzy blanket.

Gretchen quietly said, "Sorry we didn't get to go out tonight."

He quickly shook his head. "Don't be. I had a great time." And learned a great lesson. Out of the mouths of babes, right?

Chapter Seventeen

Thanksgiving came and went in a haze of too much turkey and pie. Then it was Black Friday shopping with her mom, and now getting ready for another long day of Small Business Saturday shopping with Lincoln.

He pulled into the driveway a few minutes after her dad left with Abby. They were going to hang out at the arcade while Dory wrapped presents and probably took a nap.

She grabbed her purse and hurried outside.

Lincoln hopped out of the car to open her door. When they were both back inside the car, he asked, "Get any great deals yesterday?"

Gretchen buckled her seatbelt. "Yes. I got an amazing KitchenAid mixer for Jody that was like seventy percent off. I even snagged the raspberry color she's been eyeing for months. I found a model for my dad, and I got myself a new vacuum that was dirt cheap. Get it? *Dirt* cheap?"

Lincoln groaned and then laughed. "That was bad."

"It was, wasn't it? I'm going to blame it on lack of sleep and excessive amounts of caffeine over the past couple days."

"Just one problem. You always make jokes like that."

"I'm always tired and running on too much caffeine."

"Fair enough."

She rubbed her hands together. "Do we have an agenda for today?"

"Sort of." He slowed to a stop at the light. "I have a list of places I want to go, but we'll have plenty of time to go anywhere you want, and then at some point we'll go to Holy Guacamole and eat until we explode."

"That. Right there."

"What?"

"That's why you're going to make some woman a great partner. Food is always the right answer. Mexican food is the more right answer. You always do a good job of paying attention to what the people close to you enjoy."

"Not really. I'm just guessing based on your Nachos 4 Lyfe neck tattoo."

Gretchen cackled at the idea of having a giant neck tattoo dedicated to nachos. Although, if she *were* to ever get a neck tattoo, that subject was as good as any. "It matches the massive burrito tattoo on my back."

Lincoln laughed at that. "I would expect nothing less."

"What's our first stop?"

"Beth's Boutique."

Awesome. It was one of those places she'd been meaning to visit, but hadn't gotten around to yet. "Megan's friend opened that recently, didn't she?"

"Yes and no. She ran it out of her garage for several years. I think it was right before Christmas last year that she got the actual storefront. She shares that old Victorian with the bridal shop."

"Oh, that's right, now I remember Megan saying something about the location. Isn't it all wedding stuff though?"

"No, she has a lot of different things. My mom absolutely

loves her handmade purses, so I get her a new one every year because she refuses to treat herself."

"That's really sweet."

He shrugged one shoulder.

A few minutes later, Gretchen found herself running a finger along a gorgeous handcrafted burgundy purse. She inspected the intricate stitching. "This is amazing." She wasn't one to be super "into" purses, but this one was the right size, the right weight, and the right color. She glanced down at the worn purse hanging from her shoulder. It had definitely seen better days.

Lincoln picked a sunshine yellow bag.

She noticed the style. "Wait. Are they the same? Just the color?"

Beth came out from behind the counter and smiled as she walked over. "Yes. Each year I do a new bag. Well, technically three new bags. A small, medium, and large. The design and colors are exclusive for the whole year."

Gretchen immediately appreciated the business savvy of that strategy. Exclusive, to encourage FOMO and drive sales, and smart, because only making one design would streamline the production and cut costs. Especially since each purse was handmade. "These are exquisite."

"Thank you so much. Let me know if you have any questions." She went off to help another customer.

Gretchen reluctantly put the burgundy bag back on the shelf and walked over to where Lincoln was browsing through a display of scarves.

"These are pretty." She let the silk run through her fingers as she read the sign. "'Each hand-marbled scarf is one of a kind.' These color combinations are lovely." She picked out a scarf marbled with several shades of blue and purple, with just a hint of yellow. "This would go perfectly with the purse you picked for your mom."

"You think so?" He looked skeptical.

Gretchen held the scarf against the purse. "The yellow is a perfect match."

He slowly nodded. "I think you're right. Now I need something for my Aunt Rose."

She glanced over and sucked in a breath. Another customer had picked up the burgundy bag.

Lincoln nudged her. "Once it's gone, it's gone."

"Yeah, but I'm supposed to be shopping for other people."

The lady walked away from the bag display. With the burgundy bag. "I'm too late anyway." She shrugged. "It just wasn't meant to be."

Lincoln found a green scarf for his aunt. It had colorful dots that made it look like an abstract summer field of flowers, like a Monet painting.

"Oooh, my mom would love this pink one." This scarf had about six shades of pink swirls, with a subtle thread of pale orange. She could easily envision her mom wearing it with her favorite blazer.

They paid for their purchases and after Beth handed over her bag with a smile, she said, "Megan mentioned you set up her new website. It's gorgeous. Are you taking new clients?"

"My team does have some openings. Let me give you a card." She fished a business card out of her wallet. "Do you have a pen? I'll give you my personal number."

"I probably won't have time to do anything until after the holidays, if that's okay."

"That's perfect. I can get you on the schedule for a consultation in January."

"Wonderful. Thank you so much."

Gretchen lifted the bag. "Thank *you*. My mom's going to love this."

They had to shimmy past a whole group of people to get out the door.

"I'll have to come back when it's not so busy. She had some really cute earrings but I couldn't get close to the display case."

"I got Aunt Rose a bracelet a couple years ago. It's really good quality." He popped the trunk and hesitated when he looked in his bag. "Oh, darn. I'll be right back."

Gretchen got in the car and waited for a few minutes.

Lincoln bounded down the stairs and over to the car, holding a slip of paper. "I forgot to get my receipt. I hate trying to reconcile the checkbook without receipts."

"Checkbook? I thought you used your card."

"Debit card. I don't use credit cards."

"What do you do if you need to rent a car or a hotel or something?"

He backed out of the parking space. "I *have* credit cards, but I don't use them unless it's absolutely necessary."

"I use mine for almost everything and then pay it off at the end of the month. I get cash back and airline points that add up."

"That's great. I got into some pretty major credit card debt in college–why they give plastic to students, I'll never understand. It took me too many years to dig out of that hole, so it's not something I care to repeat."

"Understandable. My parents always drilled it into my head to pay off my cards right away, but I can see how it would be easy to keep putting it off and all of a sudden the molehill is a mountain."

"Exactly." His fingers tightened on the steering wheel. "Can I ask you something?"

"Of course."

"What's it like not having to ever worry about money? I mean, I grew up without much money, so there were a lot of things we went without. I'm in a great stable place now, but I still have to sit down and do my budget every month and make sure I know where all my money's going." He grimaced. "Sorry, I'm not trying to offend you."

"I'm not offended at all." She'd definitely been asked obnoxious questions about her money that did offend her deeply, but she knew Lincoln was coming from a respectful place. And this was probably good practice for a money conversation with his future partner. "I have to credit my parents with instilling a healthy respect for money in me. My dad also didn't come from money, so I had his perspective that in some ways was completely different than my mom's, but in some ways, very similar. They both agree that you can't buy character, which was probably the biggest lesson."

"That's very true."

"I've always understood that there's immense privilege that comes with having money, and I'm fortunate to be able to organize my life and prioritize things in a way that a lot of people can't." She looked over at Lincoln and grinned. "And believe it or not, I also work on my budget monthly."

"Really?"

"Really. I always think about it. Like, am I being flashy and showing off? Am I making anyone uncomfortable? I don't want to put anyone in a position of feeling lesser, and I also don't want to be the 'rich friend' who's only along to pay the tab." She leaned back in her seat and sighed. "Money's complicated. When you have more of it, the complications are different, but it's still complicated."

"Do you worry a lot about people only wanting to be around you for your money?"

"Of course it's in the back of my mind whenever I meet

people, especially after the situation with Abby's dad." She trailed off and stared out the window.

"You okay?"

Gretchen startled. She hadn't realized she'd gotten so lost in her thoughts. "Yeah, just remembering ancient history."

"Sorry for bringing it up."

"Not your fault." She looked out the windshield at the variety of storefronts occupying the historic buildings that lined Main Street. Downtown Hickory Hollow still looked like something out of a Norman Rockwell painting or an episode of *The Andy Griffith Show*.

He changed the subject. "I need to get a gift certificate at The Color Wheel, then stop in For Pet's Sake and grab some stuff for the shelter."

They got out of the car and walked along the sidewalk. Inside The Color Wheel, a paint-your-own pottery art studio, Lincoln got a gift certificate for his grandmother.

Gretchen browsed the shelves of ceramic mugs and picture frames and ornaments. Framed pictures of customers lined the top of the walls, showcasing smiling faces with their personalized treasures.

Lincoln walked over and touched a ceramic Christmas tree. "My grandma always says she has too much crap, but she loves painting. So I bring her here for a grandma-grandson 'date' in January. She loves it. It still gives her something to sit around, but the experience is the gift."

"That's awesome. I think Abby would like doing this." She went to the counter and took advantage of the Small Business Saturday offer of buy one, get one free gift certificates.

Back out on the sidewalk, Gretchen came to a dead stop in front of a large plate glass window where colorful yarn-shaped letters spelled out "Yolanda's Yarnery" arched over a cartoon ball of yarn with knitting needles. A bright pink sign announced upcoming classes.

"What?"

"Experience as a gift. That's perfect. My mom has always said she'd love to learn how to knit."

"There you go." Lincoln pulled the door open for her to go inside.

The yarn shop was as crowded as Beth's shop. Samples of afghan squares and baby blankets and hats and scarves and socks decorated the shop. Square bins were stacked six feet high, full of skeins of yarn in every color imaginable.

"I don't really know what I'm looking at."

"Yarn," he joked.

Gretchen shot him a look and chuckled. "You sound like my dad."

"Can I help you?" A pleasant voice asked.

Gretchen turned with a smile. "I'm not sure what I'm looking for. My mom has always wanted to try knitting, but I don't know the first thing about what she might need."

The woman nodded knowingly. "Is this for a Christmas gift?"

"Yes."

"I'd recommend a spot in our January beginner class. It's a six-week class where I teach the fundamentals for people who want to try it out. It's twenty-five percent off for Small Business Saturday and it comes with a starter kit that includes needles, a stitch marker, measuring tape, folding scissors, three skeins of yarn, and one of our project tote bags. Everything she'll need to complete a whole project."

"That sounds perfect." Gretchen followed the woman to the front of the store.

She set a starter kit on the counter. "You can take a look at what's included. The class runs on Tuesday evenings or

Saturday mornings. There's information on how to get registered in the kit. I have a green kit, a tan kit, and…" she leaned back and looked at something under the counter. "A pink kit and I think that's it."

"Pink." Gretchen didn't have to think about it. Pink was her mom's favorite color, so that part was easy.

"Wonderful. Is there anything else I can help you with?"

"No, this is perfect. Thanks so much." Gretchen paid for the kit and followed Lincoln back out of the crowded store. She beamed up at him. "This was a great idea."

He nudged her arm with his elbow. "Told you so."

They stopped in For Pet's Sake and Lincoln got wrangled into helping his aunt with a bit of a situation.

"Ginger got out of her cage," Midge stage-whispered.

"Oh, no." Lincoln's eyes went wide.

Gretchen had to ask. "Who's Ginger?"

Lincoln leaned close to her ear. "Ginger's an albino ball python. About five feet long."

Gretchen sucked in a breath.

Midge waved her hands frantically. "Make sure Babs is secure."

Gretchen looked up at Lincoln questioningly.

"Babs is a rat."

"Ah. I think I'll browse while you help your aunt." Rats and snakes were just a bit too far outside her wheelhouse.

He followed Midge to the back of the store.

Gretchen picked out some toys for Walter and for her parents' cats. She'd almost forgotten about the escaped snake when someone screamed.

Chapter Eighteen

Lincoln ran out of the storeroom with Midge on his heels. A little boy was pointing up at the air vent. His mother was hysterical, trying to drag him away, but he was glued to the scene, not the least bit frightened.

"It's okay, it's okay," Lincoln said. He looked up at the vent, where Ginger's yellow and white head poked out of the opening. "Ginger. What are you doing up there?"

The woman yelled something about the store being unsafe and that the snake was going to kill them all.

"She looks scary, but I promise, she's not going to hurt anyone." He said over his shoulder, "Uncle Stan, will you bring me the stepladder?"

The woman finally dragged her son away from the scene and out the front door, vowing to never return.

Lincoln asked another customer to back up a bit, then climbed the stepladder and reached into the vent. "Come here, Ginger."

Ginger was reasonably cooperative as he pulled her out of the vent and looped her across his shoulders.

"This stunt would have been better at Halloween, you know," he told her as he got off the ladder and carried her back to her enclosure.

Ginger flicked her tongue at him.

"Rude," he said as he put her into her tank. He secured the latch and gave Midge a thumbs up.

"Thank you, thank you. I don't know how she got out."

Stan double checked the latch. "The new kid was back here. I'll have a talk with him."

Lincoln followed Midge out. She apologized profusely to the lady waiting patiently at the counter. He wound through the aisles until he found Gretchen at the cat toys.

She asked, "Operation Ginger was a success, I take it?"

"Yeah, she's back in her enclosure. Every now and then she likes to take herself for a little stroll."

She grinned and touched one of the cat toys. "What does the shelter need?"

"A little bit of everything, but especially food and cleaning supplies. Toys are great, really anything is appreciated."

"Is it better to take in food and cleaning stuff, or are gift certificates better?"

"Honestly? The best donation is cash. We have suppliers we can get stuff from at wholesale prices, so we can stretch a dollar pretty far. You can also designate cash donations to go toward supplies or veterinary care. Otherwise we just allocate it wherever it's currently needed more."

"Maybe I'll just send a check, then, if that's better."

Lincoln's chest tightened. "No, I'm sorry, I don't want to discourage you. We need toys, too, so if that's what you would rather do, please do."

"Maybe I'll do both." She picked up a package of crinkle balls and catnip mice. "And you weren't discouraging at all. I asked what was the most beneficial way to donate, and you answered me. That's all."

He shrugged. "It just felt like maybe I was saying the wrong thing."

"Not at all." She looked at his empty arms. "Did you get what you needed?"

"Oh, shoot. Ginger and Babs distracted me. My stuff's in the back. I'll just be a minute."

Gretchen went to the counter and paid for her items. By the time she was done, Lincoln was in line right behind her.

Midge waved him away. "It's already on your tab."

He shook his head and followed Gretchen back to the car.

She asked, "Did you get anything interesting?"

"Toys for my regular clients."

"That's so sweet." She clicked her seatbelt. "How are plans for opening the doggie day care going?"

"Slowly. We had a facility in mind, but it ended up falling through. So it's back to the drawing board." He pulled out of the parking lot and turned left.

"That stinks. Is there anything I can help with? I just did an update for Gloria's real estate website, maybe I could touch base with her and see if there's anything available?"

"She's the one I'm working with."

"Oh, nice. If anyone can find you a good location, it's Gloria."

Lincoln agreed. There was a reason Gloria's face was plastered on billboards across three counties. "This is a hard time of the year, too. She's said several times that we'll have better luck finding a place in the spring."

"The right place will come along at the right time."

"I'm not in a huge hurry. I still need to work out some of the details on my business plan."

"If you need help with anything, let me know."

"Of course."

She said, "Where to next?"

"Marsha's Florals."

"We're getting flowers?"

"I'm ordering flowers to be delivered to my aunt. Her birthday is three days before Christmas, and she loves getting flowers. She does not, however, like poinsettias or red and green themed bouquets, so I order early to make sure she can get non-Christmas colored flowers."

"Awesome."

"After that, Hannigan's Hardware to shop for my dad. If there's anywhere you want to stop, just let me know."

She settled back in her seat. "Nah, you've got some good places."

"Who do you have to shop for?"

"My list is pretty light. Abby, my parents, and Jody's family are the main people I shop for. I don't have any extended family. I do get some small stuff for a handful of friends, and the women who work for me."

"Did you see JM Creations is running a special for those fancy laser-engraved insulated travel mugs? That might be something your employees would like."

"I didn't, and that's a brilliant idea."

"Her shop's open until two, do you want to stop there?"

"Yes. And from now on, you're in charge of my gift giving."

Lincoln chuckled. Warmth spread through his chest. This is what he always imagined dating would be like. Enjoying time with someone, no pressure, no performance, just a nice day doing whatever. He hoped this practice would lead him to a real relationship like this.

They went down several back roads to the JM Creations shop that was housed in Jen's—the J in JM—garage.

Half an hour later, Lincoln was pleased to see how excited

Gretchen was to have ordered personalized YETI tumblers for her employees. She was beaming as she got back in the car. "I have to say it again. You're brilliant. They're going to love those cups."

"Told you so." He grinned.

"I think I'll get some gift certificates to put inside the tumblers, and maybe something else that's small."

"Like what?"

"No clue. I'll know it when I see it, I guess."

She saw it at the very next stop. While Lincoln ordered his flowers, he saw Gretchen inspecting a display of handmade wooden flowers mounted on clips.

"Those are neat," he said.

She held one up for him to see closer. "Wouldn't these be adorable clipped on the corner of a computer monitor?"

"Sure."

She selected one for each of her employees. "Now I just need gift certificates."

"Where are you getting them?"

She grinned. "Holy Guacamole."

He might not be great at catching hints, but that one was loud and clear. "Next stop, lunch."

"You read my mind."

Twenty minutes later, they were seated at a booth at Holy Guacamole.

Gretchen didn't bother opening her menu.

Lincoln wasn't sure if that meant something. "You're... not looking at the menu? Is everything okay?"

She laughed. "Everything's fine. I know exactly what I'm getting."

He glanced down over the offerings. "There are too many options. What are you getting?"

"The taco sampler. Ten tacos. Chicken, beef, shrimp, pork, and fish."

"Ten? Are you going to be able to eat ten tacos?"

Gretchen shook her head and smirked. "Wow. We're dating, but it's like you don't know me at all."

Chapter Nineteen

Gretchen leaned back in the booth and put a hand on her belly. "Told you so." To be honest, the last two tacos were really hard to finish, but Lincoln had dared her to finish them all, and backing down from a challenge just wasn't her style.

He looked at the empanada he'd abandoned after polishing off the other four. "You're my hero. I have to tap out because there's no way I can eat another bite."

"You also had most of the chips and guac. No wonder you can't finish."

The waiter came by and cleared a few of the plates. "Any dessert?"

Gretchen would have laughed at the way Lincoln blanched at the suggestion, but she was too stuffed. "No. No, thank you. No dessert."

"How about some complementary churros for the road?"

"I won't say no to that," she said with a smile. It was likely more of a grimace, because she was uncomfortably full. Probably not the best idea to inhale all ten tacos, even though they were delicious. Especially when she also had every last bit of the spicy sour cream, creamy cilantro lime dressing, and homemade pico de gallo.

The waiter brought their check and a to go box full of churros. "You can pay up front. Have a great day."

"You, too." Gretchen fished cash out of her wallet.

"I'll get it," Lincoln offered.

"Thanks. I'll leave the tip." She put some bills on the table. "I also need to get those gift certificates on the way out."

A few minutes later, they were back in the car. Gretchen stuffed the gift cards into the bag with the wooden flowers. "What are you getting your dad at the hardware store?"

"He does a lot of woodworking in the winter, so I get him a bunch of little stuff, like new drill bits and saw blades. I saw they've got a Dremel tool kit on sale. He's been wanting one for ages, so hopefully they haven't sold out."

Gretchen held up her hand and crossed her fingers.

Luckily for Lincoln, there were still two kits left on the nearly-empty display just inside the doors. He put one kit in the cart and pushed it toward the back of the store to the section of woodworking tools.

While he looked at blades and accessories, Gretchen wandered into the next aisle where she found a section of model kits and related glues and little plastic parts and tools whose purpose escaped her. She did know one thing, though. Her dad loved putting model planes together, and would definitely put them to good use. She picked a set of fancy tweezers in several sizes and a stand magnifying glass with a light built into it.

She went back to the other aisle and held the magnifier aloft. "Jackpot. This is also a Small Business Saturday deal."

"Nice." Lincoln held up his hand for a high five.

"I'll have to bring Abby here to pick out a new model kit for him. I had no idea they had a whole hobby section here."

"How did you not know that?" Avery's voice teased from behind her.

Gretchen spun, a little guilty. "I guess I don't come in often enough."

"Well, I'm glad to see you anyway." She lifted her wrist and pointed at her watch. "I'm just now heading back to take my lunch break. It's been crazy in here all day."

"That's awful and great."

"I'm definitely not complaining, but it's exhausting. I'll definitely be sleeping late tomorrow."

Lincoln said, "I'd sleep until noon and make Alex go pick up lunch."

Avery pointed at him and nodded. "Genius. You should text him and plant the seed."

Lincoln pulled out his phone.

"Tell him to make her dinner tonight, too," Gretchen joked.

Avery gave them a double thumbs up as she headed toward the back of the store. "See you later!"

They went to the front to check out. As they were loading their purchases into the trunk of Lincoln's car, he pulled his phone out of his pocket and grinned. "Alex says he's coming in to help Avery close the store at six, and he's bringing her favorite large iced coffee from Caretti's."

"Awww, that's so sweet. They make such a good team," she mused as she got in the car. "Alex seems so thoughtful and sensible. I still can't understand how on Earth he thought it was a good idea to send you on a date with an earpiece."

"Must have been having an off day."

"I wonder if he told Avery his plan before he sent you off with your fancy spy gear."

Lincoln shook his head emphatically. "No. He absolutely did not, and he got his own earful after the fact."

Gretchen laughed. "I can only imagine. And the other

guys? My goodness, what a crew and not a single functioning brain cell among you."

Lincoln shot her a side-eye. "So you've said. Many, many times."

"Sorry. Sort of. But four of you. *Four.* And not one of you thought it might not end well." She shook her head. "And those three especially should know better. Avery, Chandler, and Becky would never in a million years have gone for something like that."

"Yeah, yeah, yeah, keep rubbing it in."

She reached over and squeezed his arm. "At least you're in good hands now."

He shifted his eyes again. "That remains to be seen," he teased.

She put her hand back in her lap and leaned back in the seat. "What's next?"

"That's entirely up to you. I got everything on my list."

"Wow, does that mean your Christmas shopping is completely done?"

"Yup. It's all over but the wrapping."

"I'm really impressed."

He held up a finger. "Oh, wait, I lied. I'm waiting on the calendars. I'll buy one for everyone in the family. Except my aunt. She's a retired teacher and still gets her new calendars in August."

"I thought they came in a few weeks ago?"

"The first shipment came in two and a half weeks ago, but we sold out, so the next batch is supposed to be here Monday. Which is great because we have the booth at the winter festival next Saturday."

"I can't believe tomorrow is December already. It feels like Thanksgiving was really late this year."

"I said the same thing when we were getting dinner ready

on Thursday. Thanksgiving was the twenty-eighth, which is as late as it can be, so now Christmas feels like it's next week."

Gretchen's phone vibrated with an incoming text. She pulled it out of her pocket. "I better check this."

Lincoln adjusted the knobs on the heater.

"It's my dad. He's asking if they can take Abby to pick out their Christmas tree."

His head jerked up. "Did you want me to take you home so you can go along?"

"I hate to say yes because we're having a great day and I feel like it would be rude to cut it short."

He gave her an adorable half-smile. "We've been out for seven hours. That hardly counts as cutting it short."

Reluctantly, she said, "Okay. But how about you drop me off at the tree farm since it's closer than taking me the whole way back home."

"Sounds good." He backed out of the parking space.

"Did you get your tree?"

"Not yet."

"Do you want to get it now? My dad will have his truck so we can easily drop it off at your place."

He shrugged one shoulder. "Maybe."

Gretchen felt like there was something he wasn't saying. "Of course if you're not ready to get your tree, don't let me pressure you."

He gave a little laugh. "No, it's just… I guess this is another lesson."

"What do you mean?"

"It feels rude to say I don't want to pick my tree tonight. Especially when I don't really have a good reason." He pulled into the full parking lot of the tree farm.

Large lights had been set up throughout the field so people

could cut down their own trees. It looked like daylight even though the sun had set before five o'clock.

"It's not rude to say no, Lincoln. You don't need a reason."

"I'm not sure. I mean, maybe not for you, but what if I'm dating someone I don't know very well? She might think it's rude."

"Then *she's* rude." Gretchen reached over and put a hand on his arm. "I get it. Believe me, as a woman, we're expected to go along to get along, and set our needs aside to please the people we're with because it's the 'nice' thing to do." She put air quotes around the word. "But I've learned, and so can you, that it's not rude to say no thanks, and you don't need some great reason. You're a good friend, so you know when to do things you might not particularly want to do because the people you care about want you to. You just carry that same mindset into a romantic relationship. If she's the right person, she's not going to be a jerk because you don't want to do something."

She saw her dad's extended cab truck pull into the lot. He'd bought it brand new ten years earlier and treated it like his baby. Hand wash and wax every week, whether it needed it or not.

"My parents just got here."

The truck parked a few spaces away from Lincoln's car.

Gretchen jumped out of the car and waved at her mom. Her dad got Abby out of the back seat and they all walked over.

Abby waited until Lincoln was out of the car, then said, "Are you helping Mommy find our tree? I have to help Grandma."

Before Gretchen could jump in to say he wasn't staying, he said, "Sure."

When she looked at him curiously, he said, "I just didn't want to get *my* tree tonight."

"Ah." She shook her head and followed her parents and Abby toward the barn where they kept the saws, as well as a bunch of precut trees. One of those would have suited her fine, but Abby was all about wandering the rows of trees until she found the perfect one.

Chapter Twenty

Lincoln trudged behind Gretchen and her parents, who were following Abby. She was on a mission. Two missions, actually, since she was tasked with finding the perfect tree for her grandparents, and the perfect tree for her and her mother.

He wasn't sure why he hadn't been able to be honest with Gretchen. The fact of the matter was that he just couldn't afford the trees at this tree farm. Well, he could buy one, but they were expensive and it would mean cutting back on something else. And he just wasn't willing to do financial gymnastics for a tree that would be dragged outside as trash in a month.

He slowed. Maybe this was a practice opportunity. No matter who he was dating, there was guaranteed to be conversations about money and priorities, right? And to be honest, it was a possibility whoever he dated would have less money than him. It just so happened that he was on the lower side of the equation for this... experiment.

Christmas music piped through speakers on tall poles all around the farm. He winced as "Jingle Bell Rock" suddenly blared from a speaker right over his head.

Gretchen looked back and grabbed his hand, pulling him forward. "Pretty loud right under those speakers, isn't it?"

"Obnoxiously so."

They'd taken a few steps on the uneven ground before he realized she hadn't let go of his hand. And he hadn't let go of hers. Her parents and Abby were twenty yards ahead.

He blurted out, "I can't afford these trees."

She looked up at him, startled. "Oh."

"That's why I don't want to look for a tree tonight. Here. I mean, I could *afford* one, but we usually get any real trees from my mom's uncle. He's got a lot of land and pine trees so that's where my parents get their tree."

"Lincoln—"

"I have an artificial tree." He forced the words out like he was confessing some deep, shameful secret.

Gretchen covered her mouth with her other hand. "An... *artificial* tree? How long were you going to keep this from me? I thought we were friends."

Even he couldn't miss the amused twinkle in her eye.

"Do you at least spray it with evergreen scent?"

"No."

"I don't know how we can move on from this." She pressed the back of her hand to her forehead and pretended to be dizzy. "Thank goodness we're not dating for real."

"Mom! I found it!" Abby yelled from all the way down the row.

Gretchen tugged his hand. "Let's see what she found."

They walked over the mostly-dead brush and branches and twigs littering the row and came to stop in front of a seven-foot tree that looked like it had been attacked with a chainsaw. The branches jutted out every which way along the trunk and some huge bare spots had no branches at all.

Gretchen reached out and snapped the very end off a tiny branch and held it to her nose. "It's got a great smell."

Abby took the piece and sniffed it. "It smells like Christmas."

"Perfect."

Brian tied the plastic tag to the top of the tree. After it was tied, he hunkered down to the ground and began hacking at the trunk with the flimsy hand saw he'd been carrying. "I should have brought a chainsaw."

"You say that every year," Dory said.

He grunted and kept chopping at the trunk until there was a loud crack. He rolled out of the way and got to his feet. The tree only needed one push of encouragement to fall.

"Yay!" Abby clapped her hands and jumped up and down. "There's your tree, Grandpa!" She pointed to a tree the next row over. At a very pretty, full tree that belonged on the cover of a magazine.

Lincoln glanced down at Gretchen. She shook her head. "That's just how it goes. My parents get the tree that could go on a magazine cover, and we get the tree with 'character.'" She made air quotes around the word.

Brian cut down the second tree. He grabbed the trunk while Dory grabbed the top of the tree. Lincoln followed his example and took hold of the trunk of Abby's tree. Gretchen grabbed the top and they began the trek back to the barn.

Lincoln's arms and calves ached by the time they got back and turned their trees over to the employee who hoisted them onto the shaker, then through the machine that squished them with a binding net to make them easier to maneuver.

"Tell Sally you got a number five and a number one." He turned to the next customer.

Inside the barn, they got in line for the cash register. Sally rang up their trees, gave Brian the change, then said to Abby,

"You may choose an ornament to take home with you." She pointed to a massive tree in the corner of the room, brightly lit with white lights and decorated with all manner of ornaments. "Help yourselves to hot chocolate or spiced cider, and some home-baked cookies," she added for the adults.

Abby ran over to the tree where two other children were investigating the offerings.

Eventually, she selected a cat ornament. She asked Lincoln, "Does any of your cats look like this?"

"Do," Gretchen corrected.

Abby rolled her eyes. "*DO* any of your cats look like this?"

Lincoln looked at the ornament of a Siamese cat. "Nope, I have a black and white cat, an orange cat, and a calico."

"What's calico?"

"It's a mix of colors. Some white, some orange, some gray."

"Huh. But do you like this?"

"Very much. This is a Siamese cat. I don't have one of those, but they're very sweet and usually talk a lot."

She looked down at the ornament in her hand for a long moment, then declared, "I'm keeping it anyway. I named it Lincoln. He wants to help other cats to find good homes like you."

He swallowed hard against the sudden lump in his throat.

She carefully put the ornament in her coat pocket and zipped it shut. "Can I get a cookie?"

Gretchen reappeared at his side with a napkin and cookie in each hand. "Chocolate chip for you," she said as she handed the cookie to Abby. Then she handed the other to Lincoln. "And snickerdoodle for you."

"You remembered."

"I probably shouldn't admit this, but I only remembered because they're my favorite, too."

He glanced at her empty hands. "You didn't get yourself one?"

She flashed a guilty grin and whispered, "I already had two."

He laughed. "You're going to get us kicked out of here."

"That's okay, they're ready to leave anyway." Gretchen jerked her head toward the door, where her parents were standing.

They wound through the crowd and stopped outside to grab the trees. Lincoln tried not to huff and puff as he carried Gretchen's tree to the truck. He hefted it into the bed of the truck. Brian tossed their tree in like it weighed nothing. He had the audacity to not even be out of breath.

Lincoln made a mental note to start working out. He ran his sticky palm against his jeans, but the pine sap wouldn't come off. "Yuck."

"You'll be stuck to the steering wheel." She held up her hands and wiggled her clean fingers. "Bummer."

Lincoln grabbed her hands and smooshed his palms against hers. She squealed with laughter and tried to twist away, which only got them tangled up with her back against his chest and his arms around her. The poofball on her hat tickled his cheek.

"Mom! Are you coming or not?" Abby was already buckled into her seat.

Lincoln let go of her.

She turned, inspecting her hands. "Look what you did." She held up her palm and pointed to a streak of sap.

He grinned down at her. "I'll make it up to you."

"Darn right you will."

"Mom!"

Gretchen called back, "That's my name, don't wear it out!"

She sighed and looked up at him. "I had such a great day today."

"Me, too."

"Drive safe."

Before a single brain cell in his head–*the* single brain cell that he apparently shared with his friends–could do anything about it, before he thought, before he even knew what he was doing, Lincoln leaned down and kissed her.

A quick kiss.

Just a peck, really.

No big deal.

Her eyes went wide, but before she could speak, he launched himself into his car and waved goodbye in what he hoped was a super casual way, but judging from the way his heart was pounding and his brain was screaming, "WHAT DID YOU JUST DO???" he guessed it was anything but casual.

Gretchen raised an eyebrow, gave him a small wave, then turned and went to the truck.

Lincoln carefully backed out of his spot and slowly made his way to the exit, stopping several times for darting children and people carrying trees to their vehicles.

His mind raced. Why? Why? Why? Why had he done that? Was she mad? What if she never wanted to talk to him again? How the heck was he going to smooth this over?

He was pulling into his driveway when he realized she'd definitely be speaking to him again. At least once.

The gifts she bought were still in the trunk of his car.

Chapter Twenty-One

Gretchen was still reeling long after the tree was secure in the stand, and Abby was fast asleep in her bed. She grabbed her phone and texted Jody.

> Do you have a minute?????

A few minutes later, Jody's reply popped up.

> Sure, what's up??

> Can I call????

Her phone began buzzing with an incoming call almost immediately.

"Is everything okay?"

"Yes. I think. Maybe. Maybe not. I have no idea."

After a long pause, Jody said, "Huh?"

"Lincoln and I went shopping today. Pretty much all day."

"Okay?"

"We went to all these local places. It's Small Business Saturday or something like that, so we did Christmas shopping at all local small businesses. And then we had lunch at Holy Guacamole."

"Babe. I know all this. I handed you caffeine to get your day started."

"Oh yeah. Right." She stammered a few times.

Jody's voice went from curious to concerned. "Did something happen?"

"He..." She pressed a finger to her bottom lip. "He kissed me."

Jody's shriek of "What?!" nearly split her eardrum.

Gretchen jerked the phone away from her ear for a second.

"Wait, what? How? When? Lincoln? He *kissed* you? How did this happen? What?"

"I don't know how it happened. We went to the Christmas tree farm and we were talking about the pine sap and he smeared some on my hand and we were laughing and then all of a sudden he kissed me!"

"Soooo, like *kissed* you kissed you, or like just kissed you. Was there tongue involved?"

"No!" Gretchen shook her head. "No, it was just a quick peck."

"On the cheek or on the lips?"

"Lips."

"Wow." Jody dragged the word out for several beats. "Nobody can say I didn't warn you. What did you do?"

"I didn't do anything. As soon as he kissed me, he jumped in the car and took off."

"Wait. He kissed you, then left you stranded at the tree farm?"

"What? No, of course not."

"How did you get home?"

"My parents were there with Abby." Gretchen realized she'd skipped that part. "Let me rewind a bit. My dad called about getting the trees tonight. We were done with our shopping, so I asked Lincoln to take me to the tree lot instead of home, and I could ride with them. He ended up going along while we–well, while Abby–picked out my parents' tree and ours. We were done and put the trees in Dad's truck. I walked over to his car to say good night because it made sense to just ride home with Abby and it all just kind of happened."

"That makes a lot more sense."

"Sorry, my brain is all over the place."

"Did you kiss him back?"

She twisted a finger in the hem of her sweater. "I think so? I mean, it happened so fast."

"How do you feel about it?"

"I have no idea." That was the absolute truth. She had no idea what emotions lurked behind the shock that still took center stage.

"How does *he* feel about it?"

"No clue. He bolted. Like, I've never seen a human being get into a car so fast. I don't know if he was embarrassed, or afraid I'd slug him, or instantly filled with regret, or what."

"My money's on embarrassed. And he probably shocked himself for doing it."

That seemed very likely.

"And maybe a little bit afraid of getting slugged."

Also likely. Gretchen ran a hand through her curls. "What do you think it means?"

"Does it mean anything?"

"It's Lincoln. He doesn't do things for no reason."

Jody made a *hmm* noise. "Well, it could be that he likes you. Or maybe he was just caught up in the date. Maybe he's taking some of your lessons to heart and letting himself relax and go with the flow, just like he would–should–on a real date."

That definitely made sense. "Okay. What I'm hearing is that

I need to stop freaking out and relax because it was probably nothing."

"Oh, it was something."

"What? You just said it was nothing."

"I never said that."

Gretchen sucked in a deep breath and held it for a count of five. "Jodyyyyy. What are you saying?"

"What do you want it to mean?"

"Me? I'm just trying to figure out what he was thinking."

"Which is impossible without asking him. Now setting him aside, what do you want it to mean?"

"I don't want it to mean anything. That's ridiculous. This is Lincoln we're talking about. My *friend* Lincoln." Who she was fake dating. Not dating for real.

"Hmm."

"No hmm. This is not a hmm situation. Take your hmm back."

"What if it was just a go with the flow peck on the lips that meant absolutely nothing. Are you good with that?"

"Of course." Probably.

"What if it was something?"

"What kind of something?"

"What if he's catching feelings? Are you good with that?"

"I…" She held another breath for a count of five and let it out to a count of five. "That's not even possible."

"Well, if you want my advice, I'd say call him. Quit speculating and wondering and just ask him point blank what it meant, if anything. You're the dating coach, right?"

"I suppose."

"There you go. Tackle it like a lesson. Stick to the facts without emotion."

"Well, hopefully his feelings aren't involved."

Jody hmmed again. "I'm more worried about yours."

Chapter Twenty-Two

Lincoln arrived at Sonny's Diner well before ten thirty, when the guys typically met for a late breakfast. No, they didn't call it brunch.

He claimed the corner booth and drummed his fingers on the tabletop until everyone got there. The guys filled the booth, chattering like usual.

Lincoln waited until Corinne poured everyone's coffee and took their food orders. On the one hand, he wasn't sure how much to tell them. On the other, he needed some advice. He half-hoped someone else had some news or something interesting to talk about, but he was quickly relieved of that notion.

Oren propped his elbows on the table. "How are the dating lessons going?"

Noah, Alex, and Nate looked at him expectantly.

His brain tried to find a good starting point. His mouth just went ahead and launched the words, "I kissed her."

There was a collective gasp followed by all four men saying some version of, "What?"

"Wait, wait, wait." Alex waved his hands to quiet the group. "Start from the beginning."

He gave them a brief rundown of the day. "We put the trees in her dad's truck, and I don't know, it was cold and her cheeks and her nose were pink and she was teasing me about the sap on my hands so I grabbed her hands to get them sticky, too, and we were laughing and she had this ridiculous poofball on her hat and I didn't even think about it. I swear there was no conscious thought involved. I just leaned down and gave her a kiss, and then I got the heck out of Dodge."

"What did she say?"

Lincoln dumped another creamer into his coffee and stirred it. "I didn't give her a chance to say anything. I literally dove into my car and drove away like I robbed a bank."

Noah snickered. Oren elbowed him.

Corinne brought their breakfasts and handed out the plates.

Lincoln looked at his pancakes, but there were so many knots in his stomach he wasn't sure if he'd be able to eat.

Nate poured a massive puddle of syrup onto his French toast. "I assume you haven't talked to her yet."

"No."

Alex offered, "I wouldn't. I'd keep my mouth shut and pretend it never happened."

Oren answered around a mouth full of scrambled eggs. "Not gonna work. I've known Gretchen forever. There's a zero percent chance she lets this go without saying anything."

Noah shrugged. "Then let her bring it up."

Nate shook his head. "No, take the direct approach. Then you'll have the upper hand in the conversation and can steer it the way you want it to go."

Oren barked a laugh. "Have you *met* Gretchen? I agree, I think you should bring it up, but don't delude yourself into thinking there's any kind of tactical advantage to be had."

Lincoln drizzled the last few drops of syrup onto his

pancake. "This is weird. It's not some kind of military operation. I'll just... I'll just tell her I was caught up in the moment and it just happened and that it didn't mean anything and it won't happen again."

Alex quietly asked, "Is any of that true?"

"Of course it's true." He shoved a wedge of pancake into his mouth to buy some time. It took forever to chew, thanks to it being dry since Nate hoarded the syrup.

Too late to help, Corinne brought a fresh container of syrup and refilled their coffee cups.

"You're not catching feelings for Gretchen, are you?" Oren asked.

"Boh gorn noh," Lincoln insisted. He swallowed the wad of dry pancake and repeated, "Of course not."

From there, the conversation flew around the table with advice to call her, to not call her, to bring it up first, to not bring it up, to deal with it head on, to deflect and avoid it at all costs, and the final bit of advice that was thrown into the ring by Noah.

"Maybe you should just call this whole thing off."

The rest of the guys considered the idea.

Noah offered, "You know what this is? That thing where patients fall for their doctor or therapist."

"Transference," Oren said.

"Yeah. Transference. That's the only reason you're starting to think there's something more than there is."

Lincoln threw his hands up. "What? I never said I was getting feelings."

His friends all scoffed.

"You need to go on a real date. Not with Gretchen."

Lincoln concentrated on his pancake and the tightness in his chest. Of all the bad advice they'd ever given him–and there was a lot–that had to be the worst.

Alex said, "Avery's friend Meredith is visiting from Atlanta. You should take her out."

Okay, maybe *that* was the worst advice ever.

He snatched the syrup container before Noah could use it all. He mumbled, "Yeah, I don't think that's something I would do."

Oren bit into a strip of bacon and said, "That might be a good idea. Give you a chance to practice the stuff Gretchen's been teaching you."

Lincoln couldn't believe his ears. "You all think I should go out with someone else? That wouldn't be, I don't know, wrong?"

"Why? You and Gretchen are just friends. You probably kissed her because you're spending too much time together and you're getting too comfortable."

"Yeah. Yup. Uh-huh, that transference thing," was the chorus from around the table.

Alex bobbed his head and pulled out his phone. "Then it's a done deal. I'll see when she's available."

Lincoln went cold, then hot. This scheme was not sitting well with him. But the guys were all talking about it and making plans without his input.

"Guys, no…" His tongue felt too big for his mouth.

The conversation had taken on a life of its own.

"Guys? I don't think—"

"Done. You can pick her up at our place at six."

Lincoln choked out a noise that wasn't a word.

"Tonight."

He felt his face heat. He wanted to object, to tell Alex to call it off, to put a stop to this runaway freight train, but his tongue was glued to the roof of his mouth. His throat and chest were tight and it was all he could do to pull in breath.

The plans swirled around him. In the end, it was decided

that Lincoln would pick Meredith up at six and take her to dinner. From there, they could go to a movie, but nobody knew what might be playing.

The subject changed, once, twice, three times before Lincoln was able to get himself under control. He choked out, "Should I tell Gretchen?"

All eyes were on him. There was a quiet beat, then a round of unanimous, incredulous, "Of course not. Why would you do that? It's not like you're really dating."

He felt stupid for asking.

As he got in his car to leave, he also felt stupid for letting himself get roped into a date. His friends were amazing, supportive, loyal men who always had his back. But sometimes, like now, their big, confident personalities overwhelmed him and he found himself in a situation he didn't want to be in.

Correction, he let himself be led into a situation he didn't want to be in. Lincoln gripped the steering wheel. He had to own his part in letting his friends steamroll him.

His mind swirled in double time. Not only did he need to figure out exactly why he'd kissed Gretchen, now he needed to figure out what he was going to do about Meredith. Was there a way to gracefully cancel without being a jerk?

Even if he went with the truth–his friends set him up and he didn't want to go, he still looked like a jerk for letting it happen.

And maybe he was. He needed to practice more than dating. He needed to practice using his words so he didn't end up in these situations. For a moment, he considered calling Gretchen to get her advice, but it didn't feel right. They weren't exclusive, because they weren't actually dating. So it shouldn't be a big deal.

He parked in front of his house and sat in the car contemplating his situation. But not for long, because the cold from outside quickly overtook the lingering heat.

All afternoon, he debated what he should do, until it was time to leave. And since he hadn't canceled, he had to go, because standing her up would be even worse than going through with it.

Chapter Twenty-Three

Gretchen sat in her home office, going through her typical Sunday night routine of making her to do list for the upcoming week. And since it was December first, she sketched out her goals for the month.

As usual, she made sure her goals were manageable around the holidays, while still including those pesky business wrap-up tasks that needed to be done by the end of the year.

She'd just added a note to print out receipts and update her profit & loss statement for the accountant when her phone buzzed with an incoming text message from Jody.

> Are you busy?

> Not really, what's up?

> Bored out of my mind. Kids are diving me bananas and Stew is riding shotgun with them. BBQ Palace??? Tess can babysit.

> LOL You've got it all planned out, how can I say no??

On our way!!!!!!!!!!!!

Gretchen chuckled as she closed out of her messaging app.

Abby was watching a movie in the living room.

"Hey, kiddo. Tess is coming over to babysit while Jody and I go out for some grown-up girl time."

Abby paused the movie. "Can we get pizza?"

"Do you want pizza, or do you want me to bring you back some pulled pork?"

Abby thought about it for a minute. "Can I get pizza *and* breadsticks?"

"Sure."

"Then pizza."

"Really? No pork or chicken or wings?"

"Nah." She turned the movie back on.

Gretchen logged onto her app and ordered pizza, bread-sticks, and a giant chocolate chip cookie for delivery. She sat down and half-watched the movie and scrolled through social media until Jody and Tess arrived, followed shortly by the pizza delivery.

In the car, Jody said, "You're a life saver. Tess and Mindy are on each other's last nerve, Darren and Samantha are fighting about some boy Samantha wants to date and Darren doesn't like him. Stew was completely oblivious to everything and then had the nerve–the absolutely *audacity*–to tell me I was overreacting."

"Oh, Stew."

"Right? So clueless sometimes. I figured I should probably remove myself from the situation before I strangled someone."

"Good call."

"Besides, I need an update on the kiss situation."

"There's no update."

"What do you mean?" She put on her turn signal and

pulled into the busy BBQ Palace parking lot. "Don't tell me you haven't talked to him."

Gretchen shifted in the seat.

Before Jody could continue her interrogation, an incoming call popped up on the radio's screen. Stewart.

"I'll go ahead and grab us a table since it looks busy."

Jody heaved a sigh. "Good idea." She connected the call.

Gretchen heard Stew ask, "Where's the ketchup?" as she got out of the car. Poor Jody was probably ready to explode. Stew would have been better off to go out and buy new ketchup instead of bothering her.

The air was biting cold. Gretchen hurried along the sidewalk, pulling her coat tighter around her chin.

She glanced to the bank of windows. The restaurant was filled with a warm glow from little tea light candles on the tables. An extraordinarily pretty blonde in a booth against the windows caught her attention. Long, soft curls framed her face. The sort of curls Gretchen had always been jealous of because her own red mop of curls was unmanageable without a lot of intervention.

Her feet came to a halt before she recognized the man in the booth across from the woman.

Lincoln.

He was leaning forward, all of his attention focused on the woman. He was smiling, nodding, and maintaining eye contact. Just like she'd coached him to do.

Footsteps clicked up behind her.

"What's the holdup? It's freezing." Jody grabbed her arm and tugged her toward the door.

A second later, she said, "Oh. What the heck's going on there?"

Gretchen shook her head because she had no answer.

Jody grunted a disgusted growl. "Fine. Plan B. Let's go to Holy Guacamole. I didn't want barbecue anyway."

Gretchen let Jody nudge her toward the car. As she fastened her seatbelt, she was even more confused by what she'd seen. "I don't get it. Why wouldn't he tell me he had a date? Ask for pointers or something? Do you think it was really a date? Maybe it was just a friend or a cousin or something?"

Jody started the car and blasted the heater. "That was Meredith. Avery's friend who's visiting from Atlanta. I mean, it's possible they know each other somehow?"

"Maybe."

As they pulled into Holy Guacamole, Jody said, "Hey, worst case scenario, he's graduating early from your coaching program, right?"

Gretchen gave herself a mental shake. "Right. Exactly."

"There could be a million explanations. You'll have to ask him."

She forced herself to laugh. "For sure. I'll give him a pop quiz and see how it went. Clearly he's learned something from me since he was looking very attentive and comfortable." It shouldn't bother her. They weren't dating. It was a little annoying that she had to keep reminding herself of that fact.

After they were seated and had ordered their food, Jody broached the subject again. "If that's the case, you can just call this whole thing off, right? I told you this was a bad idea when you first mentioned it, but maybe it worked and now Lincoln can go forth and date with reckless abandon."

"Yeah."

"You can be done with it before anybody gets all into their feelings and starts thinking it was more than it was, right?"

"Right." She sounded way more convincing than she felt. Which was ridiculous because Jody was right. One hundred percent right. The entire point of this experiment was for Lincoln to learn how to date. *Other people*. That was the point. Which was a good point, because she wasn't interested in dating Lincoln or anyone else.

"Maybe since you dipped your toes back into the dating world, you'll be more inclined to find a man of your own."

"I don't want a man of my own. You know that."

"Eh, I know you say that."

Gretchen sighed. "It's kind of late, so I'll save my 'I'm a strong, independent woman and I don't need no man to be complete' speech for another time."

Jody chuckled. "I won't listen to it then, either."

She suddenly felt a little snappy. "Just because you're happily married to the man of your dreams doesn't mean every woman wants to be married."

"Yeah, okay. This isn't about fighting the patriarchy, it's about creating the life *you* want. And I know having a partner is on the list, even though it's well below your main priorities. As it should be."

"Fine. I'll concede the point. That doesn't mean I'm interested in dating."

"Eh, it's late so I'll pretend I agree with you."

"Gee, thanks."

Somewhere around the halfway point of the loaded nacho platter, it occurred to her. The news didn't upset her, per se. It was just surprising, and it was preemptive disappointment because she was looking forward to having someone to spend time with over the holidays. It was fun to go out and do things, even if they weren't real dates. That's all.

It didn't bother her at all that Lincoln might be dating someone, because that would be ridiculous. That was the clear goal from the beginning. She was just bothered that this might change some of her plans. And if there was one thing Gretchen loved, it was having all her ducks in a row, well in advance. Mentally, she'd had the rest of the holiday season planned out, so it was only natural a disruption would be an annoyance.

See? That's all it was.

An hour later, over a decimated platter of loaded nachos, Gretchen–with Jody's encouragement–had convinced herself that was the answer.

Well, almost.

Chapter Twenty-Four

Meredith was pleasant enough. Lincoln sat across the table from her, killing time by studying the menu.

After they ordered, Meredith asked the first typical first date question. "What do you do?"

"I'm a pet sitter."

She looked interested. "That sounds fun. You must love animals then, huh?" Her words had a mild Southern twang.

He expanded a little bit. "I do. I volunteer with the animal rescue, and I'm working on opening a doggie day care/dog boarding facility."

"How fun. We work with animals, too, in a different capacity."

"Oh?" He wasn't quite prepared for her next words.

"My daddy runs a taxidermy studio. He's a conservation expert and uses a lot of his taxidermies in educational programs and whatnot."

Lincoln swallowed. Taxidermy didn't quite seem like "working with animals" in the same way.

"We have some family who own a cabin not far from here. It's a great area for hunting whitetail."

"I... yeah, a lot of people go deer hunting."

"I got an eight-point a few years ago. Haven't been that lucky since. How about you? Any big ones?"

"Uuuhhh, no. No, I don't hunt. I prefer rescuing animals. Getting them good homes. Hunting is..." He trailed off.

"An ecological necessity?" Meredith supplied in a tight voice.

Well, great. He'd managed to offend her two minutes into the evening.

Their waiter brought their dinners and walked away.

Meredith inclined her head toward his plate. More accurately, toward his steak. "Since you're clearly not against eating animals, I sure hope you're not passing judgment."

He cleared his throat. "No. I'm not at all. It's just not my thing. It makes me uncomfortable to think about being out in the woods with a gun. It's not for me."

"Well, bless your heart."

Ouch. Even he knew what that meant. He didn't even disagree with her. He was very familiar with local conservation efforts and how hunting and fishing played a huge role in a healthy ecosystem. And yes, maybe it was hypocritical, but he couldn't see himself being the one to personally turn a cow into a steak, but it's not like he ground his own wheat into flour, either.

The rest of the date progressed with forced small talk and long awkward silences. Somewhere along the way, though, Lincoln realized that it wasn't his anxiety keeping him quiet. He just didn't have much to say to Meredith. They had very little in common and she seemed as disinterested as he was.

He felt like that was a step in the right direction. Acknowledging and understanding that this was going nowhere. Not because of his fears or inability to connect, but because

Meredith was not the person for him, and he most definitely was not the right person for her.

Interestingly enough, that realization made him relax and mostly enjoy the rest of the evening. He even told a joke or two that Meredith actually laughed at.

Maybe the evening wasn't the horrible mistake he'd originally thought.

Chapter Twenty-Five

By Thursday, Gretchen was ready to scream. Or run away. Or both. The entire week had been one frustration after another. No, dear client, she couldn't build a brand new website from scratch in time for Christmas shopping when it was the first week of December. It was bad enough to get one such request, but there had been three. Three people who should have been competent business owners, but couldn't understand why their requests were unreasonable.

Moments like this made her glad her main office was at home. She got up from her desk, left the room and closed the door. Her office was decorated and organized for maximum productivity, but the rest of the house was decorated for comfort and peace. Especially her happy place, the kitchen. The walls were a pale sunshine yellow with bright white cabinetry and warm wooden floors.

She got herself a fresh mug of hot chocolate and put a whole handful of mini marshmallows on top, then added a little sprinkle of cinnamon. Perfection.

She took a sip, glanced at the clock, and made a second cup. She was just swirling a hefty dollop of whipped topping on the surface of the hot chocolate when the front door burst open and Abby blasted inside. "MOM!"

Gretchen poked her head into the hallway. "In the kitchen."

Abby skipped into the kitchen. Her eyes got big. "Oooh, is that mine?"

"Of course." Gretchen slid the mug across the island as Abby climbed up onto a chair. "How was your day?"

"Terrible. Oliver's a jerk. He pulled my hair and the teacher said he just liked me and I told her she was stupid and I don't care if he likes me, he can't pull my hair. Well he did it again after recess and I yelled at him to stop touching me and then she made me clean off the whiteboard."

Gretchen's jaw clenched. Seriously? Abby got punished for setting a reasonable boundary and not letting this kid pull her hair?

"Oliver had to wipe all the tables and then he had to put all the books away nicely all by himself. Then she made him say sorry." She took a huge sip of hot chocolate and gave herself a whipped topping mustache.

"I might still give her a call. There was no reason to punish you."

Abby gave a dramatic shrug. "She said 'cos I called her stupid."

Oh. Yeah, calling the teacher stupid was probably a reasonably punishable offense. "Name calling is wrong. But telling that kid to back off was exactly right. He doesn't get to pull your hair."

"I know, Mom." Abby rolled her eyes.

Gretchen shuddered. She thought the eyerolling and sarcasm wouldn't come until Abby was a teenager. Boy was she ahead of her years. "Do you have homework?"

"Yeah." She drained the rest of her hot chocolate and set the mug down hard.

Gretchen had to stifle a laugh. Poor Abby looked like a hardened detective at the bar after wrapping up a difficult case. "Pork chops for dinner."

"Cool." Abby fished in her backpack and slapped a worksheet on the countertop. She moaned dramatically. "I don't have my pencil box."

That was an easy fix. Gretchen opened the junk drawer and got out the pencil box full of miscellaneous pencils, random logo pens, and stray crayons. She set it in front of her daughter. "Here you go."

Abby went to work on her paper while Gretchen put dinner in the oven.

Walter ambled into the kitchen and let out a wheezy bark at the back door.

Abby scrambled off her chair to take him out. "Lincoln should come take him out."

Gretchen stiffened at his name. She hadn't heard from him since Sunday. No call, no text, no nothing.

So apparently that was that.

Chapter Twenty-Six

Saturday was brisk and chilly, but the sky was bright blue and the forecast was clear. In other words, the perfect day for the Hickory Hollow Christmas Village Extravaganza.

Lincoln popped the canopy tent into place and adjusted the legs. All the side streets leading to the town square had been barricaded. Vendors were setting up canopies and tables on the sidewalks. A few residents already strolled up and down the streets, checking out the offerings before anyone was ready.

Alyssa heaved another box of calendars onto the table. "Do you think we'll get rid of all of them?"

"Let's hope." He busied himself clipping calendar pages to the front of the table.

"You have the cash box?"

"No, Ruby is bringing it with her."

"Do we have a donation jar?"

Lincoln frowned a little. "No, we'll just have the calendar sales."

Alyssa let out an exasperated grunt. "We need a donation jar. Lots of people will walk past and put a couple bucks in a jar who might not want a calendar. Or who already got their calendar."

She was absolutely right, and he felt a little stupid for not thinking of something so simple. He snapped his fingers. "I know exactly what to do. Are you okay if I run to Prescott's?"

"Sure."

He jogged off, hurrying past the other businesses who were setting up. He hustled the three blocks to Prescott's Grocery and darted across the parking lot and into the store. He made a beeline for the snack aisle and scanned the shelves until his gaze landed on what he wanted. A large clear plastic tub of cheese puffs. He snatched it off the shelf and hurried down another aisle, where he grabbed a roll of paper towels and a box of plastic zipper bags.

Instead of going back to the booth, he went to his car, where he emptied the cheese puffs into zipper bags and wiped out the container. Not wanting to take any longer than necessary, he jogged back to the booth.

"Nice. Did you eat them all on the way back?"

"Yes. They were delicious." He spied the roll of tape he'd been using earlier and quickly made a "Donations" sign for the container.

Alyssa put some dollar bills into the tub. "Seed money," she explained. "It's a psychological thing. If the container is empty, people are less likely to put money in. But if they think someone already donated, they're more likely to toss some money in themselves. It's weird."

"Very weird. People in general are weird."

The event was scheduled to start at noon, but by eleven thirty, they'd already sold five calendars, gotten a handful of bills tossed into cheese puff container, and the streets were full of people milling about, enjoying the decent weather after a long stretch of biting cold.

Ruby arrived just before twelve and surveyed the booth. "Nice job, guys. Lincoln, you're done at noon, right?"

"Yes, but I'll be back this evening to help tear down."

"Great, thanks."

He walked along the street, looking at the other booths. All the usual suspects were in attendance. Hickory Hollow Travel, a brewery and a winery, Hickory Hollow Campground, and Myers Insurance Agency, where Alex was nodding politely at an older lady who was insisting that her payment for her car insurance was withdrawn from her bank account six times.

Lincoln stood off to the side, waiting until he was done.

"Ma'am, I'm so sorry, I'm just helping out with the booth. I don't work for the insurance company."

The woman's eyes narrowed. She pointed a finger to his face. "You're a Myers."

"Yes, ma'am, my sister Holly owns the company since our parents retired. I own a security company." He pointed to his own company booth, set up next to the insurance. His business partner, Erin, was busy in their booth talking to a customer about doorbell cameras.

"There you are!" an exasperated voice called.

Lincoln turned to see a man rushing toward the elderly lady who was scolding Alex.

"Mom, what are you doing?"

"Fixing that problem with my car insurance."

"Ma, you don't have car insurance anymore." He glanced up at Alex. "Sorry."

"No problem. Free pen?" He held out one of the logo pens from the table.

The woman brightened and took the bright pink pen. "It's my favorite color." She let her son lead her away.

Lincoln walked over. "Look at you, harassing little old ladies."

He waved his hand at the booth. "It never fails. Something odd happens every time I cover for Holly."

"Uh oh, why am I hearing my name?" Holly came around the back and into the booth with Alex. He filled her in on the situation.

"Ah. Mrs. Perkins. She calls at least once a month. Poor lady. Dementia is such a horrible thing." She turned her attention to Lincoln. "How are you?"

"Good. Just popping by to see Alex before I head out."

"Head out?" Alex asked. "It's just starting."

"I know. I set up the stand for the shelter and I'll be back later to help tear down."

Alex's brow furrowed as he came around the back of the booth and joined Lincoln on the sidewalk. "I kind of figured you and Gretchen would meet up here."

Lincoln shrugged one shoulder. "I haven't heard from her all week."

"She's ghosting you?"

"No. I don't think so. I mean, I haven't reached out to her, either."

"Why?"

"I don't know. I guess I feel weird about going out with Meredith."

Alex wore a pained expression. "Sorry about that. I never should have suggested it."

"She had a terrible time, didn't she?"

They strolled down the middle of the street, mixing in with the crowd.

"She said it ended up okay, but it was pretty obvious you didn't want to be there. I wish you would have stopped me."

"I tried."

Alex nodded and kicked a small stone. "I think we all have to do a better job of backing off. I tend to get caught up in my brilliant ideas and just run with them. Sorry for steamrolling you."

"Nah, no apology needed. I need to work on speaking up. I let myself get too overwhelmed and don't open my mouth." True, he'd been annoyed with Alex, but that was the bottom line. Alex didn't force him to go out with Meredith and he had a dozen opportunities to call it off but he hadn't.

"Why do you think Gretchen hasn't contacted you? Does she know about Meredith?"

"I don't see how she could."

Chapter Twenty-Seven

The grinding roar of a chainsaw swallowed whatever Abby just said. Gretchen leaned down and shouted, "What?"

Abby yelled back, "It's a reindeer!"

Indeed, the ice sculptor was sawing away chunks of ice and shaping the remaining block into a large reindeer with massive antlers. A crowd gathered behind a rope barrier to watch the creation come to life.

He set the chainsaw down and began tapping at the ice with a chisel. Abby was transfixed by the process. Gretchen's mind wandered. She looked up and down the street, at the rows of vendors, and thought for the millionth time that she should have gotten a booth for her business. But that would have meant buying things to hand out and having people to set up and tear down and man the booth.

On a day like today, it would have been easy. Today was that comfortable kind of cold that made being outside during an event like this enjoyable. But last year's event had been miserable. Sleet and freezing rain that hadn't been forecasted started in the early afternoon, causing the event to shut down barely an hour after it started.

Unfortunately, there weren't many opportunities to get out there in the winter. Sure, she was one of the sponsors of the Ladies' Society's Valentine's Ball, and at least her business was listed as a sponsor in the shelter's calendar.

Oh.

She'd done such a good job putting Lincoln out of her mind, but now she found herself annoyed all over again. She'd left the ball in his court. He'd kissed her on Saturday and she hadn't heard from him since.

And let's not even think about his Sunday evening date.

Was he seeing this person now? He really had graduated from their little plan, hadn't they? Were they going to be official? Was he here with her right now? Was her hair still perfect?

She hated the way her head whipped around so she could scan the crowd. It wasn't like she *cared*. She was just annoyed because he hadn't bothered to tell her they weren't dating–*fake* dating–anymore. He could go see whoever he wanted, but it was rude not to give her a heads up.

Or maybe a thanks for coaching him into behavior that got him a stupid new girlfriend. Nope, she wasn't bothered at all by the idea of him dating someone else. It was his rudeness. In fact, she'd tell him so the next time she saw him.

That's why she looked through the crowd again. It was definitely not to see if he was here with what's-her-face with the perfect hair. Maybe it was a wig. Or at least salon-bought extensions. The thought comforted her a little.

Her gaze took in all the faces in the crowd. It looked like the nice weather had brought the entire county out for the event. She briefly hoped that meant the shelter would be able to sell all of their calendars and maybe even get some applications for the animals needing forever homes.

Suddenly, her eyes snapped back to a face she hadn't seen

in a handful of years. She whipped her head around, hoping she hadn't been spotted, but her skin crawled like she was being watched. The cold in the air was no match for the chill that ran down her spine and made her shudder. It definitely wasn't needed, but she reached over her shoulder and flipped her hood up to cover her head.

Her heart skipped a panicked beat when Abby wasn't against her. She'd moved a few feet away with a group of kids who were watching the ice sculptor add fine details to the reindeer.

With shaking hands, she slipped her phone out of her pocket.

> Mom where are you??

It took a few minutes for the screen to pop up a notification.

> Your dad and I are in front of the pet store.
> Where are you?

For Pet's Sake was several blocks away.

> Can you come to the hair salon please ASAP

Dory must have known something was amiss.

> What's wrong? Are you and Abby ok????

> We're fine. Please hurry.

On some level, she felt ridiculous for needing her parents to come rescue her from what was probably nothing. On many other levels, she was infinitely grateful they were on their way.

A leisurely stroll from one end of town to the other could take twenty minutes. Six minutes passed when she heard her dad's voice. He was next to her, leaning down to her ear, his arm around her shoulders. "What's up? You okay?"

Her throat constricted and all she could do was nod. She held up a finger in a "wait" gesture so she could compose herself.

Dory got to her other side a minute after Brian.

Gretchen saw her mom's gaze quickly find Abby and then sweep down over Gretchen, assessing that they were fine, physically at least.

The sculptor finished the reindeer and turned to take a bow. Everyone gave him a round of applause and started to mill away.

Gretchen reached over and snatched Abby's hand, holding it tight. Abby looked up at her, confused, so she loosened her grip and forced a smile onto her face.

A man juggling Christmas ornaments wove through the crowd, smiling and winking at the children. A woman in an elf costume made balloon animals as she walked and handed them out. She stopped in front of Abby. "Would you like a balloon turtle?"

"Yeah!" Abby clapped her hands as the woman twisted a green balloon into a turtle and used the excess length of the balloon to turn it into a bracelet.

As she worked, Gretchen looked over the crowd, but the face was gone.

"What is it?"

She kept her voice low. "I saw Carla."

Dory sucked in a sharp breath.

Brian growled, "She has no reason to be here."

"I don't know if she saw me or not. I didn't want to bother you, but I want more eyes on Abby."

The balloon artist slipped the turtle over the wrist of Abby's coat and gave a little wave as she moved on to the next child.

"Look!" Abby held her arm up.

"That's so cool!" Gretchen admired the turtle from all sides. "She even drew a smile on his face."

"I think I'll call him Shelly."

"That's a great name for a turtle," Brian said. He smoothed Abby's wild hair back while he looked around them.

Dory chimed in. "Super name for a turtle."

"Can we get hot chocolate?"

"We sure can." Brian stayed close as they strolled along the street. All of them were taking in their surroundings, the adults for very different reasons than Abby.

"Can I get whip cream?"

"If they have it," Gretchen answered absently.

"Aunt Jody!" Abby took off at a sprint, heading for the Caretti's Coffee Shoppe booth, where Jody was running things along with her younger daughters, Tess and Mindy.

"Abby, wait your turn."

Abby danced back and forth, humming Christmas carols until the customers in front of her were finished. She shimmied up to the counter and held her arm up. "This is Shelly."

"Nice to meet you, Shelly." Jody leaned over the counter to give Abby a kiss on the forehead. "Would you like to try our special peppermint hot chocolate?"

Abby's eyes got big. "Oooooh."

Jody winked at her and turned to put a small sample into a little plastic cup.

Abby tasted it, then vigorously nodded her head. "That's good!"

Gretchen relaxed enough to remember something about that drink. "Is this the special drink for the animal shelter?"

"Sure is." She tapped the sign announcing that two dollars from each five-dollar cup of the special peppermint cinnamon hot chocolate would be donated to the animal shelter.

"I'll take one, too, please." Gretchen pulled a ten dollar bill out of her pocket.

"You know I'm not charging you."

"It's for a good cause." She slid the money across the counter.

Without needing to ask, Jody put a heaping dollop of whipped topping on Abby's drink before securing the lid. "This is hot, so let it cool a little bit," she warned.

Dory ordered plain hot chocolate. "Will you be getting any more of those lemon bars?"

Jody grinned. "As a matter of fact, I put in an order yesterday. I'll have them on Tuesday."

"Excellent."

Gretchen was still on high alert, but feeling better with her parents close, and being around Jody.

"Everything okay?" Jody asked.

Before she could answer, a chill ran down her spine and a split second after, a voice she'd never forget said, "Abigail! Hi, sweetheart."

Abby took a giant side step until she was pressed into Gretchen's side.

Dory and Brian stepped between them while Gretchen pulled Abby away from the booth. The last thing she wanted was to speak to Carla. The second-to-last thing she wanted was to have any kind of scene, especially near Jody's booth.

She shuffled Abby off to the side, out of the flow of people.

Brian and Dory were close behind.

As was Carla.

"Abigail, you're getting so big." Carla's grin was wide, with lots of teeth. Not that Gretchen needed any reminder of Carla's predatory nature.

"Mommy? Who is this lady?" Abby's voice was small and unsure.

"She's no one." Gretchen put a hand across Abby's front, effectively putting herself between her daughter and Carla.

"I'm hardly no one."

"Don't speak to her."

"Oh, Gretchen, are you still holding a grudge?"

"Yes. I'm also still holding a restraining order."

"I just wanted to say hello."

Dory said, "Speaking of hello, there's our friend Sheriff Grady with Santa. Let's go say hi."

Brian scooped Abby up into his arms. "I bet he's handing out candy."

Abby's concerned frown flipped to an excited grin. "Santa!"

Gretchen watched her parents take Abby across the street. A moment later, the sheriff was looking in their direction, listening intently as Dory told him something.

"This is all very unnecessary."

"What's unnecessary is you coming anywhere near my child. What do you want?"

"I just wanted to see how she's doing. Make sure she's okay."

Gretchen snorted.

"She's my only grandchild. Believe it or not, I care about her wellbeing."

"I do not believe it."

"Gretchen, I know we've had our differences—"

"Stop it, Carla."

"Seth is no longer with us. Abigail's all I have left of him."

Gretchen sucked in a breath. As much as she might feel sympathetic for Carla's loss, and as shocking as it was to hear her ex had passed away, none of that made a bit of difference when it came to protecting Abby. Carla and her ilk had made Gretchen's life miserable, dragging her through courts and doing their best to get their claws into her money, through her daughter. None of it had ever been about any kind of love for the child. None of it.

"I'm sorry to hear that, and you have my condolences. But you are not to go near her. Not now, not ever."

Carla's face fell.

Gretchen felt a small pang of sympathy.

"Can I just—"

"No."

Dory and Sheriff Grady walked over.

"Everything okay here?"

Gretchen shook her head. "We have an active restraining order against her for myself and Abby."

Carla shoved her hands deep into her pockets. "I'm leaving."

Sheriff Grady said, "See that you do. I'd hate to leave the festival to take you to jail."

As soon as Carla walked away, he said something into his radio, then looked at Gretchen. "We'll escort her to her vehicle."

Gretchen nodded. Her heart skipped a beat when she couldn't immediately locate Abby. Her mom pointed. "They're right over there."

Abby sat on the ice throne that had been set up for photos. Brian stood right in front of her, snapping pictures with his phone. Gretchen put a hand to her chest and reminded herself to breathe before hustling across the street to where they were.

"Can we see the ponies?"

"Sure," Gretchen answered as her dad lifted Abby off the throne. She grabbed Abby's hand and tried to act casual as they walked toward the pony rides that had been set up in the alley beside For Pet's Sake.

Abby yanked her hand away. "You're squeezing too hard."

"Sorry."

"Are you mad?"

These were the moments all that acting paid off. She plastered a smile on her face that was fairly convincing. "No."

"Is that lady a bad guy?"

What a question. The simplest answer was yes, but she didn't want to make Abby afraid. "She's not a nice person. A long time ago she tried to cause some big problems for me."

"At work?"

"No." She wracked her brain for a way to explain the basics without getting into detail.

Luckily, she didn't have to think about it for long, because Abby spied the ponies. She reached out to grab Abby when she took off, but pulled her hand back. Abby was fine. She was safe. The ponies were in view, even with the crowd of people passing across her line of vision. She sped up, bumping into someone. "Sorry, Merry Christmas," she said brightly, never pausing to take her eyes off Abby's hot pink coat.

She and her parents waited off to the side with other families while Abby joined a group of kids being instructed on how to touch the ponies by the owner of the Hickory Hollow Horse Farm. A second person led the pony rides down the side street along For Pet's Sake and back.

She was uneasy, but there didn't seem to be a good reason to not let Abby take the pony ride. There was an adult right there, experienced with horses and children and safe pony rides. They held the pony's reins the entire time and just walked the length of the block and back. The side street was roped off, so other than a few people using the sidewalk to get to and from the main event, the alley was effectively closed.

She watched a few of the kids take their rides. At the end of the block, the pony went out of view for ten, maybe fifteen seconds as it was led into For Pet's Sake's back parking lot to take a nice wide turn and make the trek back.

Three or four kids took their pony rides, and then it was Abby's turn. She beamed as she climbed a set of wooden steps and slung her leg over the pony's saddle like a natural cowgirl. Her little hands clutched the horn of the saddle. Her red cheeks puffed as she grinned.

She looked out over the crowd and when she spotted her family, she gave them a wave, then quickly grabbed the horn again.

Gretchen waved and snapped a dozen photos.

There was nothing to worry about.

Nothing at all.

Chapter Twenty-Eight

After Alex headed back to his booth, Lincoln popped over to For Pet's Sake. Midge and Stan were on the sidewalk in front of their store, handing out little tchotchkes to everyone who went past. Children got pencils, plastic bead necklaces with paw print medallions, and little boxes of animal crackers. Grownups got punch cards to use in the store (with two bonus spots pre-punched), coupons, and pens.

He had to smile at his aunt and uncle. They were both in their element, chatting with everyone about the wonderful weather, the incredible turnout, and the fantastic events coming up later in the day.

"Lincoln! So nice to see you." Midge grabbed him in a massive hug while Stan clapped a hand on his back.

"Did you need help with anything?"

"Aren't you working at the shelter booth?"

"I helped set up, and I'll go back later to help tear down." He'd come a long way with his social anxiety and awkwardness, but manning a busy booth and making small talk with hundreds of people while trying to sell them calendars and ask for donations was still a bit too far out of his wheelhouse.

"We've been telling people to stop over and get a calendar."

"Or a new pet," Stan added.

"You guys are the best." He stepped off to the side as they greeted a cluster of folks walking by. When they passed, he asked, "How long are you going to be out here?"

"Until we run out of stuff to give out." Midge gestured to a half-full large cardboard box on the card table beside the front door. "Then we have to mop, feed the fish, and do the trash, and then we're going to relax and see what all's going on. And get some funnel cake. I keep seeing people walk by with it and it looks delicious."

"I can take care of most of that for you." Easy peasy. He went into the store, and like he'd done a million times since he was a young boy working here, he gathered all the trash. He took a quick walk around the aisles, looking for anything out of place, like the inevitable empty drink bottles people left in random spots on the shelves. He straightened a few crooked items, then took all the trash to the back room.

He followed the routine to feed the fish, then mopped the floors, starting at the front door and working all the way to the back storeroom.

He propped the back door open so it wouldn't lock him out as he took the trash bags down the stairs to the dumpster. He lifted the lid and slung the bags into the container.

"Lincoln! Lincoln!"

He whirled around to see Abby atop a pony. "Hey! Look at you!"

The woman led the pony in a wide turn around the parking lot. As ponies sometimes do, it left a fresh present from its backside on a pile. The woman apologized and promised to clean it up.

Abby's eyes got wide and she laughed. "He pooped!"

Working with animals, Lincoln was no stranger to poop. As

the pony ambled away, he grabbed a shovel from beside the dumpster and headed for the stairs to retrieve a heavy duty trash bag and a pair of work gloves from the storeroom.

Halfway up the stairs, a noise from behind the dumpster caught his attention. He slowly backed down the stairs and cautiously walked over, giving the dumpster a wide berth.

A woman hunkered beside the dumpster, holding her phone out in front of her.

"Excuse me?"

"Oh!" She gasped and toppled backwards onto her butt.

"What are you doing?"

She shoved her phone inside her coat. "Nothing."

Something felt off. "Were you... are you taking pictures of the kids?"

She scrambled to her feet and straightened her coat with an indignant tug. "Certainly not."

She didn't look like his idea of a homeless person, but who could know anyone's circumstances. He asked, "Do you need food?"

Her mouth flopped open, shocked and offended. "Of course not!"

"Then why are you out here?"

She flipped her hair with a quick shake of her head. "If you must know, I was simply getting a picture of my grand-daughter on the horse."

Granddaughter? Surely not. "Why not stand out front with the rest of the families taking pictures?"

She pressed her lips together. "My circumstances are unusual."

He reached to his back pocket to get his phone. "Yeaaaahhh, I'm going to call the police now."

At that, the woman took off running down the alley.

"Hey!" He took a few steps to run after her, but stopped.

Thanks to Alex's need to test security cameras, the store's property was videoed from every possible angle. He hurried back into the store and made sure the door was secure, then hustled toward the front. He wanted to catch Gretchen before Abby got off the pony and they disappeared into the festivities.

He slipped out the front door and went over to where the rides were set up just as Abby was being helped off the pony. He waited to see which direction she went before going over to find Gretchen.

She stood along the side with her parents and gave Abby a big smile as she started talking about the amazing pony.

He sidled up to her. "Hey, can I talk to you a minute?"

She still smiled, but through gritted teeth, she said, "Now's not a good time."

"I know. But this is important."

"Not a good time." She was clearly not happy to see him.

He didn't want to blurt anything out that Abby could hear, so he leaned in and as quietly and quickly as he could, said, "A strange woman was taking pictures of Abby."

Her head snapped up. "What? When? Where?" The color drained from her face as she frantically looked around at the crowd and tugged Abby against her. "Where, Lincoln?" she demanded.

Brian said, "Let's get out of the way," and steered their little group away from the growing pony crowd.

Lincoln followed Gretchen, who had a tight hold of the hood of Abby's coat. He hadn't meant to upset her.

They ended up a few blocks away, where the buildings gave way to a park with benches around the monuments dedicated to the town's fallen soldiers. A massive pine tree had been erected, covered with tons of lights and surrounded by colorful fake presents at its base.

"This is boring," Abby said with a scowl.

"Mommy needs to talk to Lincoln for a minute. Just hang out right here with Grandma and Grandpa."

She led him to a bench several yards away and sat down.

Lincoln sat beside her. "I don't know if it's anything, but it was weird. I was taking stuff out to the dumpster when Abby yelled at me to look at her on the pony, so I watched until they were back around the building. When I turned around, there was a woman behind the dumpster taking pictures. She said she was taking pictures of her granddaughter. I think she meant Abby. As soon as I said I was calling the police, she ran away."

Gretchen didn't seem surprised. Scared and concerned? Yes. Surprised? No.

"We have cameras everywhere, so it'll be no problem to get them to the police and figure out who she is."

Gretchen finally looked up at him. "I know who she is."

"Who?"

"Abby's grandmother. Carla."

Lincoln sat back. "What's she doing here?"

"She said Seth died and Abby's all she has left."

"Whoa. She just showed up here, though? That's... something's not right."

"I need to call Sheriff Grady. He escorted her off the property already." She got up and went over to talk to her parents. A minute later, Brian was on his phone.

"I'm hungry," Abby announced.

Lincoln walked over and spoke quietly so only Gretchen could hear. "If you want, you can get food and eat in the back room of the pet store so you don't have to keep looking over your shoulder."

"Thanks." Her relief was unmistakable.

Brian lifted Abby onto his shoulders and they walked back

into the crowd, stopping at various booths to put together a meal.

Back at the pet store, Midge and Stan had given away all of their trinkets and were getting ready to lock up. Lincoln ushered everyone inside and saw Gretchen's sigh of relief when he locked the door behind them.

"Not many places to sit and eat out there, are there?" Midge said. She put a finger to her chin and looked at Abby. "You have a pug, don't you?"

Abby nodded vigorously. "His name is Walter."

"Walter! That's a great name for a pug. I think I have something you can take home for Walter, if you like." She disappeared into one of the aisles.

Lincoln led everyone back to the combination storeroom/break room, where there was a big table and plenty of chairs.

Midge came back with an elf-shaped chew toy for Walter.

"Thank you! He's so cute," Abby gushed, immediately tucking the elf under her arm while she ate.

Midge beamed. "We're heading out. Be sure to lock up when you leave."

"I will." Lincoln got up to give her a hug and a kiss on the cheek. "Enjoy the festival."

They'd just finished eating and Dory said, "What do you think we should do now?"

Abby piped up, "I want to see the parade!"

Lincoln glanced at the event schedule Midge had tacked on the bulletin board. "Looks like the parade is in half an hour."

Gretchen put her head in her hands. "I don't know, honey, I was thinking we could go home."

"Why?" Abby demanded.

Dory and Brian exchanged a look. "We'll all stick together. It'll be fine."

Lincoln saw the muscles at the back of Gretchen's jaw work as she clenched her teeth.

"Mommy, please? I didn't sit on Santa's lap." Her chin quivered with disappointment.

Gretchen smiled. Lincoln recognized it as her theater smile. "Okay. But you have to stay close to me and Grandma and Grandpa all the time, do you understand?"

Abby's little brow furrowed. "Is it 'cos of that lady?"

He saw Gretchen wrestling with the answer. "Partly, yes," is what she ended up saying.

Abby seemed to take it in stride.

Brian reached over and flicked her braid. "You can watch from Grandpa's shoulders. Mommy can grab the candy for you."

"Yay! Candy!"

Lincoln said, "We can watch right out front here. The parade starts right over at the park and ends at Prescott's."

Sitting on Brian's shoulders only worked until the first float was past, then Abby wanted to be down on the ground, grabbing her own candy like the other kids who darted from the sidewalk onto the street.

Lincoln could feel Gretchen's tension. She kept an eagle-eye on Abby, tensed to leap if anyone came out of the crowd. The high school marching band had Abby enthralled, clapping her hands to the beat of the drums. Local politicians sat on the backs of convertibles, waving and tossing candy to the kids. The Boy Scouts and Girl Scouts had a float competition to see who could get the loudest cheers.

The Dairy Princess and her court tossed cow-shaped erasers instead of candy. A huge, bright red, antique farm tractor pulled an elaborately decorated flatbed trailer carrying a Christmas tree and a red bench, occupied by none other than Santa Claus, who smiled and waved and Ho-Ho-Hoed all the way through town while four elves tossed down handfuls of candy canes.

Lincoln kept an eye on Gretchen, and one on Abby, as all the floats made their way past. The junior high marching band brought up the rear of the parade with an excellent Christmas carol medley.

As they passed, the crowd folded in behind them, going back to browsing and shopping and eating.

Gretchen's forced smile was stretched tight.

Lincoln wasn't sure how to help her.

She said, "We should—"

Brian held up a hand. "Hang on, I got a message from Grady." He listened to his voicemail and grinned. "They picked her up. She'll be a 'special guest' until Monday morning at least. So we can relax and enjoy the tree lighting."

"Are they sure it's her?"

"One hundred percent."

Abby was too busy sifting through her bag of candy to pay attention to what the adults were talking about.

Dory must have seen the incoming anxiety attack the same time Lincoln did. Gretchen pulled in huge breaths that made her entire torso rise and fall, visible even under her puffy winter coat.

Lincoln was already fumbling in his pocket for the keys to the store when Brian held his hand out for Abby's. "How about we go watch the ponies some more?"

Abby squealed with excitement and shoved her candy bag at her grandma. "Ponies! Ponies!"

Lincoln unlocked the door. He and Dory practically dragged Gretchen inside. Dory said, "Would you feel better if I stay with you, or go with Dad and Abby?"

Gretchen's breathing was even heavier now. She simply pointed toward the door.

As soon as Lincoln locked the door behind Dory, Gretchen sucked in a massive sobbing breath.

He grabbed her waist and led her to the storeroom. He steered her to a chair and before she could sit, she sobbed uncontrollably. Gently, he undid her coat and tugged it off. Then he slid a chair against hers and sat down so he could pull her against his chest. He stroked her hair and said, "It's okay, she's okay, everything's okay now."

He had no idea if she could even hear him over her sobs. There were no tissues in the storeroom, but a half-used roll of paper towels was within reach.

After a few minutes, the shuddering sobs subsided and Gretchen wiped her face and blew her nose. She sat up and closed her eyes, pulling in deep breaths and releasing them slowly.

"You okay?"

She snapped, "No, I am not okay."

It really was a dumb question, wasn't it? Obviously there was more going on than he was aware of. "Do you want to talk?"

She blew her nose again, then glared at him. "To you? After you ghosted me for a week?"

"I…" He trailed off. He hadn't *meant* to ghost her, but he kind of did, didn't he?

"You what?"

"I'm sorry. Last weekend was a whole mess, and we can talk about that later. But I want to know if you're okay. What happened with that woman?"

Gretchen sighed. She wasn't sure which topic was more uncomfortable–Carla, or last weekend's events.

"You know all about Seth's parents dragging me to court, trying to get visitation–correction, trying to get joint custody. Well, we have permanent restraining orders against him and his parents. They have to stay away from Abby and from me. We haven't seen hide nor hair of any of them for almost five years."

"And she just showed up here today. That's crazy."

"She approached Abby. Just walked right up to her like it was no big deal. Dad was talking to Sheriff Grady, and he told her to leave or she'd go to jail. She said she was leaving and I stupidly thought she did."

"Hey, don't do that. Any normal person would have listened to the sheriff and been glad they weren't going to jail."

Her chin quivered. "I thought she was going to grab her."

"Hey, hey." He pulled her against his chest. "I can only imagine how terrifying it was."

She sniffled and pushed back from him. "I need to get myself together and go out there with Abby. Is there a restroom?"

"Yeah. Right there." He pointed to a doorway mostly hidden from view by two storage shelves. "I'll wait out front. Take your time."

He went out by the counter and waited. A few minutes later, she came out. The only evidence of her crying was a little redness around her eyes that could easily be mistaken for being out in the cold air all day. Must be all those years of theater and switching roles and emotions at the drop of a hat.

She zipped her coat and smiled. "Let's go."

Chapter Twenty-Nine

Gretchen knew she looked fine. Nobody would be able to see that she was still freaking out inside, or that her skin felt like it was going to crawl right off her body. Thank God for her parents, and thank God for Lincoln being handy and giving her a private place for a quick meltdown.

He turned out the store's overhead lights and locked the doors behind them.

Abby was atop the pony, on the way back up the alley to where her grandparents waited.

Gretchen snapped a few pictures.

As soon as Abby was back with them, she said, "Can we get more hot chocolate from Aunt Jody?"

"Sure." She tried not to overreact as Abby ran ahead of them. Jody's booth was in view and she got there five steps behind Abby, but still. What wouldn't have given her a second's pause three hours ago was now a scary ordeal with potentially dire consequences.

The PA system crackled and announced that the vendor hours were over, and that local bands were set up and ready to start playing on the free stage near the tree lighting area.

Stewart packed their equipment into plastic bins so they could tear down the booth. "Hey, munchkin, what are you up to?"

Abby jumped up and down. "I just rode a pony."

"A pony? That's awesome. Mindy used to have a pony named Peaches."

Mindy rolled her eyes. "I did not."

"You sure did. You talked about it all the time. Ask Uncle Eric. He'll remember."

"You had a pony?" Abby's jaw dropped.

Jody shook her head. "She had a pretend pony when she was your age."

"Oh." Abby shrugged. "I rode a real pony."

Gretchen forked over money for the last of the white chocolate peppermint drinks (with extra whipped topping).

Jody was subtly throwing eye daggers at Lincoln, who hung back, standing awkwardly off to the side.

Dory nudged Gretchen's arm. "They're starting to line up for S-A-N-T-A. We'll take her, you relax for a while. We'll meet you at the tree lighting." Gretchen knew what her mom meant. Calm down, chill out, go back to feeling like things were normal. But what was normal, anyway?

Lincoln pulled his phone out of his pocket and looked at the glowing screen. "I have to take this, I'll be right back."

Jody pulled her to the side of the booth. "Fill me in."

"There's nothing to fill in with Lincoln yet, but Carla was here."

Jody's gaze snapped to Gretchen's face. "What? Here?" She pointed to the ground. "Like *here*-here?"

"Yeah. She came up to Abby."

"Wait. That was her? The weird lady who came up to you here earlier?"

"Yeah."

Jody pressed a hand to her throat. "Oh, no. I wish I'd have recognized her."

"What could you have done?"

She flashed an evil grin. "Anything I needed to."

That made her laugh. "What would I ever do without you?"

"I don't know, but you would be very, very, bored. Seriously, though, is there anything we can do?"

Her curls bounced as she shook her head. "She's spending the weekend in jail, so I'm not even giving her another thought right now."

"Okay. Now go give Lincoln an earful about his sneaky activities last weekend and then ghosting. Then report back. And if you want me to stuff him in one of these plastic bins, I'm happy to do so."

"I'll keep that option in mind, for sure." Gretchen gave her a quick hug and looked around to see where Lincoln had gotten to.

He leaned against the brick wall, his hands shoved in his pockets.

"Hey."

"Hey. That was Ruby. Her sons came by so she got them to help tear down the booth so I don't have to."

"Oh. Good."

"We sold all the calendars."

"That's great."

"Do you want to go hear the band?"

"Sure." They started walking toward the opposite side of town. At least half of the vendors were already torn down and gone, emptying the sidewalks. Still, most of the people milling around walked on the road instead of the sidewalks that were occupied by ice sculptures.

Stars dotted the black sky, so bright even the streetlights

couldn't cancel them out. The shop windows were full of twinkling colored lights that reflected through the ice sculptures displayed in front of each store.

"What is that?" Gretchen pointed to a sculpture that was about three feet high.

"I think it's burger? With a hat?"

"There's the Hollow Dog. That's really cute." The five-foot sculpture of the radio station's mascot stood regally, pointing toward the station's window display of a Christmas village.

They passed the massive reindeer sculpture. There was still a line of people waiting their turn to sit on the reindeer and take pictures.

An ice sculpture in front of the jewelry store was a giant heart with interlocked rings chiseled onto it.

They had to step off the sidewalk to get around the massive six-foot tall ice goose in front of Stephanie's Duck, Duck, Goose Daycare, which also had a goose etched in the glass of the front door.

Lincoln said, "Are we going to talk about last weekend? Or are we just not talking anymore?"

Gretchen focused her attention on an ice hot dog holding a soda. "I didn't think there was anything to talk about."

"I think there's a lot to talk about."

"Why? We're done. You've graduated the program. You certainly don't need my help anymore because you're doing fine on your own." She shoved her hands deep into her coat pockets.

"Gretchen."

"Lincoln. It's fine."

"It's clearly not fine."

She walked faster.

"Hey. Gretchen. Come on, slow down."

"I want a good spot to watch the tree lighting."

"It's a forty-foot tree. There are no bad spots."

She stopped abruptly and spun to face him. "Okay, fine. What are we going to talk about?" When he hesitated, she yanked her hands out of her pockets and lifted her arms. "See? Nothing to talk about."

"We have a lot to talk about."

"Such as?" She crossed her arms and tapped her foot.

"A lot happened last weekend and then you kind of ghosted me."

Her eyes bugged. "Me? Ghosted you? I don't recall getting any calls or texts or emails or letters or cards or smoke signals or carrier pigeons from you. You're the one who ghosted me. Presumably because your free time was occupied?"

"No, I didn't have any free time this week. The calendars—"

"Calendars?" She couldn't believe what she was hearing. "What do the calendars have to do with the blonde?"

"Blonde? Oh. Meredith." It really seemed to take him a second to connect the dots.

"Yeah. Meredith. I don't get it. If I'm supposed to be helping you date, why wouldn't you tell me? Get some pointers or something?"

Lincoln took a small step back like he was shocked. "Pointers?"

"Pointers. Tips. Ideas. Advice."

"So you…" He ran a hand over his hair and blew out a plume of breath that rose into the night. "That's why you're mad? Because I didn't get tips from you on taking another woman out on a date?"

Gretchen glared down at the sidewalk. Nope, that was absolutely not why she was mad, but it was an easy explanation. She could just run with it and put an end to this whole situation and part ways as friends. Or she could just be honest. She decided to go with that. "No. That's not why I'm mad."

"I'm confused."

"Me, too. The whole kiss thing on Saturday caught me so off guard and I wasn't sure what to think. And then when I saw you at the restaurant it confused me even more."

"You saw me? Why didn't you say anything? Come over and say hi?"

She looked up at him like he was clueless. Which he was. "Oh, sure. The woman you're fake dating just casually strolls up to you while you're on a romantic real date? There are zero ways I don't look crazy in that scenario." She emphasized the point by making a zero with her thumb and fingers.

"It wasn't romantic."

"It sure looked like it was. I suppose I should be glad my advice has been so effective. You were doing all the things I've told you. Leaning in, smiling, making eye contact. I'd give you a gold star if I had one."

"Gretchen."

"I think what confuses me the most is, why did you kiss me on Saturday if you knew you had a date the very next day? I don't get it."

He let out a huge sigh, sending another cloud of breath into the sky. "I had not been planning to go on a date with Meredith."

That didn't make sense. "When did you ask her out?"

"I didn't."

"How does that work, exactly?"

"Alex. Oren. Noah. Nate. That's how that works. Particularly Alex. We were at Sonny's for late breakfast on Sunday and I told them about the kiss."

"You told them?" Even in the dim streetlight, she could see him blush.

"Yeah. I didn't know if I should call you and talk about it, or wait for you to bring it up. Somehow they all decided I was suffering from transference and I needed to go out with someone else and Avery's friend Meredith was in town. Next thing I know, Alex is on his phone telling me that I'm taking Meredith out. I wasn't sure how to stop that runaway freight train, and I feel like a spineless dweeb because I went along with it instead of putting my foot down."

"You're telling me that you didn't want to go out and spend an evening with that gorgeous blonde?"

"I didn't."

"It looked like you were having a good time."

"Towards the end, it wasn't so bad, but it was really awkward and uncomfortable at the start. She was nice enough, but the whole time I felt like I was doing something wrong by being there. I know this is all supposed to be fake, but it still felt like I was being dishonest and disrespectful to you." He cleared his throat. "The funny part is that somewhere along the line I realized I wasn't feeling weird because of my anxiety. It was because I just wasn't interested in her."

Gretchen wasn't sure she bought that. Meredith was stunning, and if she was a good friend of Avery's, she had to be smart and funny and generally a good person.

"The good thing is that she clearly wasn't interested in me, either. Weirdly enough, that's when I was able to relax and have a decent time."

"That is weird. What woman wouldn't like you?" She squinted up at him. "And speaking of weird, *transference*? What were they talking about?"

He snorted a laugh. "They decided I only kissed you because I had imaginary feelings like you're my therapist or something. I don't know. They had a whole convoluted theory and none of it made any sense."

"Those guys rarely make sense."

"Tell me about it."

"Hey, don't act like you agree with me. You're the one who keeps taking their bad advice."

"I know, I know."

"Their theory is stupid, but I have to ask. Why *did* you kiss me?"

"Mommy, guess what! Santa's going to bring me a pony!"

Gretchen's gaze snapped away from Lincoln and down to Abby's red-chilled face. "Sweetheart, Santa can't bring you a pony."

"Yuh-huh he is. He asked me what I want for Christmas and I said I want a pony and I'm going to name it Peaches like Mindy's pony only this one is going to be real and it can sleep in my room with me and Walter and I'll feed it pancakes and dress it up like Princess Poppy and take it to school for show and tell—"

"Whoa, whoa, slow down. Ponies don't live inside the house. And they don't eat pancakes."

"Yes they do."

"Ponies live in barns."

Abby's brow pinched inward. "Not *my* pony."

Gretchen looked at Dory over Abby's head. Dory just shrugged and put her hands up in defeat. "I tried to tell her."

Her boot stamped down onto the sidewalk. "He's bringing me a real pony!"

Gretchen braced herself. It had been a long day. Meltdown incoming in 3... 2...

Lincoln hunkered down to be eye-level with Abby. "Hey."

She glared at him.

"Unfortunately, Santa isn't allowed to bring real ponies."

"Santa can bring *anything*."

Lincoln shook his head. "It's the law. I know, because I work with animals, so I have to know the animal laws."

"Nuh-uh." She sounded a little less certain.

"Yeah. You see, regular animals aren't allowed to be up in the sky in Santa's sleigh. Only his specially trained reindeer. Even regular reindeer aren't allowed. It's a rule from the Federation of Animals."

Gretchen watched the emotions play over Abby's face as she decided whether or not to believe him.

"It's a grown-up safety rule. It kind of stinks, but Santa's hands are tied. Did you know that Blitzen almost wasn't allowed to fly the sleigh last year because his Federation of Animals clearance expired?"

Abby's eyes got wide.

"It was a whole mess. Lots of paperwork that didn't get fixed until like an hour before they had to take off. It was on the news and everything."

Gretchen bit her lips to keep from laughing until Abby turned to her and stabbed a finger in her direction. "Then *you* can get me a pony."

There would be no reasoning with this child, so Gretchen decided to deflect. "Let's go watch them light the tree."

They found a spot in the crowd. The last local band of the night exclusively played Christmas carols. The mayor walked through the crowd, encouraging everyone to join in. Before long, the whole town was singing.

At nine o'clock on the dot, the streetlights dimmed and the band played "Silent Night."

Soft white lights dotted the tree. With each line, the lights brightened. For the second verse, even more white lights turned on.

When the song ended, "Deck the Halls" began. With the festive, upbeat music, colored lights began to pop out on the tree. By the end, thousands and thousands of lights lit up not only the tree, but the whole town square and the wonderful faces of everyone who made Hickory Hollow special.

At the end of the song, the streetlights came back up to full brightness. The band played more carols, but most of the people began to peel away from the crowd and head for home.

Chapter Thirty

Lincoln was trying to figure out a way to get Gretchen alone for a few minutes when Dory dropped the solution into his lap.

"How about we take Abby home and get her to sleep?"

"I'm not tired!" Abby's eyes were heavy and rimmed with red that matched her cold cheeks.

Brian scooped her up. "How about we go change into jammies and we'll read until you *are* tired."

Abby's head was already on his shoulder. "Okay."

Dory reached over and gave Gretchen a side hug. "We'll stop and let Walter out." She shot a look at Lincoln. "Take your time."

Lincoln waited by the big carved ice goldfish in front of For Pet's Sake until Gretchen said good night to her family.

"Been a long day," he said when she walked over to him.

"Extremely."

He used the ace up his sleeve to get her to spend some time with him. "I was thinking pie might be a good idea." He was glad to see her smile at the suggestion.

"Pie is a genius idea."

"I'm parked back here." He thrust his thumb in the direction of the alley that led to the back of the pet store.

"I'm over at Prescott's. Meet you at the diner?"

"How about I give you a ride to your car? It's getting really cold." Not to mention he didn't love the idea of her–or anyone, really–walking alone in the darkness to the other side of town.

She must have been tired and cold, because she readily agreed.

A few minutes later, he'd slowly zig zagged around dozens of people who were still using the streets as sidewalks, and dropped her off at her car. A few minutes after that, they met at Sonny's, just a couple miles outside of the heart of the town.

The place was half-full. Unusually busy for a regular Saturday night at ten o'clock, but apparently a common idea for the people who'd been at the tree lighting.

Gretchen said to their waitress, "I didn't think you worked weekends."

Corinne sighed. "I don't, but we had one scheduled off and one call off. So I missed the tree lighting again. Was it nice?"

"It was."

"Good. What can I get you?"

Lincoln read whiteboard behind the counter that listed the available pies when Gretchen said, "Hot roast beef sandwich with fries."

"Gravy on the fries?"

"Of course."

He sat back and decided that was a better idea than pie. "Same for me."

When Corinne walked away, Gretchen said, "I thought you were getting pie."

He grinned. "I'm still getting pie, but actual food was a good call."

"I didn't realize how little I've eaten today. As soon as we walked in and smelled the food, I was starving."

"Same." A gurgle from his stomach punctuated the word.

Corinne set their plates down on the table a few minutes later.

They ate mostly in silence, both of them wolfing down the hot, hearty food. Finally, Lincoln sat back and put his hand on his stomach. "Much better."

Gretchen shoveled the last bite into her mouth and nodded in agreement. She swallowed and said, "Definitely. I'm not sure if it's because I was so hungry, but that was the best hot roast beef sandwich I have ever had in my whole life."

"It was." He looked down at his plate. One plop of gravy remained that would have been one perfect bite, if he'd had any fries left to scoop it up.

Now that hunger was out of the way, he thought it might be a good time for a talk. Gretchen was staring absently out the window, so maybe that was a good place to start.

"What's on your mind?"

She pulled in a long breath.

He waited, assuming she would bring up the kiss. Or his date. Or their agreement. Any of which would be a perfect lead-in to a conversation about maybe making this real.

Her hazel eyes fixed on his. "My mind is going a thousand miles an hour. I'll have to contact our attorneys, but I don't know if I should send a message tomorrow or wait until Monday. I have no idea if they monitor their inboxes over the weekend or not. Probably? I've got so many questions. Why did she just show up? How did Seth die? Or even did he? Carla didn't seem all that upset, so maybe she was lying."

This was not a direction he'd anticipated, but it made sense. Carla showing up was a much bigger deal than a kiss or a friend you're not dating getting caught on a date. He set aside all the lines he'd been rehearsing in his head. "I think you should send a message tonight when you get home. Then you can cross it off your list and get some sleep."

She sipped her soda. "That's probably a better idea."

"I would bet they check their messages over the weekend. And then they'll have a heads up that she's due to be released on Monday, so maybe that'll give them time to do whatever lawyerly things they need to do while she's still sitting in jail."

"Yeah." She nodded. "You're right. My worrying isn't going to get anything done, all I can do is contact them, and then it's out of my hands."

"Exactly."

She lifted her wrist to check her watch. "It's almost eleven. I should get home and email the attorney and get to bed. It's been a long, long day."

"You go ahead. I'll grab the check." When he saw her fumble with her purse, he waved a hand. "Don't worry about it."

"Thanks."

"You can get the next one," he joked.

She smiled and slid out of the booth.

"Drive safe," he said.

"You, too."

It wasn't until her headlights swung around and onto the main road that he realized she hadn't gotten any pie.

He ordered two slices of peanut butter cream pie to be boxed to go. After he paid the check and left a hefty tip, he drove to Gretchen's house. He waved at her camera doorbell and set the pie on the little decorative bench beside the door. When he was back in his warm car, he texted her just in case she missed the alert from her camera.

Peanut butter pie on the front porch.

> You're the best. Thank you!!

Another text with a string of heart-eye emojis popped up.

Sunday morning brought six inches of snow to Hickory Hollow. Lincoln sat at the kitchen table, drinking coffee and watching Pickles, Edith, and Jerry, his three rescue cats. They all congregated at the back door, staring out the glass at the falling snow, cek-ceking and acting like they wanted to go outside.

"It's cold out there, you wouldn't last two seconds."

Jerry cek-ceked more enthusiastically.

Lincoln finally saw the objects of their rapt attention—two bright red cardinals swooping across the back yard in some sort of territory dispute. He watched with them for a few minutes and finished his coffee.

Reluctantly, he showered and exchanged his comfy flannel pajamas for jeans and a hoodie over a t-shirt.

He waited until noon to text Gretchen.

> Good afternoon. How's everything?

It was a while before she texted him back.

> Crazy. Nothing from the atty. Now I'm trying to get this stupid website updated for a client and it's not going well.

Okay, it sounded like they weren't having a big what-are-we conversation today, either. He sighed and put the idea of The Talk on the back burner.

> Running out to Sub Shack. Want me to bring you and Abby lunch?

> That would be amazing. Thank you thank you thank you!!!!!!!

He called the order in and left a few minutes early. Since Caretti's was closed on Sundays, he stopped by the chain coffee shop to get Gretchen some caffeine, and a hot chocolate with lots of whipped topping for Abby.

Abby opened the door before he was even out of the car. He balanced the drinks and the bag of subs and carefully trudged through the snow to the front door.

In the kitchen, Gretchen typed furiously on her laptop. Her lips were pursed like she was near tears.

"Hey, what's wrong?"

She shook her head angrily and poked her hands toward the computer. "This is ridiculous. I don't know why people can't just leave things alone when they don't know what they're doing." Her voice rose an octave.

"Why don't you take a break and get some food." He held up the large coffee cup. "And some caffeine?"

He winced as she slammed the laptop shut.

"Yes. A break. You're a lifesaver."

"Did you eat anything at all today?"

She looked a little guilty. "A little bit. Mom made this breakfast casserole her neighbor lady gave her, but it tasted weird so I didn't eat much. And after we got home, I got too busy to think about food."

Abby pushed away more than half of her sub. "I had bacon and waffles and bacon and orange juice and bacon."

Lincoln couldn't help but smile. "I like bacon that's crunchy."

Abby eyed him and grinned. "Me, too!"

"I think I like pancakes better than waffles."

She considered it. "I like waffles. Waffles have syrup cups."

"That's true."

"Do you like orange juice?"

"I do. Do you like apple juice?"

"It's okay."

Walter waddled into the kitchen and whined at the back door.

"I'll get him," Lincoln offered. He grabbed his coat before Gretchen could object–which she did rather weakly–and took Walter out to snuffle through the snow in the back yard until he found the proper spot to do his business.

Walter was quick to head back to the door to go inside.

"I don't blame you, buddy." Back inside, he unclipped Walter's leash and hung it on the hook.

Walter waited expectantly until Lincoln gave him a treat.

"How come I don't get treats for going to the bathroom?" Lincoln asked, but Walter had no answer.

He sat back at the island and got a good look at Gretchen. Her face was pale with bright red spots on her cheeks. "Are you feeling okay?"

"I'm fine. Just frustrated and so much to do." She managed a tired smile. "I thought weekends were supposed to be relaxing."

Abby bounced on her heels. "Can we build a snowman?"

Lincoln could see her fighting to keep smiling as she said, "I have to shovel the walk anyway."

"Yay!" Abby jumped up and down and ran to get her boots and coat.

"I'll shovel your walk."

"You don't have to. It's not like you're my boyfriend."

"No, but I am your friend." He stood and leaned down to kiss her forehead. He straightened, concerned, and pressed a hand to her forehead. "Whoa. You feel really warm. Are you sure you're okay?"

She frowned like she was taking stock.

"Maybe you should lay down for a little bit."

"I don't have—"

He held up a hand to cut her off. "You have fifteen or twenty minutes."

"But—"

"But nothing. Abby and I will take care of the snowman and the sidewalk. Do you have salt to throw down?"

"By the garage door. Do you have gloves?"

He patted his coat pockets. "Doesn't look like it."

She stood up and put the leftovers in the fridge.

"There's extra in the coat closet for my dad. Use them. And make sure Abby keeps her hat on."

"Aye, aye, captain. You go grab a catnap."

"Aye, aye, captain." She saluted him. "Fifteen minutes."

Abby bounced from foot to foot by the front door. "Let's go, let's go."

Gretchen said, "Mommy's going to lay down for a few minutes. Listen to Lincoln and stay where he can see you."

"Fine. Let's gooooooooooo," she grumbled.

Lincoln gave her a nod. "Let's go."

She was out the door and into the yard in a flash.

He was a bit slower, getting the shovel and finding the bag of rock salt to spread when he was done. He reached down and scooped a handful of snow and pressed it into a ball. Perfect snowball snow. Nice and sticky.

He assumed Abby would get bored on her own for too long, so he helped her make a giant snowball for the snowman's base. "Now I have to shovel for a little bit, okay?"

"Okay." She flopped onto her back and swung her arms and legs wide, making a snow angel.

Maybe she wouldn't be bored after all. Lincoln grabbed the shovel and cleared the walkway and the edge of the driveway that had been missed by whoever plowed.

When he was finished, Abby had made a dozen snow angels and several stockpiles of snowballs.

He quickly spread the salt, then made the second and third snowballs to finish the snowman's body. Abby informed him that he needed to make a snowwoman companion, which he did. She then let him know that he also needed to make a snow angel.

His coat lifted as he flopped onto his back, giving him a shock as the snow hit his bare skin. "Gah!!"

Abby giggled hysterically as he flailed on the ground.

When he was about frozen, they searched the yard and found some sticks for arms and rocks to make faces on their snowpeople.

"Oh! Wait!" Abby yelled and ran into the garage. A minute later, she came back, holding a scarf and a hat aloft.

"Nice." Lincoln lifted her up to put the hat on the first snowman, then lifted her again to put the scarf around the snowwoman's neck. When he set her down, he lifted his hand for a high five. "Nice work."

"I have to pee."

"Let's head in, then."

Abby clomped up the stairs and burst through the door, leaving a trail of snow from the front door to the coat closet across the foyer. She kicked off her boots and dropped her coat and hat and gloves onto the floor. She yelled, "I'll pick it up after!" as she sprinted up the stairs.

Lincoln shut the door and shook his head. He picked up Abby's coat and shook it. Drops of melting snow flew everywhere. Learning from his mistake, he took her hat and gloves and boots out to the front porch. He clapped the boots together to get rid of the snow and ice and shook out the cloth. He stomped his feet to clear his own boots, then toed them off right outside the door.

Back inside, he hung his coat on the doorknob and hung Abby's things in the closet.

She tromped down the stairs.

"All better?"

"Yup."

"Do you know where the mop is?"

Her eyes got big with excitement and she sang, "I'll get the Swiffer. Swiffer, Swiffer, Swiffer." She ran into the kitchen and came back with the Swiffer mop. "I like to Swiffer. Swiffer, Swiffer."

Lincoln laughed. "I think you just like saying Swiffer."

"Swwwwwiffer," she sang and pushed it around the foyer, managing to get most of the wet spots cleaned up.

"Good job."

"Can I have a dollar?"

"What?" He hadn't expected that.

"Mom gives me a dollar when I do the Swiffer."

He dug in his pocket and found a dollar. "Sure. Here you go."

She giggled and ran into the living room, where she flopped onto the couch and tugged a giant fleece blanket over herself. Almost immediately, Walter waddled over and climbed up his doggie stairs to get onto the couch with her.

Lincoln had to chuckle at them. He glanced at his watch and the amusement disappeared. He'd been outside with Abby for almost three hours.

It felt odd to text Gretchen when they were both here in the house, but it was less odd than poking around.

Are you awake?

No reply. He waited five minutes, then went through the kitchen to Gretchen's office. The light was off. No Gretchen.

He hated the idea of walking through her home uninvited, but he couldn't just leave without making sure she was okay. He considered calling Brian and Dory, but that didn't make sense, either, to make them come over when he was right here. And he didn't want to send Abby to find her just in case something was wrong.

And this was uncharacteristic enough to suggest there was a good chance something might be wrong, so he decided to suck it up and go upstairs.

He peeked in on Abby. She was curled up with Walter, absently stroking his head while she watched something on television.

He padded up the carpeted stairs. He had no idea which room was Gretchen's. He lightly knocked on the closest door. When there was no answer, he cracked it open and peeked inside. Stacks of boxes labeled with different Shakespeare plays filled the room. He pulled the door shut.

The second room was Abby's. The third, a bathroom.

He lightly rapped on the fourth door and got a groan in response.

"Everything okay?"

Another groan.

"Heads up, I'm coming in." He slowly opened the door, then pushed it wide and rushed over to the bed. Gretchen was covered in a sheen of sweat. Her face was ghostly white, with two bright pink spots on her cheeks.

"So… cold…" she whispered.

He tucked the blanket around her. "Where's your thermometer?"

"Bath…room…"

He rushed into her attached bathroom and rummaged

through the medicine cabinet. There was nothing useful, so he rifled through the cabinet drawers until he found a box with cold medicines. He fished out some tablets to reduce fever and found the thermometer.

As he crossed back into the bathroom, Gretchen was struggling to pull the blankets off and get out of bed. Her white face had taken on a greenish tint. Oh, crap. He dropped the tablets and thermometer on the floor and lunged forward, snatching the trash can and getting it under her just as her lunch made an unfortunate reappearance.

Chapter Thirty-One

Well this is awesome, Gretchen thought as she heaved into the trash can. The blankets had tangled around her torso and legs, making it impossible to move. So here she was, hanging over the side of the bed, barfing into a trash can.

Lincoln held the can with one hand and held her hair with the other. All she could do was keep from sliding off the bed by gripping the sheets with one hand and the nightstand with the other.

The violent heaves felt like they were going to last forever. There was nothing left in her stomach, but her middle still clenched, trying to expel the last drops of whatever was in her stomach.

Finally it stopped and she half-rolled awkwardly back onto the bed and grabbed a tissue to wipe her mouth and nose.

Lincoln helped untangle the blankets with his free hand, then wordlessly tied the trash bag shut.

Her arms and legs shook with the effort of standing.

"Hang on." Lincoln put the trash can next to the door and came back to help her up.

"I don't know what happened. I was fine." She wanted to

insist she was fine, but the fact that she was a bit dizzy trying to cross the room to the bathroom meant she couldn't even convince herself with that nonsense.

"Food poisoning, the flu, stomach bug, could be anything." He led her into the bathroom and waited while she braced herself on the counter. "You okay by yourself?"

She nodded.

"I'll be right out here if you need me."

Another nod. She turned the water on and scooped a handful into her mouth. Gross. With shaky hands, she brushed her teeth and even swished some mouthwash. Gross, gross, gross. Throwing up was the worst.

She finished her business, then washed her hands and face and smoothed her hair back into a messy bun. She felt marginally better.

Back in the bedroom, Lincoln perched on the edge of her reading chair, ready to jump up to help her. She waved him down.

"Aww, thank you so much."

He'd remade her bed, straightening the covers and turning down the corner of the comforter.

"No problem. How are you feeling?"

"Better, actually. I'm sorry you had to witness that."

He shrugged one shoulder. "Once you've pet-sat for a pair of Saint Bernards with diarrhea, a little barf barely even registers."

She sat on the edge of the bed. "Both of them?"

"Yup."

"At the same time?"

"Poor big guys left a trail all over the house. It was a nightmare. Especially the white carpet in the master bedroom."

"Oh, no."

"Oh, yeah. It was horrible. And the smell."

She made a face that mirrored his, scrunching her nose and grimacing. "I can only imagine."

"Don't even try to imagine it."

"I need to check on Abby." She stood too fast and sat right back down, dizzy.

He came over and put a hand on her shoulder before she could get up again. "Easy."

She squeezed her eyes shut and slowly opened them, waiting for the little dots to stop swimming in her vision.

"She's watching a movie with Walter."

"Princess Poppy, no doubt." Slowly, she got up.

"You sure you're okay?"

"Yeah." Not really, but she wanted to go downstairs and see Abby. Rationally, she knew Abby was fine, but after yesterday, she wanted some reassurance with her own two eyes.

Lincoln grabbed the trash can on the way out the door and walked down the stairs with her, making sure she stayed on her feet.

"I'm not that bad."

"I'd rather err on the side of caution."

Touché. Wasn't that exactly why she was trudging down the stairs in the first place? To err on the side of caution? Yup, exactly.

She looked into the living room. Abby and Walter were snuggled together on the oversized chair beside the couch. Their heads were the only thing peeking out from under Abby's fleece blanket. Just seeing her, safe and sound, made her feel better.

"I assume you want this in the outside can?" He held up the trash can 'o barf. "In the garage, I assume?"

"Yes, I'll get it."

He gave her a look that clearly said he was taking care of it, so she chose not to argue.

While Lincoln went to the garage, she shuffled into the kitchen and got a bottle of Sprite from the pantry. She poured it over ice, got a handful of crackers, and went to the living room.

Princess Poppy, using her famous peacock feather tiara, was shooting rainbows and stars into the sky for some reason. Gretchen didn't understand half of the things Princess Poppy did, but for some reason, kids loved her.

"Did you see my snow people?"

"No, sweetie, I didn't look outside."

"Me and Lincoln made snow angels."

"You did?" She nibbled at the crackers and took a few sips of Sprite.

"It was fun."

"Good. I'm glad you had fun. I'm sorry I missed it."

"Are you sick?"

Gretchen nodded. "Yeah, my tummy doesn't feel so good."

"Did you take some medicine?"

"Not yet, but I will."

Abby sat up and gave her mom a hard look. "Medicine will make you feel better."

"Yes, Doctor Abby. I will take my medicine."

"Tell her, Lincoln."

She hadn't heard him come back in.

He walked over and sat beside her. "It's true. You should take your medicine so you feel better."

Abby looked rather smug.

"I will. I promise." She felt like she was being scolded. Which was probably fair, since Abby did nothing more than parrot her own words back at her.

Lincoln's arm stretched over the back of the couch.

Gretchen went ahead and followed the urge to settle against him, getting comfy while sipping the last of her Sprite.

"Do you want me to refill that for you?"

She sighed. "No, I'll get it. I need to grab the laptop anyway."

He gave a mildly disapproving look, which she ignored as she got up and went to the kitchen.

She popped the lid of the laptop open and sat down at the island. She quickly scanned her inbox. Nothing from the attorney. Three emails from the client, with some "helpful suggestions" on how to fix the things they'd screwed up in the first place.

Honestly, it'd probably be easier and less drama to just cancel their contract and send them on their way. She made a mental note to revise her contracts to include a massive premium for after-hours contact.

Her stomach rolled and she closed her eyes. Okay, so getting worked up was a really, really bad idea right now. She pulled a deep breath in and slowly let it out. In, out. In, out.

A sudden shiver reminded her that she hadn't miraculously overcome whatever sickness she had. In her head, her mom's voice scolded her, telling her she needed to rest and whatever was on that laptop could wait until morning.

The client's stupidity was not her emergency.

The attorney had all the information she had, so there was nothing more she could do. Obsessively checking her emails wouldn't make them respond faster.

Fine.

Gretchen closed the laptop and carried her fresh glass of Sprite to the living room. Lincoln and Abby were both laughing at something on the screen.

She settled in between them and leaned back on his arm. "Enjoy it now, because it gets less and less and less funny every time you see it."

He smirked and jutted his chin toward Abby. "Apparently not for everyone."

She tried to think of a witty retort, but her brain just wanted to shut down.

Lincoln took the glass from her hand and set it on the side table. "Do you want to go back to bed?"

No, she wanted to stay close to Abby, so she shook her head against his shoulder.

"Okay, just close your eyes for a minute."

She nodded. Good idea.

Chapter Thirty-Two

Lincoln felt Gretchen relax against him. She didn't feel as warm and some color had returned to her face, so hopefully that meant her fever had broken.

Abby helped herself to the rest of her leftover sub and most of a big bag of chips. He kind of guessed she normally wouldn't be allowed to have that many, but he wasn't about to say anything.

At some point, she went upstairs and changed into a set of flannel Princess Poppy pajamas and came back down with a bottle of pink glitter nail polish.

"Will you do my nails?" She thrust the bottle at him.

"I'll try." He shifted, shimmying out from under Gretchen. He held her head with one hand and fluffed a pillow under her with the other. "Let's sit at the table so I can see better." He slid to his butt on the floor in front of the coffee table.

Abby knelt on the other side and stretched her hands out, splaying her fingers flat on the table.

He unscrewed the cap and Abby shook her head. "You hafta shake it first."

"Oh." He tightened the cap and shook the bottle until she

seemed satisfied.

When he pulled the brush out, she yanked her hands back. "That's too much."

Lincoln didn't realize how complicated nail polish was. He slid the brush against the inside neck of the bottle. "Better?"

"Yup." She put her hands back in position.

He brushed polish onto her pinky nail. "Good?"

She gave an emphatic nod. "Yes."

He'd painted three nails when she said, "What's *cosumpslive* mean?"

"Cosumpslive? I'm not sure that's a word."

"Grandma said that weird lady is a comsumpslive liar."

Lincoln couldn't imagine Dory telling Abby that, so she must have overheard a conversation. "Compulsive," he corrected the word and wracked his brain for an explanation about the context. "It basically means someone does something a lot."

"Oh." She looked down at her nails, clearly wondering why he'd stopped polishing.

He painted another nail.

"Is she a bad lady?"

Oh, boy. He polished another nail.

"Is she?"

"Uhhhmm, I don't know her. I just know that it's super important for you to listen to your mom."

"Grandma said that lady was mean to Mommy a long, long time ago."

"That's what I heard."

"So if she was mean and she lied, she's a bad person."

Lincoln was definitely not equipped for this conversation. "I don't think it matters if she's a bad person or a good person. The important thing is that your mom doesn't want that lady around you."

"Why are you and Mommy pretending to be boyfriend and girlfriend? That's dumb."

Good thing you can't get whiplash from a subject change. Lincoln painted her last nail and screwed the lid back on the polish.

Abby flapped her hands to dry her nails. "Well?"

"Your mom and I are friends. She's being really nice and teaching me how to go on dates so I can be a good boyfriend."

"Why can't you be a good boyfriend?"

He leaned back against the couch and stretched his legs out under the coffee table. "I have trouble talking to people. Especially ladies."

Abby snorted and rolled her eyes. "I'm a lady. You're talking to me."

"How'd I do with your nails? Good?"

She stopped flapping her hands and looked at them. "Yup. Good job." A split second later, she asked, "So how come?"

"How come what?"

"How come you can't be a good boyfriend?"

"Uh, it's complicated grown-up stuff, I guess."

"Maybe you're just chicken."

Ouch. "You know what, Abby? I think that's a lot of it."

She squinted her eyes. "So stop being a chicken."

"That is excellent advice." At any rate, it was more straightforward than any of the advice he'd ever gotten from his friends.

He glanced at his phone to check the time. It was almost eight thirty. "When is your bedtime?"

Abby gave a guilty shrug. "I don't know."

"You don't know, or you don't want to tell me?"

She heaved a massive sigh. "Eight o'clock."

"Oh." He looked over at Gretchen, who was out cold. Her face was flushed.

"Mommy don't feel good."

"No," he agreed. "She's pretty sick." He wasn't sure what to do. He had no clue what Abby's bedtime routine might be, and he hated to leave in case Gretchen got worse. "Do you know your grandma's phone number?"

"Yup." Abby jumped up and in half a second had Gretchen's phone unlocked and was calling Dory.

"Hello?" a weak voice answered.

Abby said, "Hi, Grandma."

"How are you feeling, pumpkin?"

"Good. But Mommy's sick."

Dory groaned.

"Here." Abby shoved the phone at Lincoln.

"Hey, hi, um, this is Lincoln. Gretchen's got some kind of bug or food poisoning or something. Abby's fine, but I wasn't sure what to do here."

"Pretty sure it's food poisoning. Neighbor called to tell us not to eat the casserole, but she was too late. We've both got it, too."

So much for hoping one of her parents might come over and handle the situation. "Oh, no."

"Is Gretchen okay?"

"She's asleep. She had a fever earlier and was vomiting. I didn't want to wake her to get Abby to bed."

Dory groaned. "Maybe I can…" Her words were cut off by a violent retch.

"It's okay, I've got it under control. I hope you feel better. Don't worry about Gretchen or Abby at all." It came out like one long word. He hung up.

Abby climbed up on the chair with Walter and the fuzzy blanket.

"I think you're supposed to go to bed."

"Can't I just sleep here?"

Walter whined.

"He hasta pee."

"I see that. Walter, let's go."

The old pug lumbered off the chair and stretched his stubby legs before waddling toward the back door.

Lincoln grabbed his coat and went outside with Walter. He stood on the back patio in his socks, realizing his mistake as soon as his feet came in contact with the freezing concrete. He danced back and forth while Walter went into the snow-covered yard.

The snow had started again. Random flakes wafted gently toward the ground.

Walter thankfully had no interest in lingering. He did his business and hustled back toward the door.

"Good boy." Inside, Lincoln gave Walter a treat and a scratch on the head.

Walter shook a handful of snowflakes off his coat and went back to the living room. He climbed up on the chair with Abby, turned in a circle three times, then curled up and huffed a sigh.

"Will you read me a story?"

The kid had some major stalling tactics. "Sure. Where's your book?"

She pointed to the bookcase.

"Anything in particular?"

"Nah."

He walked over and squatted down to pick a book from what was clearly Abby's shelf. "How about this one?" He held up a book.

"Nah."

She rejected four books until he just picked one.

"This one looks good." He settled onto the couch at Gretchen's feet and held the book so Abby could see the pictures as he read *Don't Let the Pigeon Drive the Bus* by Mo Willems.

When he finished reading the book, she said, "Can I watch the rest of my movie?"

Lincoln shook his head. "No can do, kiddo."

Walter looked up at Lincoln, then jumped off the chair and headed for the stairs. He got to the bottom step, put his front paws on the first stair, stared pointedly at Abby, and boofed a light bark.

"Looks like he's ready for bed."

Abby flipped her blanket off and trudged to the stairs. "We coulda slept on the chair," she grumbled to Walter.

Lincoln wasn't sure if he should follow Abby to make sure she got herself into bed, but the decision was made when Gretchen groaned and shifted on the couch.

She frowned uncomfortably in her sleep. A moment later, her eyes slid open and she looked around, disconcerted. "What time is it?"

"Just after nine."

"Oh, crap." She struggled to sit up. "Abby—"

"She just went up to bed with Walter."

"She did?"

"It was Walter's idea."

She wiped her hand down her face.

"I called your mom to see what to do about Abby's bedtime. Both of them are sick, too. She said it's food poisoning because the neighbor called and told her to throw the casserole out."

"Oh, no."

"How are you feeling?"

"Marginally better. The fever seems to be gone, but I have a pretty nasty headache."

"Probably dehydration. I'll get you some water." He hurried

into the kitchen and got her a glass of ice water and two pain reliever tablets. He took them back into the living room and sat beside her on the couch.

At first, she sipped the water, then gulped it down without taking the pills. "Wow, guess I'm thirstier than I thought."

Before she could stand, he jumped up and took her glass to refill it. Handing it back to her, he said, "You have more color in your face. That's good."

She swallowed the pills. "Thanks."

"Do you need anything else?"

"No, go home. Please. I feel terrible for wasting your entire day."

"Wasn't a waste at all. I got to make snow angels, and I got some really good advice from Abby."

She gave him a half-smile. "I can only imagine."

"She told me I'm a chicken, and the way to do better is to stop being a chicken."

"I'm sorry."

"No, she's not wrong."

"Her delivery, though…"

He chuckled. "She's as subtle as her mom."

"The line between honesty and niceness is a constant work in progress."

"That's true for all of us, I think." He stood and brushed his hands across his thighs. "You sure you're okay?"

"Yeah. I'm going straight to bed." She grimaced. "Probably after I take Walter out."

Lincoln shook his head. "He was just out, not even twenty minutes ago and did all his business."

She looked so relieved. "Thank you so much. You're the best."

He wanted to ask, "The best what?" but that was a question for another day.

Chapter Thirty-Three

Luck was on Gretchen's side in the form of a two-hour school delay. Which was super convenient since she'd overslept both her alarm and her backup alarm.

She threw on a pair of jeans and a hoodie before checking her phone and seeing the alert for the delay. Halleluia. She slowed down and brushed her teeth and took a few minutes to untangle her curls before giving up (like usual) and pulling it all back with an elastic band.

Abby was already sitting up in bed. "Are we late?" She didn't seem particularly upset at the prospect.

"There's a delay, so we're on time. Time to get up and get dressed. Do you want waffles?"

"Yeah." Abby trudged to her bathroom.

Walter jumped down off the bed and headed for the stairs.

Gretchen followed to let him outside. Another inch or two of snow had accumulated overnight. She hugged her arms over her chest until Walter was satisfied and ready to go back inside.

She popped waffles into the toaster and set the bottle of syrup on the table.

Abby bounded into the kitchen.

"Did you brush your teeth?"

"Yup."

"Did you wash your hands?"

"Yup."

"Did you make your bed?"

"Nope."

"I guess two out of three isn't bad. At least that's what Meatloaf says."

Abby scrunched up her nose. "Meatloaf says?"

"Never mind, you're too young to get my lame joke."

The waffles popped up. Gretchen hurried to toss them onto a plate without burning her fingers.

Abby rolled her eyes and squeezed half the bottle of syrup onto her waffles.

"Now I'm hungry for meatloaf. I think that's what I'll make for supper."

"Eeeew, I hate meatloaf."

"You do not. Last time you ate three big pieces."

"Did not."

"Did too. And two big scoops of mashed potatoes."

"I like mashed potatoes."

"You like meatloaf, too."

"Nuh uh."

"Okay then, I'll eat all the meatloaf and you can just eat potatoes."

"Fine." Abby shoveled a chunk of waffle into her mouth, dripping blueberry syrup onto her chin and shirt.

Gretchen glanced at the clock. "Twenty minutes until the bus comes. Finish up."

While Abby finished her waffles, Gretchen made sure her backpack was ready to go.

"Abigail. You have more syrup on your shirt than you had

on your waffles. Run upstairs and change your shirt."

"I like this shirt."

Gretchen glanced at the clock. "Come here." She grabbed the damp dishcloth from the sink and wiped at the syrup. "Did you paint your nails? You know you're not supposed to play with the nail polish by yourself."

Abby glared, offended. "I didn't. Lincoln painted my nails."

"He did?"

A familiar rumble came from outside.

"Oh, crap. Get your shoes, get your shoes." Gretchen tossed the dishcloth toward the sink and missed. It landed in a heap on the floor.

Abby sprinted toward the door and shoved her foot into a boot while Gretchen pulled the door open to wave at the bus.

"I can't!" Abby dropped to her bottom on the floor and yanked the boot off, then pulled it onto the correct foot.

The bus honked once.

"We're coming!" Gretchen yelled. She tugged the second boot onto Abby's foot and grabbed her arms to pull her up.

Abby grabbed her coat and shoved her arm through.

Gretchen snatched Abby's backpack and dashed onto the front porch.

Just as the bus pulled away.

"Dang it!" she yelled and went back inside. She looked down at Abby's feet and laughed. "I guess it's a good thing you didn't make it to the bus."

Abby looked down and started laughing, too. She was wearing one black boot and one boot with shimmery white glitter.

"Okay, kiddo, fix your feet and we'll get going. I'm already late, might as well stop at Caretti's and be even later, huh?"

She hated the thought of starting work late, especially after being derailed over the weekend, but maybe that break was just what she needed to recharge and attack her clients' problems with a fresh perspective.

Not that she wanted to deal with another bout of food poisoning or whatever had troubled her yesterday, but it had certainly been effective in making her take a break.

When Abby's footwear situation was sorted, Gretchen grabbed her purse and keys and herded Abby to the garage.

"Bye, Walter," Abby called on her way out the door.

A few minutes later, Gretchen pulled away from the school and headed for Caretti's.

A few customers sat at tables with their laptops, but the café was mostly empty.

Jody brightened as she walked to the counter. "What are you doing out and about this morning?"

"Abby missed the bus, so I had to drop her off. Figured I'd stop and caffeinate before I started work."

"Always a solid plan. The usual?"

"Of course." She looked up at the menu board. "And get me one of those iced peppermint latte things."

Jody raised an eyebrow. "Really?"

"I'm going to drop it off for Lincoln. He loves those minty things you come up with."

"So you guys are..." Jody waved her hands and shrugged. "What?"

"I have no idea. We never really got a chance to talk about anything. He brought lunch over yesterday and I think he planned to have The Conversation, and then I got sick. Like *bleeeeht* sick." She mimed barfing.

"Oh, no."

"Pretty sure it was food poisoning. Both my parents had it, too. We all had the same thing for Sunday breakfast, which included some questionable eggs. I'm glad Abby's on a bacon and waffle kick right now and she didn't get sick."

"That's good. Are you feeling better now?"

"I feel fine today, thanks. Mostly thanks to Lincoln because when I got sick he told me to go take a nap. I got to sleep while he shoveled my driveway and made snowmen with Abby."

"Aww, that's so sweet."

"He even painted her nails."

Jody froze in place and spun around to face her. "He painted her nails. After building her a snowman and shoveling your driveway."

"Yeah."

"I don't know how to tell you this, but you have a boyfriend."

"Stop. You know Lincoln. He's super thoughtful and he'd do the same for any of his friends."

Jody snorted. "I didn't see him out there shoveling my driveway, so you keep telling yourself that."

Gretchen wasn't sure *what* she was telling herself. She liked Lincoln. And it seemed like he was starting to hint that he liked her. Or maybe she was reading too much into things he hadn't even said. "In any event, I need to get going. What do I owe you?"

Jody handed over the two cups. "An oath of fealty."

Gretchen took the cups and laughed. "Didn't I already swear one of those?"

With a one-shouldered shrug, Jody said, "Eh, probably."

"Thanks."

"Let me know how your boyfriend likes his latte."

"Yeah, yeah."

As she popped the cups into her cupholder, it occurred to her that the idea of Lincoln being her boyfriend was kind of nice.

No, actually, the idea was kind of great.

She just had no idea what *he* might think about it.

Chapter Thirty-Four

Lincoln slung the last massive bag of dog food onto the shelf and stepped down off the stool when the front door jingled with an incoming customer. He ignored it, grabbing the stool to return to the stockroom.

"Hey. I was hoping you were here this morning."

He spun, happily surprised to hear Gretchen's voice. "Hey yourself. How are you feeling?"

"Good as new. Abby missed the bus so I had to take her to school. Since I was already out, I stopped for caffeine and thought I'd get you a fancy latte as a thanks for helping me out yesterday."

"No need to thank me."

"Baloney. You spent your whole day babysitting and doing manual labor and taking Walter out. And you even did a manicure."

He grinned. "A pretty good one, if I do say so myself."

"Abby was thrilled."

"Good." He gestured to the stool. "I need to put this back, then I'm done—"

Gretchen's phone chirped from her purse. She pulled it out and gasped. "It's the attorney." She turned and hurried outside.

Lincoln put the stool away, then paused at the counter. "Need anything else?"

His aunt Midge reached over and patted his hand. "That's all for today. Thank you, dear."

"No problem." He went outside and looked up and down the sidewalk. He didn't see anything, but he heard a voice nearby. After setting his latte on the roof of his car, he peeked around the corner into the alley, where Gretchen stood, one hand pressing her phone to her ear, her other hand moving excitedly.

"Yes. Yes. Yes, thank you so much. Okay, perfect. Thank you." She hung up and dropped her phone into her purse, then stood, staring at the ground with her hands pressed to her chest.

"You okay?"

She gasped out an almost-laugh, sort-of-sigh, exclamation of excitement. "I'm great!"

"What hap—" His inquiry was cut off as Gretchen threw her arms around his neck. He lifted her off the ground and squeezed her back as hard as she was squeezing him. When he set her down, her face was wet with tears.

"I—I—I—I'm not even sure what just happened." Her voice was an octave higher and twice as fast as normal. "That was the attorney. Carla's being extradited–I'm not even sure where they said, out west somewhere I think, but she's got charges in seven different states and something federal. I—I—can't even process it all. Embezzlement, identity theft, fraud, all kinds of stuff. Warrants… I couldn't even hear all the details because I was just stuck on that she's going to prison for a long, long time and the attorney thinks she'll be locked up for a mini-mum–*bare minimum*–of fifteen years, but probably more like twenty-five." She gasped in a breath and shuddered. "My hands are shaking. I'm so relieved. I'm so relieved." She pressed a hand to her mouth to cover a sob.

Lincoln pulled her into his arms. "That's the best news ever."

"I can't stop shaking. I hope I don't throw up again."

"I hope you don't, either."

She half-sobbed, half-laughed. "Oh, gosh, I didn't realize how scared I've been."

"I'm sure."

"They're going to make sure the restraining order violation gets thrown in there, too, I guess to get as much against her as possible."

"Good." He just held her, waiting as the shaking slowed and finally stopped.

Her breath eventually slowed to normal and she pulled back. "I'm so relieved."

Lincoln wiped her cheeks with his thumbs.

"I'm also freezing."

He looked down at her snow- and slush-covered shoes. "No wonder."

"I need to talk to my parents."

"They'll be thrilled."

She pulled in a deep breath and blew it out.

From her purse, her phone vibrated several times in rapid succession. She yanked it out, then made a face. "Crap. Client messages. I guess I need to quit celebrating and get my butt to work."

Lincoln looked at his watch. They walked toward their cars. Hers was parked behind his. "Yeah, me too. I have triplet mastiffs to get in half an hour."

"I bet they're a handful."

"Great dogs, massive poops."

She laughed. "I can only imagine."

"You don't want to imagine that, I promise you."

She pointed to the cup on the roof of his car. "Don't leave your latte up there."

"Not a chance."

They reached her car. She opened the door and tossed her purse over onto the passenger seat.

"Thanks for the latte."

"Thanks for taking care of me yesterday. And Abby. And Walter. I really appreciate it."

"Any time."

"Don't tell me that. I'll put you into the regular babysitter rotation."

"I'd be happy to babysit if you want to do something with your mom or have a girls' day out with your friends. Probably not going to babysit so you can go out with some great new guy."

Gretchen laughed and put her hand on his chest. "Awww, I was going to start a new dating coach business." Her phone vibrated again. "I really have to go."

Lincoln put his hand over hers and held it against him. "Just one more thing."

"What?"

He tipped his head and leaned down.

Her eyes widened in surprise, just for a second, then drifted shut as his lips touched hers.

After a long moment, he pulled back and smiled. "That one was on purpose."

Chapter Thirty-Five

She couldn't stop grinning. She grinned the entire drive home. She grinned while telling her parents about the news from the attorney. She grinned while responding to the frantic angry messages from her clients. She even grinned while making a quick sandwich for a late lunch.

This day couldn't possibly get any better.

At three thirty, Abby burst through the door and ran into the kitchen. "Hey, Mom, guess what!"

"Whoa, close the front door."

Abby ran back, slammed the door, chucked her backpack on the floor, and skipped back into the kitchen. "Guess what."

"What?"

"What's *espelled* mean?

"Espelled? Do you mean expelled?"

"Yeah. Member that mean boy at the food thing and I punched him and he lied?"

"Yes, I remember."

Abby hoisted herself up on her favorite stool at the island. "Well guess what."

Gretchen slid a glass of water over to her. "Hmm. Was someone expelled?"

Abby snickered gleefully. "I hadda pee. I tried to held it until after recess but I couldn't anymore so the lunch lady sent me in."

"The lunch lady?"

Abby rolled her eyes like it should be obvious. "She was recess monitor."

"Okay. Anyway, so you go inside to pee."

"Yeah. So. Then. I like went in and had to put my coat on the hook and there was snow on it so the floor got wet but it wasn't my fault because I couldn't put it in my cubby because I had to pee *so bad*."

Gretchen tried to follow the story.

"And then there was only this much toilet paper." She held her fingers about two inches apart. "So. Then. I washed my hands and I did the soap twice because the new soap they put in the bathrooms smells really good and I like it. So. Then. My coat was stuck backwards and I was pulling it and I was in the hallway and I heard Mr. Stephens yelling from the office and so I kind of squished my coat back backwards and then Mrs. Flannery came out to help me and then. Guess what."

"I have no idea."

Abby leaned forward and stage whispered like she was about to impart a big secret. "Billy got es—ex—escpelled."

"Expelled. How do you know?"

"Because his mom was yelling at Mr. Stephens and she was saying lots of bad words and yelling really loud about they can't es-ex-exscpel Billy cuz he's a good kid and that's when Mrs. Flannery made me go back outside." She crossed her arms, affronted that her teacher had put a stop to her nosiness.

"Rude."

She flung her hands in the air. "I know, right?!"

Gretchen bit her lips to keep from laughing. No question Abby was following in her dramatic footsteps. "That's quite a day."

"So. Then. Mr. Stephens walks by when I was in the bus line and I said to him, I said, 'Hey, Mr. Stephens,' and he said, 'What?' and then I said, I said to him, 'Billy's mom lies.' And he was like what do you mean and I was like I punched him in the stomach at the food thing because he pushed down a little girl and he kicked me and he lied because he's mean."

Gretchen bit her lips again. She could only imagine what the principal was thinking upon hearing Abby's declaration.

"So. Then. He was like," Abby made her voice deep, "Oh, we shouldn't punch people."

"Which is true."

"So I said, I said to Mr. Stephens, well we shouldn't push down little girls and kick them neither and he was like no, we shouldn't do that neither and then they called my bus and Mr. Stephens said to have a good evening and don't punch nobody."

Gretchen tried to imagine working in the elementary school and dealing with a hundred kids with similar story-telling skills. Every. Day. It must be exhausting. She made a mental note to get Mrs. Flannery a big fat gift card to Caretti's in addition to the basket of school supplies she'd already gotten from her Christmas wish list.

"That is quite the story."

Her eyes narrowed. "I knew he was a bad kid."

Gretchen bit her lip and changed the subject. "Do you have any homework?"

"Yeah, I have two worksheets."

"I still have some work I need to get done today. Do you want a snack?"

"Animal crackers!"

Gretchen got a pack of animal crackers from the pantry. "Here you go."

"Can I work with you?"

"Sure." She grabbed her own pack of animal crackers.

A few minutes later, they were both at Gretchen's desk snacking on animal crackers. Abby did her worksheets while Gretchen worked on her laptop.

At some point, Abby left to take Walter outside and Gretchen got an email from her attorney. It turned out Carla hadn't only been involved in fraud and theft, she was also a liar.

Seth was very much alive.

The week flew by in a flurry of work and… well, mostly work. Something about the holidays–and maybe the fact that it was Friday the thirteenth–brought website issues out of the wood-work. As Gretchen put out fires all week, she didn't have much time to consider that Seth was alive, or that Lincoln had kissed her. Again. On purpose.

Everyone was so busy with holiday preparations or work that she hadn't even had time to talk it out with Jody.

That was about to change.

It was Friday evening after a long week for everyone, about to be a little longer for Jody's daughters, Tess and Mindy, who were tasked with babysitting Abby, Chandler's kids, Maddie and Finn, and Becky's son, Wyatt.

Because, oh yeah, it was girls' night.

Gretchen, Chandler, and Becky met at Jody's house to drop off the kids. From there, they rode together to Holy Guacamole, where Sarah had reserved the small banquet room.

Sarah and Megan were already at the restaurant. Avery and Kim arrived a few minutes later, and at twenty after seven, a harried Margo arrived, still in her scrubs. "Sorry, guys, I got held up when one of my patients decided to have a little of puppies literally two seconds after the owner swore up and down the dog was just fat."

A round of sympathetic groans went up from the table.

"I'll see your puppies and raise you a drunk guy trying to steal a chainsaw," Avery said with a laugh.

"Oh, no, what happened?"

She waved a hand. "Ridiculousness is what happened. My brother Jimmy had to escort him out of the store."

They started sharing the week's horror stories until the waiter popped into the room. "Are we waiting for anyone else?"

"Nope, we're all here."

"Great." He handed out menus. "I'm Dakota, I'll be taking care of you this evening. What can I get you to drink?"

Chandler said, "Nine margaritas to start!"

"Yes! You're going to be a fun group, I can tell," he joked.

A few minutes later, he came back with a tray of margaritas, a pitcher of ice water, and a few bowls of chips and salsa. They gave an order for an obscene amount of food, and when he left, Chandler stood and held her margarita up.

"I can't believe we managed to all get here tonight. I'm ridiculously happy about it, so I'm making a toast." She cleared her throat as everyone raised their glass. "To our husbands, our kids and/or animals, which are sometimes the same thing, our obligations, and to not dealing with any of them tonight. To girls' night!"

They cheered and gave several enthusiastic "hear, hear" responses.

"Okay, okay, okay," Sarah waved her hands to get everyone's attention. "Thirty second updates. We'll go around the table. I'll start." She made a show up pulling her hot pink stopwatch out of her bag and clicking the start button, then quickly updated the group on her life.

When she finished, everyone clapped and cheered.

Avery went next, then Margo, then Chandler, then Becky.

Kim's eyes welled with tears when her turn started. "You guys... tonight's on me. Nate and I just had our highest grossing film ever, and... you guys..." She stopped and squealed. "JARED AND ISOBEL ARE GETTING MARRIED!"

The room erupted with congratulations and chairs were abandoned as everyone scrambled to hug Kim.

Megan was still wiping happy tears when they settled back into their seats. "Wow, I don't know how to follow that. Eric and I are super excited to be finalizing a two-month trip to Africa. He found some excellent coffee connections, so we're going to be visiting Tanzania, Kenya, and Uganda. We've wanted to visit Africa for some time, so we're both really excited for this trip."

When the cheers subsided, Jody shrugged at her sister-in-law. "My update is so lame. I'm just glad I didn't have to follow Kim." Everyone laughed. "Stew and I finally got the plans approved and got all the permits for expanding the back end of the coffee shop. They said they'll be able to get the framing done in January, depending on snow, of course. That's about it."

Gretchen cheered louder than anyone. Poor Jody had been waiting to get the plans approved for almost a year, but there was always something small that held it up.

Sarah held up her stopwatch. "And last but certainly not least, Gretchen, what's your thirty-second update?"

"Okay, no pressure, huh? Let's see. Abby told the principal she punched a boy, I finished all my Christmas shopping, for the first time ever I fired a client, and Lincoln kissed me again."

"Again?! When did he kiss you the first time?"

"What? When?"

"Lincoln?"

"Whoa."

"Was it good?"

"I thought you were fake dating, like coaching him to date other people."

"I told you so."

The last from Jody.

She was saved from answering by the appearance of food.

"Dakotaaaa!!!" The women all cheered his arrival, even though, let's be real, they were mostly excited for what he had on his tray.

Dakota expertly handed out the platters of tacos and empanadas and quesadillas with rice and beans and then set a bunch of little bowls of salsa and sour cream and guacamole and queso on the table. "Let me know if you need extras."

Chandler laughed. "We're all a little extra in here."

Dakota laughed along with her. "Nothing wrong with that. How does everything look? Did I miss anything?"

Everyone confirmed they had everything they needed. He set a stack of extra napkins on the table and said, "I'll be back to check on you."

"Gretchen," Sarah sing-songed. "Are you and Lincoln dating?"

She had a mouth full of taco. She wiped a dap of sour cream from the corner of her mouth and chewed fast to swallow. "No. Not really. I don't think so. I don't know."

"Well, as long as you're sure," Avery joked.

Someone else said, "We need to know everything. Start at the beginning, please."

"Lincoln was getting dating advice from Oren, Alex, and Noah."

"Oh, geez."

"Exactly. So after a spectacularly botched date, I offered to go out with him and kind of coach him."

"And then somebody caught feeeeeeeelings," Chandler said, with some added kissy noises.

"Well, no, I mean, not exactly. We were picking out a Christmas tree and he kissed me, like super quick, and then bailed. The next evening he went on a date with Avery's friend from Atlanta."

"Which I had nothing to do with, by the way." Avery held up a hand. "That was all my genius husband's idea. If I had known he kissed you, I never would have allowed it."

"It was a big misunderstanding, but then I had the issue with Seth's mother coming back and violating the restraining order—"

"What?"

"Oh my goodness, when was this?"

"What happened?"

"She showed up at the festival last week and tried to talk to Abby and take pictures of her. She was taken to jail for violating the restraining order. I contacted my attorneys and they found she's got a ton of warrants and stuff in other states. She'll be in jail for a long, long time."

"Thank goodness."

"She should have been in prison in the first place."

"She's nuts."

"I'm glad your lawyers are on top of it."

"So Lincoln came over to my place to talk on Sunday, and I ended up sick. Food poisoning. I slept all afternoon and he helped Abby build snowmen and he shoveled my driveway and took the dog out. He was so sweet." She left out the part about him seeing her barf, even though this crowd would see it as the height of practical romance. "Then on Monday Abby missed the bus so after I took her to school I got him one of Jody's amazing iced peppermint latte things. We talked for a little bit and I had to get to work and he kissed me on purpose."

"Awwww."

"That's so cute."

"Was it good?"

"He's such a sweet guy."

"Then what?"

"Then nothing. We've texted a few times, but we've both been so busy this week. I'm seeing him tomorrow, though. We're going to the theater for their opening *Nutcracker* performance. I have to be there to make sure everything goes smoothly, anyway, so he's meeting me there."

"And you'll have a big talk and make it all official afterward, right?" Jody smirked.

"Let's not get ahead of ourselves. It was just a kiss."

Margo snorted. "Yeah, but for Lincoln one kiss might as well be a declaration of undying love."

Avery agreed. "She's not wrong."

"You guys." Gretchen picked up another taco and steered the room to even better gossip. "Kim, tell us more about the upcoming wedding."

"Where do I even start?"

Gretchen was glad her turn in the hot seat was over. She listened and chimed in here and there as her friends took turns expanding on their thirty-second updates.

Somewhere in there another round of margaritas appeared and then magically disappeared, along with enough chips and salsa to fill a football stadium.

Dakota appeared in the doorway. "What are we having for

dessert?"

After a moment of weak protests, Dakota headed back to the kitchen with orders for chocolate cake, tiramisu, and cheesecake.

And more margaritas.

By the time the check came, which Kim grabbed and insisted she would fight anyone who tried to give her money, Gretchen was feeling stuffed, fulfilled, and rather tipsy.

She leaned over to Jody. "I don't think I should drive."

Jody chuckled. "None of us should drive. That's why I messaged Stew. He's rounding up the guys to get everyone home."

"You have such a good guy. No, really, he's great."

"He is pretty great. Doesn't mean I won't murder him if I find one more pair of smelly socks balled up under the bed."

Several of the women's phones dinged almost simultaneously.

"Ha! We're getting chauffeurs."

"Until they get here, I have some ideas for Gretchen," Sarah said.

"Oooh, yeah."

Gretchen grimaced. She'd hoped the food and tequila had made them forget about her situation. Apparently not.

"You should call him. Like right now. Put it on speaker," Margo suggested.

"Absolutely not."

"On it!" Avery waved her phone.

"Wait, what? What are you doing?"

"Hello?"

"Linnnnnncolnnnnnn, hey!" Avery yelled.

"Having a good girls' night, I take it."

Gretchen called, "I had nothing to do with this!"

Lincoln's laugh came across the line.

"We all think you guys should be dating," Megan said.

Exclamations of agreement went around the table.

"You should just get married and have babies," Sarah suggested. "My cousin works at the courthouse. I could get you a marriage license tonight, I bet."

Gretchen choked on her last swallow of margarita.

Lincoln chuckled. "I think tonight is a little soon."

Gretchen set her glass on the table a little too hard. "No! We can't anyway. We have to plan Jared and Isobel's wedding first."

"Oh, yeah."

"Good point."

"OH MY GOSH," Chandler yelled. "DOUBLE WEDDING!"

Becky gasped and then laughed. "How drunk are you?"

"Pretty drunk," Chandler agreed. "No double wedding."

"So like, Lincoln," Sarah began.

"Yes?"

"Are you in love with Gretchen? You should be, because she's amazing. If I was a dude I'd be in love with her."

"Me, too."

"Yup."

"I'd be in love with all of you!" Chandler said.

"Uhhh, that's a conversation Gretchen and I should probably have privately."

"Boooo, that's no fun," Avery said.

"I'm so sorry," Gretchen said in the general direction of the phone.

"Are you gonna kiss her again?"

"She totally wants you to."

Megan made kissing noises.

Gretchen leaned her forehead on Jody's shoulder, which was shaking from laughter. "Make it stop."

Becky said, "Hey, Lincoln. We had margaritas."

"A bunch of them," Margo added.

Lincoln said, "I hear. Sounds like you're having a great time."

"We'd have a better time if we leave here knowing you guys are together," Avery insisted. "Like officially official."

Lincoln laughed again. "I'm not making any promises over the phone, but how about this: I can assure you with a great deal of certainty that whatever Gretchen and I end up doing, you guys will be the first to find out."

Avery thought about it for a second, then said, "Yeah, that sounds okay."

Several others added murmurs of assent and nodded.

Suddenly, Megan yelled, "Stewart!" and cheered.

All heads swiveled toward the door, where Stewart looked a little surprised and embarrassed. He waved. "Hello, ladies."

Connor, Alex, and Rowan came into the room behind him, followed by Nate and Eric.

"Holy cow, it's a party now," Becky yelled.

The guys had pretty ingeniously worked out a carpool scheme, where Stewart picked the guys up in the coffee shop's van, then brought them to the restaurant so none of the cars would be left behind.

Oren and Nate were back at Stewart and Jody's to drive home with the kids.

Gretchen felt a twinge of something close to jealousy that she didn't have a partner. Yeah, there was something going on here with Lincoln, but they weren't at the drive-your-drunk-behind-home stage. Oh, well. At least she could count on her parents to step in and help her. She knew how lucky she was to have them so close.

It was probably the tequila—and the weight of a dozen tacos—but she felt a bit melancholy as she settled into the back row of Stew's van.

When they pulled into the driveway and all poured out, she said to Jody, "I'll give my parents a call to come get us."

She gave her a weird look and said, "Don't worry about it. I told you Stew was in charge of getting everybody home safe." She nudged her toward the front door, which Stewart held open.

Inside, Oren and Noah were bundling up their kids. Tess said, "Abby's in the bathroom."

When Oren and Chandler and their kids moved toward the door, Gretchen froze. Lincoln sat on the couch. He lifted a hand in a little wave.

Before she could say anything, Chandler grabbed her in a massive hug. "I love you so much." She let go abruptly and hugged Jody. "And I love you." And then Becky. "And I love you." And then Stew. And then Lincoln. And then Becky again.

Oren laughed and shook his head. "Let's go, babe."

"I love you most of all."

"I know you do." He steered her toward the door.

Becky and Noah left with Wyatt.

Abby came down the stairs and beamed. "Did you have fun, Mommy?"

"I had a lot of fun."

"Me, too. Tess curled my hair. I didn't touch the hot curler iron, I promise." She skipped across the room. "Guess what me and Mindy did." The bright red lips and bright purple eye shadow weren't much of a mystery.

"I bet you did makeup. You look beautiful."

Lincoln stood up and held a hand out. "Keys?"

Gretchen fished in her purse until she found her ring of keys. "Thanks."

"Any time."

"You said that before, and now look where it's gotten you."

He chuckled. "Nowhere I'd rather be."

Chapter Thirty-Six

"How is your car already here?"

Lincoln slowed to pull into Gretchen's driveway. His car was parked in front of the second garage door. He pushed the button on her visor and pulled into her spot in the garage. "Stew followed me here and picked me up. Same with the other guys, so everybody got their cars home tonight instead of figuring it out in the morning."

"I'm impressed."

Truth be told, he was, too. It wasn't simple to coordinate for nine cars to get home, but Stew had a plan and it worked.

Maybe Stew was the one he should have been getting advice from all along.

Lincoln opened Abby's door so she could hop out, then went around and opened Gretchen's door. She seemed more relaxed than she'd been in a while. Girls' night had definitely been a much-needed success.

She opened the door to the house and pushed it open. "Why don't you go in and take Walter out," she said to Abby.

Abby groaned and stomped into the house. "I have to do *everything*."

Gretchen pulled the door most of the way closed. "Thanks. Again."

"Happy to help."

"You did not have to come out in the freezing cold to drive my tipsy behind home."

He shrugged one shoulder. "Did you have fun?"

"I had a blast. It's been like six months since we've been able to all go out together. I really, really needed this."

"Good."

She leaned closer. "And I think I really, really need to kiss you."

Lincoln took a step back and eyed her. "Hold up, how drunk are you?"

Gretchen rolled her eyes. "I drank too much to drive. I should definitely not operate any heavy machinery and probably shouldn't sign any contracts. I'm fully coherent and competent, although I am feeling a wee bit bolder. Which I totally attribute to the margaritas. But I'd want to kiss you even if I was stone cold sober."

"Compelling." He let her pull him close to her.

"Not even slurring my speech."

"Not much, anyway."

"Not at all."

He nodded. "Not at all."

"I had three margaritas, or maybe four, but I also had a million tacos, some quesadilla that Jody couldn't finish, most of a slice of chocolate cake, and like four times my body weight in chips and salsa."

"It's a wonder you're even tipsy."

"I know, right?" She slipped her arms around his neck.

Her puffy coat prevented him from putting his arms all the way around her. "I'm convinced."

"Good."

Lincoln tasted the spices on her lips. They were so like her personality–spicy pepper, tangy lime, sweet chocolate.

Something crashed inside the house, followed by Abby impatiently yelling, "MOOOOOM!!"

"I guess that's my cue to head inside."

"Do you need—"

"No. I don't need rescued from little everything, I promise. Thank you for the ride home." She went up on her tiptoes and kissed him again. "I'll see you tomorrow."

"Okay, okay. I'll see you tomorrow. Good night."

She gave his shoulder a playful shove. "Go."

"One sec." He leaned down and kissed her again, then backed up and headed for the open garage door. "Tomorrow."

As soon as he was outside, Gretchen hit a button next to the door. He jumped in his car and watched the door slide down until it met the ground.

He was almost home when he felt his phone vibrate in his pocket. He slid into his parking space and kept the heater on full blast while he looked to see who had messaged him.

It was a photo from Gretchen, showing her kitchen floor with an array of plates and cups strewn about along with an overturned dish drainer.

Figured out what the crash was.

Yikes, what happened?

She tried to get cereal bowl and it caught on the little hook so everything went flying.

I bet it's a setup. Walter probably mad being home alone tonight.

Sounds like something he'd do.

A second later, she messaged again.

Abby is totally on board with that theory.

I bet she is.

There was no response for a few minutes, so he turned the car off and went upstairs and let himself into his apartment. Edith and Jerry ran over and wound around his legs.

"Hey, guys. Where's Pickles?"

A scratching noise answered his question.

"Ah, he's in the bathroom."

He tossed his keys and wallet on the side table and hung his coat up. As he slipped his shoes off, he told his cats, "She kissed me. Of course, she was three or four margaritas deep, so it's possible she'll regret it in the morning."

Edith meowed.

"Thanks."

Jerry froze, whipped his head to the side, then sprinted off at top speed.

Lincoln scooped Edith up. "Ready for bed?"

She purred her answer.

Morning came too early, when Pickles decided it was time for breakfast an hour before the automatic feeder was set to go off. He announced his demands with a loud wailing meows, which he delivered from the top of the dresser so he couldn't be swayed by a few head scratches.

"Dude, it's Saturday."

Pickles yowled.

Jerry decided Pickles was right, so he jumped off the bed and meowed in the doorway.

Edith opened one annoyed eye and curled onto her side.

Lincoln sighed and got out of bed. "Fine. I'm up. But the joke's on you, because I'm not giving you food."

Pickles and Jerry dashed toward the kitchen. Lincoln went the opposite way, into the bathroom.

Two minutes later, a set of white paws appeared under the door and curled upward, catching the door and violently shaking it so it rattled against the latch.

"Jerry, knock it off."

The rattling stopped for a second, then enthusiastically resumed.

That's pretty much how Lincoln's morning went until it was time to leave for the theater.

He got there early and parked beside Gretchen's car. The lobby was a flurry of activity.

Oren spotted him and called him over. "Could I get a hand with this?"

"Sure."

"Grab that box. I'll get these." Oren took two gold posts toward the counter. "There were a lot more ticket presales than I thought, so we're going to make two lines—one for people who have their tickets already, and one for people who need to buy tickets."

"Good idea."

They set up the posts and Lincoln took the velvet ropes out of the box and clipped them to the posts. Oren stood back and considered for a moment, then shifted the posts to where he wanted them. "That should be good. There's a message board thing somewhere."

Gretchen came rushing from the back room with a letter-board on a stand. She set it between the new rope lines and handed something to Oren. "Arrows. I wasn't sure which lane was which."

She looked amazing, in a black velvety dress that made her red corkscrew curls stand out.

"Perfect." Oren answered, but she was already moving off to take care of something else. He put one arrow with the words "Ticket Holders This Way" and the other one pointing the opposite direction with the words "Ticket Sales This Way."

A young man in a tuxedo asked where he was supposed to be. Gretchen took him to the closed entrance to the theater, where he would punch tickets. A team of four tuxedoed volunteers would show people to their seats. Another young man was stationed at the cash register.

Lincoln stood back and just admired the smoothness of the operation. More accurately, he admired Gretchen as she flitted from spot to spot, pointing and giving directions and taking care of every last detail.

A solid five minutes passed before Gretchen finally saw him. Her face immediately brightened. She came over and put a hand on his arm. "I didn't realize you were here. Have you been waiting long?"

"Just got here. Anything I can help with?"

She scanned the room a final time. "Nope, I think we're ready."

The first of the spectators came through the main door. Gretchen tugged his arm. "Let's get our seats."

They went through the line. Gretchen gave her tickets to the young man, who clipped the corner and handed them back. Then a young woman in a tuxedo showed them to their seats that were about a third of the way back from the stage, in the exact middle of the theater.

"Perk of running the place. We get the best seats."

He raised an eyebrow. "These are the best? Not those?" He pointed to the front row.

"Acoustics are perfect here." She tilted her head back and

pointed up at the ceiling. "We had those panels installed so the acoustics are good no matter where you sit, but this is the very best spot."

"You're the expert. I'll take your word for it."

The theater filled fast.

"Abby didn't want to come?"

"No. They'd never say it, but I think my parents were glad to skip the theater this year. They're taking Abby to the mall and out to eat."

"Nice. It's great that you guys have such a great relationship with your parents."

"I honestly don't know what I'd do without them."

"Same here."

Miss Judith, owner of the dance studio, crossed the stage in front of the closed velvet curtains. She approached the microphone and beamed at the audience. She raised a hand and the murmuring conversation quickly went quiet.

Gretchen reached over and took his hand. She whispered, "Pay attention to what she says."

He doubted there could be anything in Miss Judith's introduction that was very important to him, but he listened anyway.

A spotlight cast a bright light on Miss Judith. "Thank you all for coming to our production of *The Nutcracker*. The students have worked very hard on this production, and we're all very excited to present it to you. Special thanks to the amazing Hickory Hollow Theater for allowing us to use this incredible facility. In exchange for the use of the facility, including the theater's wonderful volunteer staff, they only asked that we donate a portion of our ticket and merchandise sales to the Hickory Hollow Animal Rescue in lieu of payment. We will be donating twenty percent of all those sales to the

Hickory Hollow Animal Rescue, that does so much amazing work for our community."

"What?" Lincoln whispered.

"Surprise." Gretchen grinned up at him. "Merry Christmas," she whispered back.

Miss Judith continued her opening speech, but Lincoln didn't hear a word of it. He was beyond touched that Gretchen had arranged for the rescue to benefit from this event.

Two hours later, the ballet finished to thunderous applause and a standing ovation.

"That was *incredible*," Gretchen said. "Magical."

Lincoln nodded. Sure, it was enjoyable, but ballet was definitely not his first choice in entertainment. "Do you have to stay and help with anything?"

"Nope, I just have to get my coat and we can get out of here."

Easier said than done. The theater-goers were in no great hurry to leave, blocking the aisles in little clusters of conversation.

Gretchen grabbed his hand and tugged him to the far aisle. "Secret shortcut."

"You're like Batman with a super secret cave."

She laughed. "Something like that."

He followed her around the stage to a door he'd never noticed. It led them into a hallway that connected to all the back rooms of the theater. She pushed open a door marked "Employees Only" and reached inside to grab her coat and purse.

From there, he followed her out a side door to the parking lot.

"Meet you at the restaurant?" she asked.

"Yup. See you there in a few minutes."

It wasn't long before they were seated at Sonny's Diner, in a cozy booth in a quiet section.

"I guess Corinne's not working today," Lincoln said.

"I actually saw her and Derek at the theater when we were trying to get out. They must have been seated farther back."

"I didn't see them."

They chatted about the ballet and the theater crowd until the waitress brought their drinks and left with their orders.

"I had no idea you had arranged for the dance company to make a donation to the rescue."

"I know. That's why they call it a surprise."

"Doesn't the theater need that money?"

She gave him an exasperated sigh. "We're already covered for the expenses for *Merchant* in the spring, not even including ticket sales for the show. I suggested it to Oren and the rest of our board and they all thought it was a great idea."

"I'm touched. Thank you." The words seemed so inadequate next to her gesture.

"Besides, I had no idea what to get you for Christmas. I was thinking of getting things for the shelter, but I'm guessing you can order a lot of their stuff wholesale through the pet store. So I thought, what better way to do something that shows you that what's important to you is important to me. And the whole community helping community thing. It's a win-win-win all around."

"You're the best." He couldn't think of anything else to say.

"I really am," she said with a laugh.

Now he was second-guessing the gift he'd gotten her, because it was just a thing. A regular old present wrapped up in paper with a bow. Hers was a grand gesture. His was a... regular old Christmas gift. He hoped she wouldn't be too disappointed, especially since there was only a little more than a week until Christmas, and his holiday budget was gone.

"What are you thinking about?" she asked.

"Nothing. My train of thought just jumped the track and I glitched out for a minute."

"Happens to me all the time. I saw this thing that said something like, 'My life is on track, but there are six trains speeding toward the intersection and all the conductors are screaming.'"

"That is unbelievably accurate."

"Here you are," the waitress said as she set their plates down.

"Thank you," they both answered.

Lincoln squirted ketchup on his plate for his fries. "Now seems as good a time as any to have a conversation."

She looked up at him, her brow raised in confusion. "Is that not what we were doing?"

"I meant a big conversation. About moving forward?"

"Oh. You mean The Conversation."

"Yeah."

"Sure."

"This is not my forte, as you well know." He stared down into his fries.

He kind of hoped she'd jump in and steer the conversation, but it soon became apparent she was waiting for him to speak. Another lesson in dating, he supposed.

He figured he might as well start strong. "I think we should date for real. First, we enjoy a lot of the same things. Two, we get along really well. C, we understand each other's situations. D, um, crap." He sighed. "I had a whole list of good reasons."

"I think you're right. We should start dating for real."

Even though he had been pretty sure she felt the same, he was surprised and relieved to hear her say the words. "You do?"

"Yeah. I mean, if our fake dating has shown me anything,

it's that we're good together, that we can learn from each other, and we the kissing part seems to be going pretty well. So it seems like a no-brainer to give it a shot for real."

He sat back in the booth, stunned. This incredible, beautiful woman actually said that it was a no-brainer to date him. Him! The guy who needed intensive therapy to learn how to have normal conversations. And here was Gretchen, so naturally outgoing and vivacious and talented and amazing, acting like it was the most obvious thing in the world that she'd want to be with him.

Practice dating had not prepared him for this.

She froze with her fork halfway to her mouth. "Was that not what you were thinking?"

"No, yeah, I mean, yes, it was, I'm just… it's just hard to believe someone like you would want to be with someone like me."

She set her fork down on her plate and fixed her gaze directly on him. "Sure. I mean, why on Earth would I want to be with someone hardworking and honest and thoughtful and kind and considerate and loyal who loves animals and builds snowmen with my daughter and paints her nails and holds my hair when I barf and comes out in the cold to make sure I get home safely when I've had too much to drink and attractive to boot. Makes zero sense why I might be interested in a guy like that."

He was flabbergasted.

Attractive? She really thought he was attractive?

Chapter Thirty-Seven

Gretchen wasn't sure what thoughts were coursing through Lincoln's mind, but clearly there was an overwhelming amount of them, so she patiently poked at her fries while he processed whatever was in his head and waited for him to speak.

A few minutes passed.

He huffed out an uncertain laugh. "I think you broke my brain."

"Unintentional, I assure you." She watched his neck redden and then his cheeks.

"I'm just kind of floored that you would be interested in me. You're..." he waved a hand up and down to encompass her entire being. "Amazing and so far out of my league."

"You sell yourself short. I think maybe because you didn't go through all the regular dating when you were younger, you missed picking up some confidence." She set her fork down again. "There aren't any leagues, Lincoln, and if there are, I promise you I'm not out of yours." She took a deep breath. "I know you feel like you're too quiet or too anxious or too what-ever. Believe me, I get it because for my whole life, I've always been the opposite. Too loud, too pushy, too talkative, too *much*." She blinked back some tears that threatened to form.

"I think you're perfect."

"I'm far from perfect."

"Okay, I think you're amazing."

She reached across the table and slid her hand under his. "I think you're amazing, too."

"This is really happening, huh?" He grinned.

She matched his wide smile. "This is really happening."

"Maybe we should talk about dealbreakers?"

The waitress brought them drink refills. "Can I get you anything?"

"No, thanks," Gretchen said. After the waitress was gone, she leaned toward Lincoln. "Dealbreakers? The basics are a good start. No lying, cheating, et cetera."

He shifted and looked a little uncomfortable. "I was thinking more about money. You've got a bunch and I've got just enough. Sometimes there are things I just can't afford."

"We'll definitely have to sit down and talk about it in depth. It seems like we have similar money *styles*, like I'm not out dropping unnecessary money on stuff. I get that we have a significant difference, but for instance, I love to travel. I'll be honest, it would frustrate me if you expected me to stop travel-ing, or never allow me to cover some of your travel expenses. Like, I'm not okay with it being a pride or ego issue. I don't have money *at* you."

"I can probably live with that. I just don't like flashy and over the top."

"No brand new pickup truck with a giant bow for Christmas?"

"Definitely not."

She pulled out her phone and pretended to send a message. "Hang on, I have to cancel something. Totally unrelated."

They laughed a bit and Lincoln took her hand in both of his. "I do have one serious dealbreaker. I've thought a lot about it."

"Okay, of course."

"I know this is premature, I get that. But I might as well just put it out there now. If this ends up being long term and serious, like if we're ever to the point of talking about marriage."

She cocked her head. It felt a bit soon to discuss even the hypothetical, but yay on Lincoln for drawing a line in the sand that was important to him.

"Okay?"

"I have to insist on getting a prenup."

She had no idea how to respond to that. "A prenup?"

He stared down at their hands, a sure sign he was very uncomfortable. "I'm never going to be the provider for you. I know this. I love what I do, but we both know it's never going to make me rich. But the best way I *can* provide for you is to help make sure that you're protected not just by protecting your financial interests, but by giving you the peace of mind that there is no part of me that is motivated by your money."

She swallowed hard. "I know that." She couldn't imagine a scenario where she ever thought Lincoln was after her money.

"Good. But I feel like having that piece of paper will reassure both of us no matter what ever happens. That's my dealbreaker."

"Okay." Her phone vibrated on the table. She hadn't turned it facedown like she usually did, so she saw the caller ID. "Sorry, it's my attorney."

He gestured to her plate. "Are you done eating? I'll get the check and meet you outside?"

"Sure." She answered the call. "Hold on one second, please." She grabbed her purse and coat and rushed for the exit.

The cold air smacked her as she went outside. "Hi, sorry, I was having dinner."

Athena, her attorney, said, "No problem, I just wanted to touch base with you. We received a call from Seth Aston."

She sucked in a lungful of stinging cold air. "I don't understand why Carla said he was dead."

Athena had been there through the entire mess his family had created. "I had my team verify his identity, and then I personally had a nice long chat with him. Apparently he claims he had an abrupt change of heart a couple of years ago and decided to distance himself from Carla. She had turned on him and racked up tens of thousands of dollars in debt in Seth's name. When he found out, he cut all ties and moved to Canada."

"Canada?"

"Yes. He's living in Vancouver with a wife and two young children."

"I still don't understand. Why now?" She wrestled her coat on with one arm.

"It sounds like Carla reached out to him after her arrest, begging for money. He did a little digging and saw what she'd been up to. He contacted us to basically say that he had nothing to do with any of her actions, that he's sorry she contacted you, and if there's anything he can do, he'll be cooperative."

Gretchen pulled her coat tighter around her middle.

"He sounded sincere enough, and I give him a tiny bit of credit that he contacted us instead of violating the order and trying to contact you directly."

"Unlike his mother."

"This is purely informational. Nothing for you to do, no need to respond."

"Thanks so much, Athena."

"Any time."

Footsteps crunched behind her. She turned and looked up at Lincoln.

"Everything okay?"

"Yeah. I'm just a little blindsided. Seth contacted my attorney. He just wanted to let us know he had nothing to do with his mother's actions. He's living in Canada now with a wife and two kids."

"Canada? Was he trying to get away from his mother?"

Gretchen nodded. "It kind of sounds like it."

"Wow." He put a hand on her arm. "You're shivering."

"It's freezing out here." Her words were punctuated with a full body shudder.

"Head home. I'll text you later, okay?" He leaned down and gave her a quick kiss.

Gretchen jumped into the car and willed the lukewarm heater to work faster. It decided to blast hot air as she pulled into the garage.

She hoped Jody wasn't too busy to talk, because this update was a doozy.

Chapter Thirty-Eight

Lincoln could hardly wait to see Gretchen. It had been an incredibly busy week for both of them. He'd had all his regular clients and put in extra hours helping out at the store. It was amazing how many people did last minute shopping for their furry family members as well as their human ones.

Despite their original plan to spend the holidays together, it just wasn't working out in a way that wouldn't disrupt Abby's regular holidays. And the last thing Lincoln wanted to do was disrupt anything for Abby.

So they were doing the next-best thing. Sunday dinner with his parents, three days before Christmas. His mother was beside herself with excitement and nervous about making a good impression. She'd outdone herself making her famous melt-in-your-mouth pot roast and mashed potatoes and carrots, both of which had come from her own garden. For dessert, she'd made an apple crumb pie and homemade vanilla ice cream.

Shelby wrung her hands. "Are you sure she likes apple pie?"

"I'm sure."

"And you're sure Abby likes pot roast?"

"I'm less sure about that, but if not I can make her a sandwich. It'll be fine."

The doorbell rang. His mom smoothed the front of her apron down.

"I got it. Mom, relax." He went over and opened the door.

"Hi!" Abby said loudly.

"Hi, yourself. Are those for me?" He pointed at the bouquet of flowers in her hand.

"Noooo. They're for your mom." Abby went past Lincoln and held the flowers up to Shelby. "These are for you. Thank you for inviting us for dinner."

Lincoln bit his lip to keep from smiling too broadly at Abby's clearly rehearsed speech.

"Thank you very much, Abby. I'm so glad you're here." Shelby took the flowers and reached to give Gretchen a one-armed hug. "Come on in. Make yourselves at home while I put these in some water."

Lincoln took their coats and hung them on the hooks next to the door.

"Is there anything I can help with?" Gretchen asked his mom.

"Nothing at all except finding a seat at the dining room table."

Lincoln ushered Gretchen and Abby into the dining room and pointed out which chairs his parents had occupied forever. "I'll help her bring food in."

A minute later, Lincoln carried the platter of roast into the dining room and set it on the table. His dad followed with the mashed potatoes and carrots, while his mom brought up the rear with the gravy boat and a bowl of green beans.

Once they were all seated, Dan said grace. As soon as she said, "Amen," Shelby jumped back up. "I forgot the rolls."

Lincoln sat with his dad on his left, Gretchen on his right.

He barely managed to stifle a laugh when Abby selected a tiny half-inch long bit of green bean and set it on the edge of her plate. Gretchen must have instructed her to try everything.

Shelby sighed. "Sorry, it looks like the roast is just falling apart."

Gretchen smiled at her. "That's when it's best, as far as I'm concerned. Nothing better than tender, melt-in-your-mouth roast."

He was glad to see his mother relax over the course of the meal.

"Did you get a chance to see *The Nutcracker*? Lincoln said you were thinking about going." Gretchen asked.

"We did. Dan and I went yesterday. They did a wonderful job."

"They really did."

Shelby said, "Lincoln said you organized the donation for the shelter. That was very thoughtful."

"He sets the bar pretty high for thoughtfulness, so that was the best gift I could think of."

"You chose well. That's all he talked about for three days, I swear."

"I'm glad. I know how important the rescue is to him."

"Did you see the calendars? They turned out wonderfully. I have one hanging in the kitchen."

"They really did. I have one in my office. I was going to get another one for the kitchen but they were all sold out by then."

"The one puppy looks like Walter," Abby said.

Shelby turned a warm smile to Abby. "What kind of dog is Walter?"

"He's a bug."

"Pug," Gretchen mildly corrected.

Abby shrugged. "He has big eyes so he kind of looks like a bug."

"Pugs do sort of look like bugs, don't they?" Dan laughed.

"May I please have more potatoes, please?"

"Of course you may." Lincoln's mom scooped a dollop of potatoes on Abby's plate. "Would you like more gravy?"

"Nah. I mean, no thank you."

Dan got himself another serving of everything. "Help yourselves. There's plenty."

"But save room for dessert," Shelby warned.

Dan patted his belly. "I have a separate dessert stomach. How about you, Abby? Do you have a dessert stomach?"

She giggled and nodded her head.

Lincoln could hardly swallow the last bite of potatoes around the lump in his throat. This, right here, was everything he had ever wanted and everything he thought he could never have. A nice family meal, no drama, no nonsense, just a calm, relaxed afternoon with silly jokes and laughter and warmth among the people he cared most about in the world.

When everyone was finished eating, Shelby said, "I made warm apple crumb pie for dessert. I hope you both like apple pie and homemade ice cream."

"Pie *and* ice cream?" Abby's eyes widened.

Shelby beamed. "Pie *and* ice cream. Do you like apple pie?"

Abby nodded, then said, "Yes, ma'am, I like apple pie."

"Oh goodness, thank you for being so polite, but you don't need to call me ma'am."

"Okay."

"Can I help with dessert?" Gretchen offered.

Dan stood and waved a hand. "You just relax and be a guest. Next time we'll put you to work." He winked at Abby. "Next time you'll have to wash all the dishes."

Abby shrugged. "Okay."

Gretchen laughed. "For some reason, she loves doing dishes. It works out great, because it's my least favorite chore."

Shelby and Dan went into the kitchen and came back a few minutes later carrying plates with pie and ice cream.

Abby cleaned her plate and sat back in her chair with a thump. She grabbed her middle. "My regular belly and my dessert belly are *stuffed*."

Everyone laughed and Dan agreed. "Mine, too. Stuffed to the gills."

They moved into the living room, where Gretchen gave Shelby a small bag. "This is just a little thank you for dinner. My mom is addicted to these lemon bars, so I thought you might like them, too."

Abby handed a second bag to Dan.

Gretchen said, "And I have it on good authority that you enjoy a certain handmade salted caramel."

"Oooh, I sure do," Dan said as he pulled the package of caramels out of the bag. "They're my favorite. I'll hide them until after Christmas."

Shelby laughed. "He'll put them somewhere safe and never be able to find them."

Dan nodded. "Guilty." He walked over to the Christmas tree and put a finger to his lips. "Hmmm. One of these gifts seems to have a tag for an 'Abby' on it. Might that be you?"

Abby sat up straight. "Me?"

He picked up a brightly wrapped box and gave it to her. "Yes, indeed, it's a gift for you."

Lincoln put his arm around Gretchen's shoulders.

"Go ahead, open it," Dan encouraged.

Abby looked at her mom for approval.

"Sure."

She tore the paper, gingerly at first, then with enthusiasm

until she revealed a plain cardboard box. She pulled the top open and gasped.

"One of Santa's elves said you like ponies."

She carefully lifted a wooden horse from the box. It was the perfect size for her dolls to ride on.

Gretchen gasped. "Did you make that?"

"I carved the horse. Shelby made it pretty."

The horse was painted light brown, with a slightly glittery sheen. The mane and tail were bright pink with glitter highlights.

"That's amazing."

"I love it! Thank you!" Abby hugged the horse to her chest. "See, Mommy? I told you I'd get a pony."

"What's your pony's name?" Shelby asked.

Abby stared hard at the horse for a long minute. "Sprinkles. Her name is Sprinkles."

"That's a fine name for a horse," Dan said.

The afternoon passed faster than Lincoln expected. Before long, he was holding Gretchen's car door open. "Did you have a good time?"

She put her arms around his middle. "I had a wonderful time. And I can't tell you how much I appreciate them giving Abby a gift. She's over the moon with that horse."

"Dad was excited to make it for her."

"It's pretty easy to see where you get your thoughtfulness from."

"Aw, shucks," he joked.

Abby yelled from the back seat, "Thanks, Lincoln!"

He poked his head in the driver's door and said, "Thank *you* for being so polite. My mom and dad really enjoyed having you here."

"I love Sprinkles." She held the horse up.

He gave her a thumbs up.

"Okay, I'm freezing." Gretchen playfully nudged him out of the way. "I'll see you Tuesday after church?"

"I'll see you then."

He watched her back down the driveway and pull out onto the street before dashing back inside.

Both of his parents gave him a sappy look. "Well?"

"I think you two are perfect together."

"To be fair, you'd say that as long as she had a pulse."

"Lincoln!" Shelby smacked his arm.

He laughed at her outrage. "You blew her away by giving Abby that horse. The quickest way to her heart is to be good to Abby."

Shelby pressed her hands to her heart. "She was just lovely. Such a sweet, polite little thing. Her mother's done a wonderful job with her."

"She does her best."

"It's great that she has support from her parents. Family's the most important thing in the world."

Chapter Thirty-Nine

Gretchen finished her last-minute wrapping and made a quick stop at the grocery store before they closed at noon on Christmas Eve. Along with everyone else in Hickory Hollow. She clutched her bags tightly and scurried against the wind to her car that felt like it was parked six miles away.

She got to her parents' house and burst into the kitchen. "My goodness, I swear everyone in the entire county was at the grocery store." She plopped the bags onto the table.

"Excellent," Dory said, pulling out the bottle of cinnamon. "Thank you. I didn't realize I was so low."

She and Abby mixed up some cinnamon sugar and rolled dough balls in it, then squished the balls on a cookie sheet.

"Snickerdoodles are my favorite," Gretchen said.

"Grandma let me put kisses on." She pointed to a rack full of peanut butter cookies with Hershey's kisses on them.

"Those are my favorite, too."

Abby giggled. "You can't have both favorite."

"Sure I can." She pointed to the sugar cookies with green sprinkles. "Those are my favorite, too. And those." She picked up a chocolate chip cookie and took a bite out of it. "Mmm-mmm, still warm."

They spent the afternoon boxing up cookies into variety packs that her mom would hand out to her neighbors like she did every year.

After cookies, they watched a Christmas movie, and after that, they got ready and headed to church for Christmas Eve service.

Brian had been at the church all afternoon, helping to sort toys that would be handed out to all the kids.

Somewhere in the middle of *Silent Night*, Gretchen felt all the tension drain from her shoulders. She kept an eye on the candle Abby carefully held in front of her. The lights in the church dimmed until the only light was the soft glow of candlelight. She let the meaning and the peace of the season wash over her, and for a little while, she refused to let her brain turn to all the things that needed to be done. There would be plenty of time for that later.

After the candles were extinguished, everyone enjoyed a moment of quiet reflection. Until the newest member of the congregation, a two-month-old baby, made her presence known with a sudden wail. A low rumble of chuckling was the perfect way to end the peaceful moment and transition back into lights and noise.

The service ended with a cheerful rendition of *Joy to the World*. At the end, Gretchen and Abby gave Dory and Brian hugs. "See you tomorrow."

Abby gleefully announced, "Santa's coming tonight!"

"He sure is. You better get right to sleep." Dory gave her a kiss on the forehead.

Gretchen kept a hand on Abby's hood as they made their way out into the parking lot. They were almost to the car when she bumped into Abby's back. She had come to a stop and was staring up to the sky. "Does Santa ever bump into the stars?"

Gretchen looked up at the perfectly clear sky dotted with bright, twinkling stars. Her breath danced upward. "Nope, the stars are way, way higher than Santa flies."

A few people walked past and wished them a Merry Christmas.

"Merry Christmas!" Abby called as she climbed into her seat.

Back home, Gretchen made three mugs of hot chocolate.

Lincoln came a few minutes later with three gift bags.

They all settled into the living room. Gretchen took one of the gifts from under the tree and explained to Lincoln, "Abby's allowed to open one gift on Christmas Eve. It's something my parents always did with me, so I kept the tradition going."

Abby carefully set her hot chocolate on the coffee table and sat cross-legged next to Walter. "Can I open it now?"

"Go ahead."

She ripped the paper and popped the box open. "Yay!" She yelled as she lifted a set of Princess Poppy pajamas out of the box. "I love it, Mommy!"

"There's one more thing in the box."

Abby tossed the tissue paper aside to find a new book.

"That's a great tradition."

"My mom confessed one time that it was for pictures. This way nobody's wearing ratty old pajamas on Christmas morning." She laughed.

"Makes sense to me." He leaned close. His breath was warm against her ear. "Can I give her this?"

"Sure."

He handed a gift bag to Abby. "Since I won't get to see you tomorrow, your mom says you can open this tonight, too."

Her eyes shone with excitement. She pulled the tissue

paper out of the bag and tossed it aside. A second later she was holding a Princess Poppy pillow head with a gaudy sequin felt peacock feather tiara. "Wow, I love it!" She hugged it close.

Gretchen made a face Abby couldn't see. She whispered, "That's creepy."

"Very. Now here's yours." He slid a bag to her.

"This is a big bag. I only got you a little bag."

"Yes, but you did a grand gesture as part of my gift, so I wasn't expecting a bag at all."

She laughed quietly as she handed him a gift bag.

"You first," he said.

She could tell he was excited for her to open whatever he'd gotten her. "Okay. Here we go." She pulled a wad of shimmery tissue paper out of the bag. "Wait. Is this..?" She lifted the burgundy purse out of the gift bag. "How did you...? I love it, thank you so much."

"Look inside."

"There cannot be more." She unzipped the purse and laughed. "I gotta tell you, this is the best gift ever." She pulled out a bag of Reese's peanut butter trees. Something jangled at the bottom of the purse. "What's this?" She pulled out two quarters and held them up, confused.

"My grandmother always said that you never give a purse or a wallet as a gift without putting money inside. It's a wish for good fortune that they'll never be empty. So I found a quarter from the year you were born and one from the year Abby was born."

She looked at the dates on the quarters. It was so ridiculously sweet she had to swallow back a lump in her throat. "Now I feel even worse about this." She cocked her head toward his gift bag.

Lincoln peered into the bag. "What are you talking about? This is awesome." He pulled out the variety of local chocolates.

At the bottom of the bag was a plastic container. "Are these what I think they are?" He grinned and popped the lid off. "Snickerdoodles! Did you make these?"

Abby bounced on her seat. "I made them!"

"You did? That's awesome because these are my favorite. Thank you, Abby." He snapped the lid back on. "I'll have some for breakfast."

"I made the balls like this." She rubbed her palms together. "And then we shook the balls in a bag with sugar."

"And cinnamon," Gretchen added.

"Yeah. Grandma ran out so Mommy had to go to the store with everybody else in this stupid town."

Gretchen snorted. "Apparently I complained about it once or twice."

Abby sat up straight and asked, "Where are the cookies for Santa?"

"In the kitchen."

"And chocolate milk, right? And carrots for the reindeer?"

"Of course."

"Are reindeer allowed to eat carrots when they fly?"

"I'm sure they are."

She turned to Lincoln, concerned. "Do them all have their papers this year?"

He looked confused for a second, then remembered what he'd told her at the winter festival. "Yes. Yeah, all the reindeer had their papers processed through the, uh... Allianc—"

"Federation," Gretchen hurried to correct.

"Yeah. Through the Federation of Animals. All certifications are up to date and ready to go."

"Where is Santa now?"

He lifted his shoulders. "I don't know."

Gretchen unlocked her phone and tapped to the NORAD site. She held the screen over for Abby to see. "He's flying over the Atlantic Ocean right now, headed to Canada. Then he'll come to the United States."

Abby clapped her hands. "That's where we live!"

Gretchen leaned over to show Lincoln. "NORAD tracks Santa's route every year. It's amazing how he can do the whole world in one night."

"Okay, this is the coolest thing I've ever seen."

Abby settled back against the chair. "Is that another present?"

Gretchen shook her head. Before she could say anything about that being rude, Lincoln scooped the gift up.

"It is. This one's for Walter, so I was thinking maybe you could help him open it."

Abby sat cross-legged with Walter next to her. "Here, doggie, this one is for you."

Walter yawned and watched her tear the paper and open the box.

"Look, Walter. Tennis balls." She held one of the balls out for him to sniff. "And a bag of treats. I can only give you one because you don't want a tummy ache for Santa."

Walter accepted his treat, but ignored her advice and looked longingly at the bag.

"Here's a bunny."

He ignored the stuffed bunny and leaned ever so subtly toward the treat bag.

"Thank you, Lincoln. Walter loves his presents."

"You're welcome, Abby. You're welcome, Walter."

Gretchen looked at the clock. "And now it's time for you and Walter to get to bed. Santa will be here before we know it."

"But we didn't read my new story." Abby fished around on the chair and produced *Christmas in Camelot*, her new Magic Tree House book.

"After I take Walter out and we get changed—"

Lincoln popped up to his feet. "I'm on in. Walter, let's go pee."

Walter huffed and only got off the chair because Abby did.

Gretchen took Abby upstairs and changed into her new pajamas. She snuggled down into her bed, hugging her creepy new Princess Poppy pillow.

Gretchen deliberately read slowly, her voice soothing and melodic.

Abby's eyes slipped shut, then popped open. "I didn't say good night to Lincoln." She sat upright and hollered, "Lincoln!"

Gretchen winced at the loudness.

Footsteps thumped and he peeked in the doorway. "Yes?"

"Good night. Thank you for the pillow. I love it."

"That makes me happy. Good night, Abby. Merry Christmas."

"Merry Christmas, Lincoln."

Walter climbed up the doggie steps at the end of Abby's bed and made his way up beside her.

Chapter Forty

Lincoln went back downstairs and sat on the couch. Gretchen tiptoed downstairs a few minutes later. She whispered, "Okay, I have to do the cookies and the fireplace."

"The fireplace?" he asked. Which is how he found himself sprinkling powdered sugar mixed with glitter over a set of paper footprints as though Santa left the marks on his way out of the fireplace. "Wouldn't it make more sense if the footprint was the sugar stuff?"

Gretchen's head whipped around. "You don't question the things you find on Pinterest."

"My bad. How many of these should I make?"

"Just a couple like he walked over to get a cookie."

Lincoln made a few more footprints that ended at the coffee table. "Wouldn't he walk to the tree first?"

Gretchen gaped at him.

He held up a hand. "Okay, okay, no questioning Pinterest."

"Do you like chocolate milk?"

"Love it, why?"

She held up a finger in a "wait" gesture, so he waited while she ran into the kitchen. She came back with a plate and a small bottle of chocolate milk. "Drink this."

"All of it?"

"If you don't mind."

He chugged the milk and screwed the top back on.

"No, leave it off."

He unscrewed the cap and watched her precisely stage the coffee table with a plate. She took two big bites out of a peanut butter cookie, then sprinkled a handful of crumbs around the plate with the last bite of the peanut butter cookie.

She placed the plate just so, then set the empty milk bottle and the lid next to the plate. "Carrots next."

A minute later, he was tasked with eating half a carrot and leaving the uneaten half on the table for Abby to find in the morning.

After she was satisfied with the table, she enlisted his help to bring an armload of gifts out of her office closet and arrange them under the tree.

"There aren't any tags," he whispered.

"I know. Instead of tags, I wrap by color. All the blue gifts are for my dad, all the pink ones are for my mom, and everything with Princess Poppy wrap is for Abby."

"Smart."

She set the largest gift in the front. It was the only one with a tag, wrapped in green paper different from all the others.

"What's this one?" he asked.

"That's the gift from Santa."

"They aren't all from Santa?"

She shook her head.

He figured she wasn't going to explain when she focused on arranging all the gifts just so under the tree.

Finally, she stepped back, took a few pictures with her phone, then settled onto the couch.

Very quietly, she explained. "We always buy gifts from the angel trees, and two or three years ago, Abby said it was stupid because Santa could just bring those kids gifts. I had to think fast, so I decided that Santa only brings one gift. The rest come from parents or grandparents, and lots of grownups can't afford to buy a lot of gifts. So I explained that she was very lucky to get a lot of gifts from us, but some kids only got one present from Santa. It seemed to make sense to her." She stifled a laugh. "A good friend of mine handled it by telling her kids that Santa sends a bill to the parents."

"And all this?" He waved a hand at the plate and footprints.

She leaned back into his shoulder. "I wanted to go all out this year. I'm not totally sure she still believes in Santa now, but by next year she definitely won't. I figure this is my last chance to make a magical childhood Christmas."

"Are you sad about that?"

"Kinda."

The question popped out. "Do you want more kids?"

He felt her shrug against him. "At this point I've accepted that it's not going to happen. I'm almost forty, she's already six, which would already be a big gap."

"Did you plan to have more kids?" he asked.

"When I thought about my life, yes, I always assumed I'd have two or three kids. Of course I also assumed I'd have a husband and not a sperm donor who bailed when he couldn't get his hands on my money, so there's that."

"I'm sorry it didn't work out."

"Nah, I'm not sorry. Abby is the light of my life and I'd go through every bit of it all over again to have her. And if I did have a husband, he probably wouldn't like me sitting here cuddling with you." She laughed softly.

"Didn't think of that. I hope he's not a big guy that could beat me up."

Somewhere, among the quiet laughter and twinkling lights from the tree and magical footprints, their lips found each other.

In a million years, Lincoln wouldn't have thought he'd be making out with Gretchen on her couch on Christmas Eve, but here they were.

He pulled himself back and hugged her close to him. "I should go. I'm sure you'll be up bright and early."

She looked up and kissed him again. "Merry Christmas, Lincoln."

"Merry Christmas, Gretchen."

Epilogue

Christmas Day
  Four Years Later

Gretchen sat on the edge of the bed and took a few deep breaths. "I cannot be sick on Christmas. I will not be sick on Christmas."

Lincoln handed her a glass of water. "Probably all those snickerdoodles last night."

"Probably." She couldn't be sick. She had too many plans for today. This would be the first year she'd be one hundred percent out-gifting her husband. The manila packet of papers she'd wrapped as his gift would blow him away. Opening it would come second only to the moment he overheard Abby six months ago, on her tenth birthday, blowing out her candles and making a wish that Lincoln could adopt her and be her dad for real.

He had sobbed like a baby and made her love him even more. Yes, even more than she did when he'd made vows to Abby at their wedding to be the best dad he could.

If there was one thing she hated, it was keeping something under wraps. So having this secret pack of papers was driving her bananas.

Just a few more hours. She had it all planned out. After they spent the afternoon with her family and the evening with his, when Abby and Walter crashed into bed after the day's excitement, she'd take him aside and give him the papers from her attorney.

Papers that Seth happily signed—not because he was spiteful, but because he was happy Abby finally had the dad he never could have been to her. Papers that cleared the way for Lincoln to legally become her father.

Her stomach was still unsettled, so she sipped on some Sprite while Abby opened her and Walter's gifts. At ten and a half, she no longer believed in Santa, but she definitely still believed in the magic of Christmas. It was her favorite holiday by far.

She watched Lincoln sit cross-legged on the floor with Abby, removing packaging and inserting batteries as needed. Thankfully the animated princess craze was over. For the moment, she was into making friendship bracelets and bath bombs.

"Are Poppy and Nonny coming over here?"

Gretchen caught Lincoln's smile. One day, Abby had just decided to give Lincoln's parents new names. They loved it, she loved it, and Lincoln definitely loved it.

By lunchtime when her parents arrived, Gretchen was feeling a little better. By the time they headed out to Poppy and Nonny's, she felt perfectly fine.

When Lincoln was loading the car to head home late in the evening, the busy day crashed down on her and she suddenly felt exhausted.

On the way home, she jolted upright with a sharp suspicion. "Can you stop at the convenience store, please?"

"Sure, what's up?"

She tried to act casual. "I just really want some Twizzlers."

"Twizzlers. Right now."

"Yeah." No, she did not want Twizzlers. She was stuffed from two huge Christmas meals on top of an unsettled stomach.

He pulled into a parking place.

She practically dove out of the car. "I'll be right back. You want anything?"

"Cherry slushie!" Abby said.

"Nah, I'm good." He looked a little confused.

Inside, along with half the town, of course, Gretchen got a cherry slushie and a pack of Twizzlers, then scanned the aisles for what she'd really come in for.

As soon as they got home, she ran upstairs and locked herself in the bathroom.

The seconds ticked by. She didn't allow herself to turn around until five full minutes had passed. Slowly, she turned.

Oh, boy.

It looked like she would be *double* outdoing her husband's usual gifting.

A quiet knock on the door startled her.

"You okay?"

"Yeah."

"I brought you some Sprite and some Pepto Bismol."

"Okay, thanks." She hid the box in the bottom of the trash can. She washed the stick off and put it in her pocket. Now what?

Back downstairs, Lincoln kept eyeing her. She knew he thought she was sick, so she sat on the couch, trying to relax while her mind raced a million miles an hour. She couldn't help the spikes of anxiety. Holy crap, she was forty-three. He was forty-two. This was bananas.

Would he still want to adopt Abby if he had a biological kid of his own?

Abby yawned and came over for a hug. "Night, Mom."

"Night, sweetheart. I love you. Merry Christmas."

"Merry Christmas. Love you, too."

Lincoln went upstairs with Abby to read her a story. They were followed by a furry parade. Walter went first, followed by Pickles, Jerry, and finally Edith, who had finally made her peace with Walter's existence.

Gretchen wasn't sure how to proceed. This was definitely a monkey wrench in her original plans.

Time was up when Lincoln sat down beside her. "What's going on?"

"What?"

He smoothed her unruly hair back from her face. "I know you're not feeling well, but it looks like more than that. What's on your mind?"

She swallowed hard and abandoned her plan. "I'm out-gifting you this year."

His brow scrunched.

She slipped the plastic stick out of her pocket and handed it to him.

He took the stick and blinked a few times. "Is this? Does this? Are we?" He looked at her. "Does this mean…?"

She nodded.

He launched himself over and hugged her tight.

"There's more."

He sat back in wonder. "What more could there possibly be?"

"The last gift under the tree is yours."

"It's yellow. I thought yellow was for Jody this year."

"Sneaky, huh?" She went over and got the gift and brought it back over to him.

He unceremoniously ripped the paper off and tossed the box lid halfway across the room. He froze when he saw the manila envelope. "What is this?"

"Open it," she whispered.

He carefully opened the envelope and slid the papers out. His eyes darted back and forth as he read. When he finished the last page, he went back and looked at them again. "Does this mean…?" Tears spilled down his cheeks. "I can finally adopt her? Officially?"

Gretchen nodded, trying to control her own tears.

He slid off the couch onto his knees and hugged her middle for a long, long time. Finally, he held up two fingers. "I'm going to have *two* kids. I mean, we. *We*'re going to have two kids." He put a hand against her belly. "I wonder if we'll end up with one of each? Wouldn't that be cool? Or maybe another girl. That would be amazing, too." He looked up at her. "I can't believe I'm going to be a dad again."

Again.

With that one word, Gretchen broke down and sobbed. Each tear washed away every bit of the doubts that had reared their ugly heads.

They–*they*–were going to be parents.

Again.

Enjoyed this trip to Hickory Hollow? Be sure to check out Everything's Under Control, Book 1 in the Willow Creek series!

Summer Sullivan comes back home after her life falls apart, only to find her family's farm-turned-event-venue is also falling apart. As she works to fix Willow Creek, her brother's best friend tries his best to fix her broken heart.

Order Now!

Author's Note

Dear Reader,

I had so much fun writing this book!

I knew Gretchen would show up with her own story after she delivered Chandler's baby on stage (!!!) in Mending Fences, and of course sweet Lincoln stole my heart after Empurror Poofington J. Poof put him through the wringer in Cat Burglar.

I thoroughly enjoyed writing Lincoln's first date, even though I felt bad for him. But let's be honest, it was a really, really bad idea for him to follow Alex's advice and wear an earpiece. And I felt worse for his poor unsuspecting date!

This book has a couple of Easter eggs from my real life in it. First of all, JM Creations is a real business, run by a real Jen, one of my real besties. She does some super cool laser engraving and awesome wood designs. Check her out at facebook.com/JSMJPMCreations or Instagram.com/jsmjpmcreations

Secondly, I was challenged by my friend Stephanie Desaulniers to write a goose into the story. I included not one, not two, but three geese – an ice sculpture goose, a goose on the window, and a goose in the title of Steph's daycare business. In real life, Steph does not run a daycare. Instead of wrangling toddlers, she is a business consultant who wrangles small business owners, such as myself. You can check her out at businessbydezign.com.

I hope you enjoyed this visit to Hickory Hollow. Bad

Advice is the last Hickory Hollow book – *for now* – because we're starting a whole new series in a whole new setting! Willow Creek has a lot of similarities to Hickory Hollow, and I'm confident you'll love visiting there just as much!

To keep up with all the latest updates and news, be sure to sign up for my newsletter at carriejacobs.com! You'll get exclusive sneak peeks, behind-the-scenes info, notice of upcoming releases, and all that jazz. You can also follow me on Facebook facebook.com/writercarriejacobs for updates, notice of my upcoming events and more importantly, pictures of my furry editorial assistants.

If you enjoyed Gretchen and Lincoln's story and have a moment to spare, leaving a review online would be very helpful to me. (Even if you didn't buy it online, you can still leave a review.)

Until next time, be careful who you take advice from! 😉

Best,

Carrie

About the Author

Carrie's love of storytelling began in early childhood and never wavered as time marched onward. She reads in pretty much every genre imaginable, but found her writing happy place in small town contemporary romance and romantic comedy.

From that love came Hickory Hollow, a mashup of her hometown and places she's either visited or would like to. Her favorite part of Hickory Hollow? The residents don't have to drive an hour to get to Target, like she does in real life.

Carrie lives in beautiful central Pennsylvania with her family and very spoiled furry editorial assistants.

Connect with Carrie through her newsletter or social media!

Website: carriejacobs.com

facebook.com/writercarriejacobs

instagram.com/carriejacobsauthor

goodreads.com/carriejacobs